ROMANCING THE CROWN

The royal heir to the kingdom of Montebello is safe. But a traitor lurks in the heart of the neighboring kingdom of Tamir, waiting to destroy the countries' newfound alliance!

Meet the major players in this royal mystery…

Princess Nadia Kamal: The eldest Tamiri princess hides her passions behind a veil of gentility. But when a handsome stranger uncovers her secrets, there's nowhere left to hide.…

Duke Gage Weston of Penwyck: Playing an everyday average Joe is second nature to this sought-after spy. But royalty is in his blood—as is a certain standoffish princess!

Butrus Dabir: Nadia's fiancé is her father the sheik's most trusted advisor. His position is of the highest power—with the most opportunity for betrayal.…

Sheik Ahmed Kamal: After his youngest daughter's hasty marriage, the sheik is joyous to hear that his sensible oldest daughter will marry as befits her station. But his new son-in-law may not be the man he expects.…

Dear Reader,

The warm weather is upon us, and things are heating up to match here at Silhouette Intimate Moments. Candace Camp returns to A LITTLE TOWN IN TEXAS with *Smooth-Talking Texan*, featuring another of her fabulous Western heroes. Town sheriff Quinn Sutton is one irresistible guy—as attorney Lisa Mendoza is about to learn.

We're now halfway through ROMANCING THE CROWN, our suspenseful royal continuity. In Valerie Parv's *Royal Spy*, a courtship of convenience quickly becomes the real thing—but is either the commoner or the princess what they seem? Marie Ferrarella begins THE BACHELORS OF BLAIR MEMORIAL with *In Graywolf's Hands*, featuring a Native American doctor and the FBI agent who ends up falling for him. Linda Winstead Jones is back with *In Bed With Boone,* a thrillingly romantic kidnapping story—of course with a happy ending. Then go *Beneath the Silk* with author Wendy Rosnau, whose newest is sensuous and suspenseful, and completely enthralling. Finally, welcome brand-new author Catherine Mann. *Wedding at White Sands* is her first book, but we've already got more—including an exciting trilogy—lined up from this talented newcomer.

Enjoy all six of this month's offerings, then come back next month for even more excitement as Intimate Moments continues to present some of the best romance reading you'll find anywhere.

Leslie J. Wainger
Executive Senior Editor

Please address questions and book requests to:
Silhouette Reader Service
U.S.: 3010 Walden Ave., P.O. Box 1325, Buffalo, NY 14269
Canadian: P.O. Box 609, Fort Erie, Ont. L2A 5X3

Royal Spy
VALERIE PARV

Silhouette®

INTIMATE MOMENTS™

Published by Silhouette Books

America's Publisher of Contemporary Romance

Special thanks and acknowledgment are given
to Valerie Parv for her contribution to the
ROMANCING THE CROWN series.

To the authors and editors at Silhouette who helped me
bring the worlds in this book to life, and to Melissa B.
who inspired me to live in them.

 SILHOUETTE BOOKS

ISBN 0-373-27224-3

ROYAL SPY

Copyright © 2002 by Harlequin Books S.A.

Visit Silhouette at www.eHarlequin.com

Printed in U.S.A.

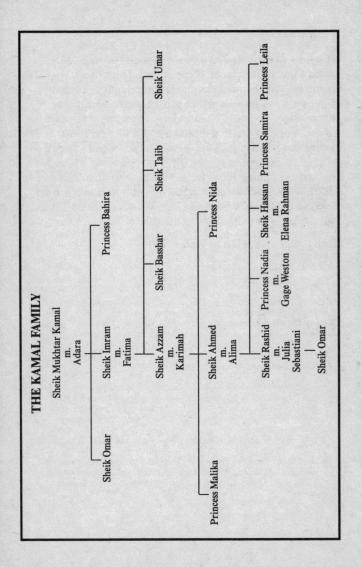

THE KAMAL FAMILY

Sheik Mukhtar Kamal
m.
Adara

- Sheik Omar

Sheik Imram
m.
Fatima

- Princess Bahira

Sheik Azzam
m.
Karimah

Sheik Basshar

Sheik Talib

Sheik Umar

Sheik Ahmed
m.
Alima

Princess Nida

Princess Malika

Sheik Rashid
m.
Julia
Sebastiani

Sheik Omar

Princess Nadia
m.
Gage Weston

Sheik Hassan
m.
Elena Rahman

Princess Samira

Princess Leila

Dear Reader,

It seems to me that when you're a member of a royal family, life can be complicated. Duty must come before personal choice. Business before pleasure. Finding ways to be together privately can be almost impossible. You only have to look at the royal families of the world to see that a crown and a fortune can't guarantee happiness. This is the double-edged sword I set out to explore in *Royal Spy*. In the process I found myself examining the drive we all have to choose our destinies. Like Princess Nadia, we want to rule our own lives, although like her and Gage Weston, we don't mind surrendering provided it's to the rule of love.

Long may love reign in your life.

All the best,

Valerie

Chapter 1

Gage Weston could think of worse ways to spend an afternoon than watching a princess get undressed. Sights like that were rare, even in his profession, but made putting his life on the line to spy for his country even more worthwhile. What other job in the world could offer such a bonus, where he wouldn't be considered some kind of Peeping Tom? Fortunately he only peeped by invitation or in the line of duty, as he was doing now.

He was determined to find out what the princess was up to. Certainly not legitimate royal business, or she would have left her father's palace dressed for her task, instead of waiting until she was out of sight to furtively exchange clothes with her maid.

Princess Nadia Kamal was the eldest daughter of Sheik Ahmed Kamal, ruler of Tamir, who was famous for his old-fashioned morality. Nadia was equally well known for pushing the boundaries of convention, but Gage would bet her father knew nothing about this little caper.

Not that Gage planned to tell him. He wasn't working for the sheik, but for his opposite number, King Marcus of Mon-

tebello. Marcus needed to know who in Sheik Ahmed's circle
had ties with the terrorist group known as the Brothers of
Darkness, to prevent the Brothers from derailing the fledgling
peace process between Tamir and Montebello.

Gage had a more personal reason for spying on the princess. The traitor was also involved in the murder of his best
friend, Conrad Drake. This ranked as a higher priority with
Gage than even the king's mission.

With luck, he could trap the traitor and Conrad's murderer
while on the one assignment.

He tightened his grip on the binoculars, a sense of loss
sweeping over him as he thought of Conrad, who should have
been at his side at this moment.

They'd been like brothers. Conrad hadn't been a member
of royalty, as Gage was, but then Gage rarely used his ducal
title, so the issue had never come between them. They had
grown up together, studied economics and law at university,
flown side by side in the Royal Penwyck Air Force and eventually become partners.

With Conrad's cool temperament moderating Gage's hot-
headedness, they had conquered the stock market almost as
a game, amassing a fortune that continued to snowball.

Just as well their finances were sound, because they had
discovered their talent for undercover work when the head
of a company they had invested in was kidnapped and held
for ransom. Gage had known the man well, and had made it
his business to track down the kidnappers, free their client
and bring the perpetrators to justice.

Word had spread until Weston Drake Enterprises became
the cover for a wide range of intelligence operations on behalf of major corporations and world leaders.

Now Conrad was gone, gunned down while feeding information back to Gage from the United States, where Conrad
had been covertly investigating the Brothers of Darkness,
searching for clues to help Gage identify King Marcus's traitor.

Gage sighed. Conrad hadn't completed the mission. Anger
gripped Gage as he thought of his friend's life ending on a

back road in Texas where a bullet had been put through his head. The only clue to his assailant had been the word that Conrad had scrawled in the dust as he lay dying beside his car, the engine still running when he was found: DOT.

Road rage, the American police concluded, not knowing that Conrad was any more than the tourist he posed as. They thought he'd tried to scratch out a message to his fiancée, Dorothy Gillespie in Penwyck, but Gage knew better. He'd introduced the couple, and Conrad had never called Dorothy anything but Doro. She hated the nickname Dot. The letters had to mean something else.

As boys, they'd made up their own code using initial letters, challenging each other to decode the message. Gage invariably won, and Conrad used to say it was because he had the more devious mind.

It worked in his favor now. After hours of sifting through alternatives, Gage had linked the *O* to Octopus, the symbol used by the younger, more reckless members of the Brothers of Darkness. The *T* was more of a challenge—until he settled on Tamir, the country the Brothers stood to gain the most from destabilizing.

The *D* had kept him up for many sleepless nights. Finally Gage went with his gut feeling that it stood for Butrus Dabir, attorney and key adviser to Tamir's ruler. Conrad had told him he was suspicious of Dabir, whose associates included underworld figures reputed to be involved with the Brothers. That was good enough for Gage.

Dabir. Octopus. Tamir. Three words that could be clues to Conrad's killer. Gage was determined to find the person responsible.

Could he be looking at her now?

He trained the high-powered glasses on the princess again. She was the most beautiful sight he'd had in the crosshairs for some time. Her short, raven-colored hair was feathered around her face, making her look a lot different from the other women in her family. With her tall athletic figure, from a distance she might have been taken for an American. Close up, her exotic features and high cheekbones belonged to a heroine of an *Arabian Nights* tale.

It wasn't hard to picture her reclining on a bank of embroidered cushions, veiled and clad in brightly colored silks. It would be a pity to veil such a tempting mouth. No veil, then, but keep the cushions and the silks. The same untamed imagination insisted he paint himself into the scene, resting on more cushions while she popped succulent dates into his mouth. His heart picked up speed at the notion.

When did you become so fanciful, Weston? he asked himself on a swell of annoyance. Her behavior was downright suspicious. He couldn't afford to be distracted by her looks, nor by the dazzling smile he saw her exchange with her maid. The reminder didn't stop him from imagining how he would feel if she smiled at him like that.

Princess Nadia was talking to the maid, both of them shielded from any eyes but Gage's by a thick screen of bushes, but she didn't stop moving, swiftly shedding her culottes and white silk shirt until she was clad only in a lacy camisole and panties that left her legs bare.

They had to be the longest legs in the sheikdom, Gage thought. Movements like hers, so graceful and unconsciously seductive, while she was clad in so little, should be outlawed in Tamir. Come to think of it, they probably were.

Pleasure shafted through him, as inappropriate as it was unexpected. Instead of seeming furtive, as befitted a potential traitor, her movements and ready smile made her look young and carefree, as if she had shed her cares with her clothes.

He frowned as the maid slid out of the traditional Tamir long dress called a *galabiya,* which she'd worn to accompany the princess from the palace. The maid took the culottes and shirt and put them on, while the princess pulled the *galabiya* over her head and settled the folds around her slender body. The two women were of a similar size, so everything fit. And the movements were so slick that Gage guessed this was a regular routine.

Within minutes, the maid was the image of her mistress, except for the long hair she tucked away under a wide-brimmed straw hat. The princess draped the maid's floaty silk scarf over her cropped tresses and shoulders. Both women popped dark glasses over their eyes. Voilà. Instant transformation.

From his research, Gage knew that the maid's name was Tahani. She was a cousin of Nadia's personal attendant, Nargis. Hearing that Tahani had artistic talent, the princess had agreed to teach her to paint in exchange for her services. At least that was the official story. Seeing them together now, Gage suspected that the maid's resemblance to the princess had a lot to do with Nadia wanting Tahani at her side.

Gage panned the glasses in a wide arc. Where the devil was the princess's bodyguard while all this was taking place? Or was the man in league with his mistress? Seconds later he had his answer. On the other side of the bushes, the bodyguard was unloading a heap of equipment from the back of the princess's car. As Gage watched, the man carried the load back to the two women. They kept their faces averted, pretending to talk, so the man didn't notice anything amiss.

The equipment turned out to be painting gear, Gage saw as the man set up an easel, stool and other artist's paraphernalia. Immediately the maid, in the princess's clothes, settled herself on the stool and began to sketch. The princess gave a low bow to her supposed mistress, then hurried away.

Nicely done, Gage thought with a twinge of professional jealousy. As far as the bodyguard knew, he was still keeping an eye on the princess while her maid was sent off on some errand. Gage decided to find out what the errand was.

She had aroused more than his curiosity, he admitted, not convinced that his interest was as professional as he wished.

He gave himself a few seconds to see in which direction her car was headed, then retrieved his rental car from where he'd secreted it in a grove of trees after following the group from the palace.

Being careful to stay out of sight of the painting pair, he found a track he could use to cut through an olive grove and come out slightly ahead of the princess on the only main road in the area—the one she had to take, unless she was heading back to the palace. Gage would stake his inheritance that she wasn't going home.

He was right. By the time she drove carefully around the bend behind him—taking no chances on breaking any laws that got her noticed, he assumed—he was in position. His car was half off the road, the front wheels in a ditch, and his forehead resting against the steering wheel. He'd used the trick a half dozen times in his covert career, and it never failed to get a result. Who could resist a lone motorist in trouble?

Not the princess. He slitted one eye in time to see her pull up ahead of him and get out. When she reached his open window, he gave a convincing groan and lifted his head. She touched a hand to his forehead. "Don't move, you could be seriously injured."

Her hand against his skin felt blissfully cool, her touch feather-light. He was tempted to do as she commanded and stay where he was, hoping she'd go right on caressing his fevered brow. But if he did, she'd probably insist on calling an ambulance, ending his chance of speaking to her alone. Given the usually restricted life led by the princess of Tamir, he might not get another chance to decide for himself whether she was traitor material or not. The opportunity was too good to waste.

He opened his eyes, finding that she was every bit as lovely close up as she had appeared in his field glasses. Something twisted inside him. She was more than lovely. She was breathtaking. His hand itched to remove the dark glasses so he could get a good look at her eyes. Black as the pits of Hades, he told himself. Black as the night, with the light of a thousand stars in them, his errant mind insisted.

He resisted the image. Black nights could hide deadly secrets, like the identity of his friend's killer. However tempting the idea, for Conrad's sake and for King Marcus, Gage couldn't afford to let himself fall under Nadia's spell.

Still, poetic images insisted on forming in his mind as he looked at the princess. Not the princess—her maid, he reminded himself. He wasn't supposed to know that they'd traded places. He made himself rub his eyes as if dazed. "I ran the blasted car off the road. I was too tired to be driving."

He saw her assess the car, one of the more expensive Branxton sports models, and guessed she was theorizing about him and how he came to be here. "You're not from Tamir," she said.

"England," he supplied, quoting from his cover story. He saw her forehead crinkle above the glasses. He added, "I'm here to head up a British trade mission to your country, although I won't present my credentials to Sheik Ahmed Kamal until tomorrow."

His home country of Penwyck retained enough historic ties with the English monarchy that his own Hugh Grant-like accent was utterly convincing. It wouldn't have mattered. Gage could do several American accents, broad Australian or Italian equally well. But he felt comfortable reverting to his native accent and was pleased to see by her expression that she had accepted his cover completely. Mentally he thanked his godfather, the British ambassador to Tamir, who had agreed to let Gage use the embassy as the base for his fictional trade mission.

"Welcome to Tamir, Mr...."

"Gage Weston. Please, call me Gage." He offered her his hand through the car window and saw her smile at the foolishness of the gesture, given the circumstances.

"Tahani Kadil. I work for the Kamal family," she said. "We should save the rest of the formalities for later. Right now you need an ambulance."

"Really, I'm perfectly all right," he assured her. "If you could just help me out so I can get some air..."

She levered the door open with difficulty, since she was pulling uphill. Strong, as well as lovely, he thought, struggling against the admiration that threatened to cloud his judgment. A wonderful jasmine scent filled his nostrils as she leaned across him to undo his seat belt, her full breasts brushing across his chest. He wasn't entirely acting as he worked to catch his breath.

Nadia slid an arm around Gage and helped him out, becoming aware of the strength in him and the fast beating of his heart, which she blamed on his accident. Her own was beating a touch too fast, she noticed, not wanting to think that the stranger was the cause.

He wasn't handsome enough to turn her head, even had she been susceptible. His features were a touch too well defined, his jaw too thrusting, his lips too full and sensuous. Too arrogant and self-assured to be her type, although she accepted that the collective effect stamped him as a man to be reckoned with.

She felt the heat from his body steaming through her, pushing up her internal temperature. The air seemed to crackle with warmth and energy, and she sensed it had little to do with the balmy summer day. At least, she hadn't noticed the charged atmosphere until she touched Gage.

What had she unleashed by stopping to assist him?

Nothing she couldn't handle, she told herself firmly. After her one tragic experience of love, she had vowed never to be swept off her feet again. So it mattered little if Gage was or wasn't handsome, could or couldn't cause her heart to race, did or didn't force visions into her mind of being held in strong arms, kissed with a tenderness that brought tears to her eyes, loved as only a real man could love.

Stop this, she commanded herself before her imagination could run away with her completely. Gage was a diplomat. Her father's court was awash with his kind. They were charming, sometimes flirtatious, but ultimately out to achieve their country's aims by whatever means they had.

She had been courted before by men wanting to gain her father's ear. Probably would be again. Her resistance should be well developed by now, she thought as she assisted Gage to the side of the car before releasing him.

So why did he make her feel as though she had no resistance at all?

Gage rested his back against the car, making a show of recovering slowly. "Lucky for me that you stopped by. I was looking for the road to the British Embassy and must have taken a wrong turning."

"You certainly did. You're headed in the opposite direction." Her smile was the epitome of innocence and beauty. Maybe beauty, but not innocence, he thought, hardening his heart. Innocent people didn't parade around in disguise, using false names.

"Perhaps you'd be good enough to point me in the right direction," he said.

She looked shocked. "You can't mean to get behind the wheel again, can you? You could have a concussion. Even if your car is drivable, which I doubt."

He glanced at it and nodded agreement. The Branxton was perfectly drivable, but he had no intention of telling her that. He wanted her to do exactly what she did next. "I'll take you to Marhaba. I'm meeting someone there who can check you over. Marhaba is a large town, so once we know you're all right, you can have your car towed there for repairs and hire another car to take you to the embassy."

Meeting someone? A contact with whom she shared state secrets? A lover? Gage was surprised at the intensity of his resistance to the idea. It was the most logical one, next to her being a traitor, but he found he didn't like to think of her being either. Hardly a professional assessment, he knew, but he couldn't seem to avoid it.

He had the feeling that Princess Nadia was the most dangerous woman he had ever met. With a nature that screamed seduction without any effort on her part, and looks to distract any man, she could start a war—or finish one—and not even know she'd done it, he thought. Tamir's answer to Helen of Troy.

Minutes later he was settled in the passenger seat of her car. They were riding in half-a-million dollars' worth of customized Bentley, he calculated, appreciating the elegance of the leather seats and burred-walnut paneling. As he got in, he'd noticed a bar and television in the back seat, where presumably the princess usually traveled.

If he'd been the bodyguard, he'd have had a few qualms about letting the maid take off in such a valuable car, Gage mused. Tamir had no prohibitions against women driving, but a princess would normally have a chauffeur. He wondered how Nadia came to be so competent behind the wheel.

"What do you do at the palace?" he asked

She kept her attention on the road while she spoke to him. "Have you heard of Princess Nadia?"

"Sheik Ahmed's eldest daughter," he supplied, knowing she'd expect a diplomat to have been briefed on such details.

"Tahani Kadil is her personal maid," Nadia went on.

She was careful not to compound the lie, he noticed. A late rush of conscience, or a wish to stick to the truth as much as she could? He found himself hoping the latter was true. He pushed the thought aside, annoyed. Much more of this and he'd be writing her an alibi himself, rather than facing facts. Her actions today had shot her to the top of his list of suspects.

Since starting this investigation four months ago, Gage had come to agree with Conrad that the most likely traitor in the Kamal circle was the sheik's closest adviser and attorney, Butrus Dabir.

Was it coincidence that Nadia was engaged to marry Dabir? And how much of an accomplice did it make her?

Gage didn't believe in coincidence, so either Nadia was a traitor or Dabir was, and he was using her in some way, or planned to. The more Gage learned about the people Dabir did business with, the more he accepted Conrad's dying suggestion, carved in the dust, that Dabir had ties with the Brothers of Darkness. All Gage needed was evidence.

Nadia could be in league with her fiancé. Until he had some answers, Gage couldn't afford to let himself get sidetracked by her, although he recognized how easily that could happen.

He hadn't been sidetracked by a beautiful woman in a long time. Five years, his statistics-loving mind supplied. Five years since he'd fallen hook, line and sinker for the daughter of a man he'd been investigating on suspicion of selling government secrets to his country's enemies. The man had been caught with enough evidence to put him away for life, but Gage had found nothing to implicate the daughter, Jenice.

Gage had believed her story that her father had blackmailed her into helping him, threatening to kill her if she betrayed him.

She had seemed so frightened, so impossibly lovely and fragile, that all of Gage's protective instincts had been aroused. He had taken Jenice home with him to Penwyck, introduced her to his family and his uncle Morgan, the king. They had taken the lovely, fey creature into their hearts, and the king had promised to grant her asylum. Gage had been there every step of the way, helping her adjust to life in his country, knowing he was falling in love with her but unable to stop himself.

What was the saying about a fool for love? Conrad had accused Gage of behaving like a giddy teenager, instead of an experienced intelligence specialist who should have known better. He should have listened to his friend.

Jenice had promised to marry him as soon as he came home from his latest assignment. He still didn't know what would have happened if he hadn't returned a week early to find her in the arms of the man who had hired Gage to put her father away. Under relentless interrogation, the pair admitted that they had set her father up so they could get their hands on his considerable assets, at which point they planned to run away together.

In floods of tears, Jenice had sworn that she loved Gage, that none of this had been meant to happen. He presumed she meant the nights she'd spent in his bed, vowing her undying love, and wondered whether she had intended to tell him the truth before or after they were married.

He hadn't waited to find out. Ignoring her pleas, he'd escorted them back to their own country, leaving them to the mercy of the local authorities. Then he'd returned to Penwyck and gone on a bender that lasted a week, or so Conrad told him afterward.

When the headache had cleared, Gage had promised himself that never again would he fall for a woman's wiles. If he married, it would be to a Penwyck woman whose pedigree he knew as far back as his own. Love wouldn't enter into the bargain. He would provide for her to the best of his ability, and in return, she would give him the children he wanted.

Belatedly he became aware that Nadia was speaking to him. "What is your area of interest, Gage? Aerospace products? Electronics? Chemicals?"

He masked his surprise. A Tamir princess with an interest in trade? "The invisible economy," he said, testing her.

She nodded. "Stockbroking, banking, insurance, worth over a hundred billion pounds to your country last year."

This time he couldn't hide his astonishment. "You're remarkably well informed for…"

"A woman?" she queried, sounding defensive.

"I was going to say for someone who must lead a relatively sheltered life at the palace," he said, impressed in spite of himself. Brains, as well as beauty. Even more reason to watch himself.

Her hands tightened on the wheel. "In Tamir, education is for all."

But not equal opportunity for women, especially royal women, he knew from his research. Obviously it was a sore point with the princess. Sore enough to make her turn to the Brothers of Darkness to fulfill her need for greater challenge? Or perhaps to get even with her father for holding her back? Gage knew he couldn't discount either possibility.

"Will you get into trouble for picking me up?" he asked, thinking of the restrictions he knew applied to women in her country. Tamir was more liberal than most of its neighbors, but being born male was still a definite advantage.

She shrugged. "It wouldn't be the first time."

"You make a habit of collecting stray motorists?"

"Hardly. And this was an emergency."

"Hardly," he echoed her tone. "I could have waited until a male driver came along."

He saw her hands tense on the wheel. "He couldn't have done any more."

So he had hit a nerve. Good. Gage decided to press the point, hoping to learn more. "He could have helped me push my car back onto the road."

Her dark gaze flickered over him, then back to the road. "Male chauvinism? I thought you British believed in equality."

"You know the saying about some being more equal than others?"

"Only too well."

He winced at her bitter tone. "I didn't say I believe it."

"What do you believe in, Gage?"

Her question caught him unprepared. "The usual virtues."

"Money, power and status?"

He found he didn't like being thought so shallow, even by a possible traitor. "They have their uses. But I wouldn't call them virtues. I was speaking of the right to live your own life your way, provided you don't harm anyone else."

"Your wife is a lucky woman," she observed dryly.

Fishing? he wondered, at the same time feeling foolishly flattered by her interest. "I'm not married. What about you?" he asked, although he already knew the answer.

She gave a quick shake of her head. "Not yet."

Her tone said *Not ever.* Interesting, given what he knew about her and Butrus Dabir. "But you have plans?" he persisted.

"I'm engaged to be married, yes."

He wondered what her resigned sigh said about her relationship. "Your fiancé won't object to me driving with you?"

"He's away a lot of the time."

What Dabir didn't know wouldn't hurt him, Gage read into her comment. He tensed. He might have his suspicions about the man, but he was entitled to the truth from his fiancée. Having suffered at the hands of a scheming woman himself, Gage didn't wish the experience on anyone else.

The princess didn't look like a scheming woman, he thought. With the breeze from the open window tugging strands of raven hair out from under her scarf and bringing a flush of peach to her cheeks, she looked beautiful, exotic, kissable.

He subdued the notion. He couldn't afford to feel anything

for her when the lifestyle she obviously resisted might have
driven her to extremes. Even to being in league with Conrad's killers? The sooner he found out for sure, the better.

"We've arrived," she said.

He looked around with interest. Expecting a village, he
was surprised to find them approaching the shell of an old
fort set on a hill overlooking a large modern town. Marhaba,
he assumed. The big faceless fort, with its whitewashed
walls, would have looked at home against a backdrop of reed
and mud-brick huts a century ago. Thick stands of greenery
surrounded the approach to the fort.

The princess drove the car into a walled courtyard, and he
saw that the outward appearance of the building was decep-
tive. Inside, apart from the cobblestones and whitewash, the
building had been completely modernized.

The other thing he noticed was the throng of children who
rushed to the car. They ranged in age from about four to
eleven or twelve. All of them seemed to want to be close to
Nadia.

"Who are all these children?" he asked as they got out.

She was immediately surrounded. Over the heads of the
youngsters vying for her attention, she smiled. "They're orphans from Marhaba's poorest families, waiting to be
adopted or placed in foster homes." She hugged each child
in turn.

"Who's this?" Gage pointed to the toddler peeping at him
from behind her skirt.

"Samir. I call him Sammy. He doesn't care for strangers."

"You going to say hello, Sammy?"

The boy buried his face in Nadia's skirt. Gage squatted at
child level. "Hey, I don't bite." He reached behind Sammy's
ear and pulled out a coin. It was the oldest trick in the book,
one Gage had taught himself when he was only a few years
older than Sammy. The toddler's eyes went round as saucers.

"More."

This time Gage made the coin disappear. Sammy shook
his head and felt his hair, obviously mystified. Gage reached
behind the child's other ear and plucked out the coin, then

placed it in the small hand. The other children watched in fascination.

Sammy giggled and held out the coin to give it back. Gage closed the toddler's fingers around it. "You keep it. Every kid needs a magic coin."

About as much as they needed parents, he thought. How had Sammy lost his? Gage was surprised by how much he wanted to know. He also wanted to know what Nadia was doing here. Not playing Lady Bountiful, or she'd have arrived as a princess. The children's welcome suggested she was a regular—and popular—visitor. What in blazes was she up to?

Sammy held out his arms and Nadia picked him up. "What do you say to Mr. Weston?"

"'Tank you.'" The little boy tugged at Nadia's concealing scarf, almost dislodging it. "Candy for Sammy?"

She tucked the scarf back into place. "Later, sweetheart, after you eat all your lunch." She glanced at Gage. "You're welcome to join us."

"You've done enough for me already," he said. "I can walk to the town from here, so I'll be on my way." In the town he might be able to find out more about this place and Nadia's role in it. If it was a front for the Brothers of Darkness, it was amazingly convincing.

Like the princess herself. Seeing her with Sammy in her arms, Gage had trouble believing she was anything but what she seemed, a caring compassionate friend to these children. Maybe dodging her royal role was the only way she could get to see them.

And maybe it wasn't.

Over Sammy's objections, she set the child down. The toddler grabbed a handful of her skirt and hung on, making Gage smile in spite of himself.

"You're not going anywhere until Warren has checked you over," Nadia insisted. "If you collapse on the way to town, I'll never forgive myself."

He was more likely to die of curiosity than anything else,

but she believed he had injured himself running his car off the road, so he murmured a reluctant assent.

She untangled Sammy from her skirt and sent him off to play with the others, the coin clutched tightly in his fingers. Then she led Gage through a double set of carved wooden doors that looked as old as the fort.

Beyond them was a spacious room set up as an infirmary. A tall, thin, red-haired man with an abundance of freckles was putting a dressing on a little girl's grazed knee. From the state of the room, the girl was the last of a long line of patients. Gage felt a stab of guilt, wondering if Nadia would have been helping out here if she hadn't been delayed by his staged accident.

The little girl smiled when she saw Nadia. "Hello, Addie."

The doctor looked up. "Hi there, running late today?"

"I picked up a passenger on the way," she said.

Addie? How many names did this woman go by? Gage gathered that Warren was a doctor, but how did he—and this place—fit into Nadia's secret life?

The doctor washed his hands, then lifted the child off the examination table. "There you go, Drina. Next time try walking across the courtyard, instead of tearing across at ninety miles an hour."

The little girl giggled. "Thank you, Dr. Warren."

The doctor shepherded the child out and closed the door, then held out his hand to Gage. "Welcome. I'm Warren Walsh. I gather you're a friend of Addie's?"

Gage shook the man's hand. "Gage Weston. I had a little accident on the way, and…Addie was kind enough to give me a lift."

"Gage ran his car into a ditch and knocked himself out on the steering wheel," she supplied helpfully. "I thought you should take a look at him before we let him wander off."

"Quite right. Sit yourself on the table."

Gage hesitated. "I'm perfectly fine now."

Warren frowned. "A period of unconsciousness, however brief, is always cause for concern."

Nadia gave Gage a little push. "You should be at least as brave as Drina."

Gage found he didn't care for the way she lumped him in with her young charge. He moved stiffly to the table, perched on the edge and submitted to the doctor's checkup, trying not to grit his teeth too obviously.

"You're in pretty good shape," the doctor said after giving him a cursory going-over. "Are you an athlete?"

"A diplomat," he amended.

"With the British Trade Delegation," Nadia added.

Gage knew he had to get out of here before the doctor stumbled across any of the battle scars he carried. Considering his line of work, he hadn't done too badly, but the number of scars would arouse any doctor's curiosity.

He slid off the table. "See, I told you I was fine."

"I'm inclined to agree," the doctor said. "You're in the best shape of any diplomat I've ever met."

"I work out a lot," Gage explained, deciding it was time for a change of subject. "What do you call this place?"

"The Marhaba Children's Shelter," Nadia explained. "The children live here until homes can be found for them."

"Which sometimes takes longer than we like," Warren contributed. "These children are the poorest of the poor. Better-off families are sometimes reluctant to adopt them."

Nadia nodded. "Although they are the most delightful children you could ever wish to meet."

Like Sammy, Gage thought. The little fellow couldn't be more than four, but he had bright eyes and a radiant smile. He was obviously attached to Nadia, or Addie or whatever name she went by here.

"How did you get involved with this place?" he asked Nadia.

Warren laughed. "She doesn't have enough to do back home."

Nadia shot Gage a quick look. "Don't worry, Warren knows who I am, but once I drive through the gates, I'm simply Addie, the children's friend. I come as often as I can to help out."

That explained two of the multiple identities, Gage thought. Did Warren know her as Tahani, the maid, or Nadia, the princess? Since he wasn't supposed to know about her royal identity, he couldn't very well ask. He pulled out his wallet. "In return for your help today, I'm happy to make a contribution."

"We don't need your money," Nadia said. "The children are provided with everything they require. What they don't have are loving homes."

Gage felt a ripple of something he couldn't pin down. Nadia couldn't possibly know that he wanted children of his own. "In my job, I'm hardly in a position to give a child a home," he said.

"Then we'll settle for your money, Gage," Warren said cheerfully. "The infirmary could use some new equipment."

Nadia frowned at him. "You should have told me."

The doctor rested a hand on her arm. "You do enough as it is. Risk enough as it is."

Gage's professional instincts went on alert. Now what did the doctor mean by that? Was the place a front for something underhand, after all? Gage peeled off some notes, hoping he wasn't making a donation to the Brothers of Darkness. He handed them to the doctor, who nodded his thanks.

"Now that I know I'll live, I'll be on my way," Gage said. "Thank you, both of you, for your help."

The doctor tucked the money into his shirt pocket. "You're welcome."

Nadia smiled. "Try not to fall asleep at the wheel next time."

"Good advice. Maybe I'll see you at the palace sometime."

A shadow fell over her lovely features. He couldn't see her eyes behind the dark glasses, and he found himself wishing he could. He had a feeling her eyes were her most beautiful feature. Time to get out of here, he told himself. The lady was trouble.

"I don't usually have much to do with the diplomatic corps," she said. "Sheik Ahmed will no doubt receive you in the reception hall. My place is usually in the family apart-ments.''

No wonder she wasn't worried that he'd spot her and rec-ognize that the princess and ''Tahani'' were one and the same. She was counting on him being kept out of her way. He'd have to do something about that. A bit of research should turn up the ways and means. He gathered that no one except her maid knew about her extracurricular activities, so he'd have an edge when they met again.

He was determined they *would* meet again. In fact, he was looking forward to it. He still didn't know whether she had any connection with Conrad's death or with the Brothers of Darkness, but she was definitely up to something. Unmasking her was going to be a pleasure.

Chapter 2

"Aren't you concerned that your British diplomat will blow the whistle on you at the palace?" the doctor asked as soon as the infirmary door closed behind Gage.

Nadia frowned. "He thinks I'm Tahani, the ladies' maid. As long as I stay out of his way when he presents his credentials at court, there's no reason for him to think I'm Princess Nadia."

The doctor tidied away his instruments. "I still don't understand why you don't simply tell your father what you're doing here. Sheik Ahmed should approve of you doing charity work with orphans."

Nadia began to help him restore order in the infirmary. "I don't want my father's approval. I want this work to be my own, independent of my royal status. If my father found out, he'd expect me to come here as Princess Nadia, with the full entourage. As plain old Addie, I can relax and be myself, get my hands dirty without someone rushing to take over and let the children rush up to me without a minder going into guard-dog mode."

The doctor's expression softened. "You could never be described as plain or old. And I can understand your guards wanting to protect you."

His tone made Nadia look at him in astonishment. "You aren't getting soft on me, are you, Warren?"

"Me, soft? You know me better than that."

His quick denial sounded unconvincing, and for the first time Nadia asked herself if she was doing the right thing working so closely with Warren when she had no interest in him romantically. She had thought he felt the same, but now she began to wonder.

"Don't worry, I'm not terminally lovesick yet," he assured her, as if reading her mind. "As long as you know I'm here for you anytime."

"I know," she agreed, her conscience troubled. Warren was a good man. After qualifying as a doctor, he had left his native Australia to work in parts of the world where his skill could make a difference. He had come to Tamir on holiday and fallen in love with the island kingdom, he had told her when they were introduced at an art gallery two years ago.

Hiking around the hills, he had stumbled upon a group of children living by themselves in the ruined fort and had contacted the princess to see what could be done for them. With her help and money from her private allowance, they had made the fort into a comfortable facility that now housed more than a dozen children at a time until homes were found for them. Warren had recruited a team of women from Marhaba to take care of the children on a roster system.

"You should be proud of what you've done here," Warren said.

"Not as much as you should be."

"I don't have to deal with the same restrictions that you do."

Of course not, he was a man. She didn't want Warren to know, but he was the main reason she couldn't tell her father what she did here. The sheik would be furious if he knew his eldest daughter was working side by side with a man, not to mention an unmarried one. He would probably forbid her to set foot in the orphanage again.

She gave a deep sigh. "I wish I could do more. By now I should be running my own show, not living at the palace like a dutiful daughter, having to sneak around in my maid's clothes to have the freedom to pursue my own interests. If I was a man, I'd be a minister in my father's cabinet by now."

Warren squeezed her shoulder. "The government's loss is the children's gain."

"I suppose so. When I was twenty-five and approached my father about a real job, he said my time would come. I never dreamed I'd still be waiting around a decade later."

"You haven't exactly been waiting around," Warren pointed out. "Between the sculptures you created for the royal palaces and your paintings, you have a body of work any artist would envy."

"Try telling my father that." She had tried many times, but the sheik seemed unable or unwilling to understand the importance of her art in her life. He tolerated her activities as a hobby, even allowing her to exhibit her work to raise money for charity, but plainly didn't regard her the way she saw herself, as a serious artist.

"Your father probably thought you'd be married by now, and the question would have resolved itself," Warren said.

With a savage gesture, she shook out a clean sheet for the examination table. "He tried hard enough, until I told him if he paraded one more minor royal in front of me like cattle at a livestock sale, I was going to throw a tantrum right in the middle of the Grand Ballroom. I wouldn't marry a princeling if he was the last man on earth."

Warren laughed. "Why ever not?"

"The only reason any of them want to marry me is because of who I am."

With the ease of long practice, Warren returned instruments to their respective trays. "You underestimate yourself, Addie. You're one of the most beautiful women in the kingdom, also one of the most intelligent."

"That's my problem. Most of the marriage prospects my father has dredged up don't want intelligence. They want compliance. Can you imagine me, compliant?"

Warren masked his smile. "It is rather difficult."

She felt her temper reach boiling point. "I'd sooner marry that…that British diplomat who can't even keep his car on a perfectly straight road."

"Gage Weston? He hardly seems your type."

"Precisely my point. He'd be the sort of man I could manage, instead of having him manage me."

Warren closed the instrument cabinet. "Are you sure about that? When I was checking him over, he didn't strike me as the manageable type."

Nadia had to concede that Gage hadn't seemed especially compliant to her, either. His accident had been foolish, but then, he had admitted to being exhausted. He hadn't told her where he'd flown in from before Tamir, so he could easily have been suffering from jet lag.

As the doctor had observed, Gage Weston was in superb physical condition. Helping him out of the car had made her aware of how lean and muscular he was, a rarity among diplomats, who spent much of their time behind a desk or socializing after dark. She had a feeling that socializing wasn't what Gage preferred doing after dark. What he might prefer, she didn't want to think about.

He had compassion, too, also rare in her experience. Most men wouldn't have bothered trying to win Sammy's trust, but Gage had taken the trouble. And on the way to Marhaba, he had said he believed in equality between men and women. Accepting her help proved he wasn't just paying lip service to the belief.

Altogether a formidable man.

Why was she letting him disturb her so? If she saw him again, it would be from a distance, at some royal function with hundreds of other members of the diplomatic community. She didn't even have to talk to him if she didn't want to.

The thought was oddly bothersome.

"If you're so against marriage, why did you agree to your father's wish that you marry Butrus Dabir?" the doctor asked. "Surely he couldn't force you?"

She wasn't fooled by his casual tone. Now that she knew Warren was attracted to her, she resolved to be careful not to hurt his feelings. "I'm not in love with him, if that's what you're asking. And he doesn't love me. We respect one another, and his position as my father's closest adviser makes him a suitable match."

"It sounds a bit coldhearted."

"Royal marriages are frequently arranged for reasons other than love. If I must marry, I'd rather it be to a man like Butrus, who doesn't dress up his reasons for proposing."

The doctor looked surprised. "He actually told you he doesn't love you?"

"Not in so many words, but I've known him for many years. He's more interested in money and power than in love. Marrying me guarantees him both. Don't worry," she assured the doctor, who looked more and more unhappy, "as a married woman, I also gain independence from my father."

"Surely any husband could have freed you from your father."

She nodded. "Unlike Butrus, most men aren't traveling much of the time. While he's away, I'll have the freedom to do as I please."

She straightened. "I'd better round up the children for their lunch. I have to return to the palace early today. Father wants to see me about something."

"Tahani will be disappointed. I gather she likes taking your place and dabbling in art while you're here."

Nadia frowned. "Sometimes I wish I could be in two places at once. Then I could spend more time painting, as well as looking after the children."

"Beats me how you get so much done as it is. I saw your new show at the Alcamira Gallery and the work is wonderful."

Nadia bit her lip. She was her own toughest critic and knew Warren's praise wasn't empty flattery. She *did* have talent. She only wished she could have attended one of the world's fine art schools, instead of studying subjects her father considered more appropriate. Like her siblings, she had been sent abroad, carefully chaperoned, to complete her education. In between her approved courses, she had studied art as best she could by visiting galleries, talking to the artists and convincing her father that attending hobby classes was a harmless indulgence.

Some hobby, she thought and grimaced. "I work twice as hard when I do get time to paint."

"As long as you don't burn yourself out."

"I won't." Her patience would give out before her energy.

"While I was at the gallery, I was tempted to buy one of your watercolors of the hills near here. They're wonderful," Warren said.

"I'll arrange for you to have one as a gift," Nadia said, glad that there was something she could do for Warren, since she couldn't give him what he plainly wanted.

His face flushed. "I'll treasure it, both for artistic excellence and because you painted it."

"You always know how to cheer me up." She wished she could do the same for him, but knew she could never feel more for the doctor than friendship.

"I'll live, you know," he said quietly.

She stared at him. Had he been reading her mind? "I'm glad, because you're very special to me," she said. "You're the first man I've met with whom I can simply be myself."

Gage Weston had also treated her like a normal person, came the unexpected thought. But he'd believed she was Ta-hani Kadil, the maid. He was bound to behave differently if he knew she was Princess Nadia. All the same, she found herself wishing she could meet him again, if only to see his reaction when he found out who she was.

Nadia should have remembered the saying about being careful what you wish for. She had barely returned to her apartments in the royal palace and changed into a gold-embroidered *galabiya,* when she received a summons from her father.

Anxiety rippled through her. Had he somehow discovered where she'd been? She lifted her head. If he had, she would deal with it. She was a woman, not a child to be dragged over the carpet for some misdemeanor.

In this rebellious frame of mind, she stalked past the guard holding open the massive door for her and into her father's study. Actually, "study" was a misnomer. The room was larger than the living rooms in most ordinary households. The sheik's long mahogany desk stood at the far end of a vast, hand-woven carpet that depicted aspects of Tamir's history.

Automatically Nadia's glance went to the chair next to the sheik's desk, where her mother frequently sat, silently supportive as she worked at her embroidery. Alima would never be so indiscreet as to disagree with her husband overtly, but her gentle smile was always encouraging, and she held strong opinions of her own that she shared with the sheik in private. Today the padded chair by the tall arched window was empty and Nadia was on her own.

She tried to moderate her stride to a more womanly walk as she crossed to his desk, then abandoned the attempt when the Sheik didn't look up.

"You wanted to see me, Father?" she said to gain his attention.

He signed a document with a flourish, added the royal seal and handed the paper to a hovering attendant with a few words of instruction. Naturally her father would finish whatever state business was on hand before attending to her. Ahmed had been on the throne of Tamir since he was twenty, and he put his country ahead of everything, even family concerns.

He looked every inch a ruler, she thought with a contrary feeling of pride. Well into his sixties, his once-dark hair and beard now almost white, he still lived up to his nickname, the Lion of Tamir. Just sometimes, she wished he could be more father than monarch.

Without waiting for an invitation, she seated herself in one of the leather armchairs opposite the desk. Sheik Ahmed looked up at last, a frown etching his forehead.

She knew exactly why he was frowning. "Father, I like my hair this way. I think it suits me."

"That is a matter of opinion, my daughter."

"And yours is very clear on the subject."

"Nadia," the Sheik said on a heavy sigh, "why does our slightest interaction have to involve confrontation?"

Why couldn't she be more compliant like Samira and Leila? she read between the lines. "I am as I am," she said with a typically Tamir shrug.

Ahmed's hawklike features softened. "And your mother and I cherish you as you are."

She heard the "but," although he didn't say it. She also saw the deepening lines around his eyes, and the shadows under them. When he had spoken of giving up the throne in favor of Nadia's brother, Rashid, Nadia had thought it unlikely that the sheik would actually step down. Now she started to wonder if Rashid had interests of his own he wanted to pursue. That she might not be the only member of the family chafing at the restrictions of her position was food for thought.

"Are you well, Father?" she asked.

"Worried about me, Nadia?"

"Of course. I love you."

He looked pleased. "I know you do, in spite of our differences. And I love you, my daughter."

She felt a momentary pang at the thought that he wouldn't always be there for her and had to blink away the moisture that sprang to her eyes. "I don't suppose you summoned me with an exciting project you want me to undertake," she said in an effort to lighten the moment.

He massaged his eyes. "One day I might surprise you."

She knew better than to take him seriously. "Is something wrong?"

"Relations with our neighbors in Montebello aren't as smooth as I wish they could be, but as you would say, what else is new?"

"I thought King Marcus's attitude toward Tamir had improved greatly since Hassan saved the life of the king's son and restored him to his home." On that occasion, her brother had been a true hero, she thought.

The sheik nodded. "My sons possess great qualities of leadership. Having Rashid married to Marcus's daughter has also improved relations between our two countries, so there is hope yet." He smiled, some of his usual vigor infusing his strong features. "I actually want to discuss a more personal matter with you—Butrus has petitioned me to nominate your wedding date."

"He asked you, instead of me?"

"Butrus knows the value of following protocol."

He would, she thought in annoyance. As an attorney, Butrus did most things by the book.

She thought of her conversation with Warren, reminding herself that Butrus was handsome, worldly and intelligent. She subdued the voice insisting that love should come into the bargain somewhere. Once had been enough for that.

His name was Gordon Perry. He was British, and five years younger than Nadia. Gordon had been an art teacher on sabbatical in Tamir with a backpack filled with sketchbooks and pencils. Nadia remembered their meeting vividly. Six years ago she had decided to go to the seashore to sketch. Unbeknownst to her, Gordon had the same plan.

With her bodyguard watching, she couldn't talk openly to a strange man, so they had started to exchange furtive notes. Like a couple of schoolchildren in class, she thought, feeling her mouth curve into a smile of nostalgia. She had no doubt that the enforced silence had added to his allure. A wealth of meaning could be contained in a look, she had found.

Their friendship grew, starting with written notes about

each other's work and blossoming into more personal matters. Lulled by the apparent innocence of the meetings, the bodyguard relaxed his vigilance enough that they could talk briefly. She still treasured the encouragement Gordon had given her, and the advice he had offered about her work.

After several supposedly chance meetings outdoors, they had arranged to meet at her studio, in the guise of Gordon giving her and her sisters art lessons. With her father's approval, she had engaged Gordon to redesign the studio so they could spend more time together.

No one had suspected that she was in love with the handsome art teacher until her father had surprised her by paying a rare visit to her studio and found them kissing. Gordon had been dismissed from the palace and she had endured long lectures about honor and duty. Instead of stemming her father's fury, telling him she wanted to marry Gordon had fired the sheik's wrath to new heights.

She had been agonizing over how she could contact Gordon when she saw on the television news that he had drowned while swimming off a notoriously dangerous stretch of the coastline. She would never know whether the ending of their affair had affected his judgment, but it had certainly affected hers. His body had been flown home to his family in England for burial, leaving her no ritual way to assuage her grief.

Instead, she had painted his portrait with all the love searing her soul. Then she had burned the painting as a symbol of the futility of someone in her position wanting to marry for love.

The acceptance hadn't been enough to make her look kindly on any of the men her father paraded before her over the next few years. Her feelings for Gordon had been too precious, too raw. But time and her father's persistence had finally worn her down.

When the sheik had suggested that Butrus would make a suitable husband for her, she was beyond caring. The man she loved was gone forever. She might as well marry Butrus and make her father happy. Butrus's involvement in state business meant she would be free of his supervision a lot of the time.

"Have you decided on a wedding date?" she asked her father, wrenching her thoughts back to the present.

"Three months from now should give you time to make the final preparations. Your mother already has her plans in hand, I understand."

The sheik sounded uninterested, as most men were when wedding plans were mentioned, she had noticed. Not unlike herself, she thought. She submitted to discussions and dress fittings to please her mother, but wanted only to get the formalities over with.

She knew her attitude bewildered her sister, Samira, who was far more enthusiastic than Nadia. Samira should marry Butrus, Nadia thought, knowing it wasn't possible. There was already a man in Samira's life. Her eyes sparkled whenever Nadia brought up the question, but so far Samira was remarkably closemouthed about the details.

"There is something else," Sheik Ahmed went on, recapturing her attention.

"Yes, Father?"

"England has sent a new emissary to lead their trade delegation to Tamir. He presents his credentials to me tomorrow. Following the formal proceedings, I have arranged a gathering to welcome the delegation. Since many of the delegates will be accompanied by their wives, I should like you to act as hostess on this occasion. Butrus will be there."

A huge lump rose in her throat. "The emissary's name?"

"Gage Weston. He is the godson of the British ambassador, and his credentials are of the highest. Have you heard of him?"

She had done far worse, but she couldn't very well say so to her father. She struggled to find her voice. "Wouldn't Mother be a more suitable hostess?"

The sheik looked irritated with her for stating the obvious.

"Naturally, but Alima has decided to spend another few days in Montebello with Rashid and Julia and our grandson."

Nadia thought fast. She couldn't simply attend the party as Princess Nadia and expect the Englishman not to react. When he did, Butrus would want to know how they'd met, and her cover would be blown.

No longer would she be able go out as Tahani without anyone being the wiser. Nadia should have known the scheme couldn't go on indefinitely, but she was surprised at how keenly she felt the prospective loss.

How would the orphans feel when she was no longer their benefactor? Little Sammy already had to deal with losing his real parents in the fire that had also destroyed his family's farm. He clung to Nadia—his Addie—as to a lifeline. How could she let him think she had abandoned him? Her heart constricted at the thought of being cut off from him and all the other children. Visiting them in her official capacity would be a poor substitute, she knew.

"Samira would make a better hostess. You know I'm likely to say or do something to offend someone," she said on a note of desperation.

Ahmed gave her a knowing look. "Perhaps you should consider this additional practice. As Butrus's wife, you will be his hostess, so you may as well accustom yourself to the role."

"Very well, Father," she said on a note of resignation, and got up to leave.

Her father's voice stayed her a moment longer. "You may be cheered to hear that Gage Weston asked the British ambassador to request an introduction. Evidently Mr. Weston purchased one of your paintings and wishes to meet the artist in person."

Alarm coiled through her. "Surely you don't approve of such a request."

The sheik smiled. "Your reticence is commendable, but your talent is God-given and entitled to be celebrated."

What a time for her father to decide to be conciliatory,

Nadia thought in frustration. Her dislike for Gage Weston grew. "Butrus may object to my having a male admirer," she said.

"An admirer of your work," the sheik corrected. "Butrus wisely knows the difference." He added, "You tell me you wish to be useful, yet when I seek to involve you in state affairs, you're still unhappy."

"Making small talk and ensuring everyone's glass remains full hardly qualifies as state affairs," she said bitterly. "Any competent servant can do that."

"But a servant cannot smooth the way between nations with a smile. Or listen to what is and is not being said, and share his or her thoughts with me afterward."

She was forced to smile. "You make hostessing sound like undercover work."

He nodded. "Diplomacy involves more than overt negotiation. The social route may be indirect, but it is often the oil that lubricates relations between countries."

She knew he was trying to make her feel better about her role and gave a wan smile. Her father couldn't know that her reluctance wasn't to acting as his hostess, at least not this time, but to the prospect of facing Gage Weston again.

His image sprang to her mind much more vividly than she expected. He was taller than she was by a head, with green eyes that looked as if they could see all the way to her soul. Warren had said that Gage was in superb physical condition. Thinking of the muscles rippling under her touch and the energy that had enveloped her as she'd helped him out of the car, she could hardly argue. But what was he like as a man? Could she prevail on him to keep her secret? What would he expect in return?

She wasn't melodramatic enough to think she had saved his life. The accident had been a minor one, and her assistance inconsiderable. But as a diplomat he would want her family's favor. Surely that alone would be enough to buy his silence?

At the same time, she couldn't subdue her fear that Gage Weston was not a man to be bought so easily.

Chapter 3

Samira Kamal bounced into her sister's bedroom and stopped short. "Nadia, what on earth are you wearing that for?"

"Father wants me to act as hostess at tonight's party. I decided to look the part," Nadia told her sister with a calmness she was far from feeling. The prospect of confronting Gage Weston again weighed on her mind and had influenced her choice of dress for the occasion.

Samira looked nonplussed. "But isn't national dress a bit over the top, especially for you?"

Nadia's hands stilled on the veil she was adjusting. "What do you mean, especially for me?"

Samira hesitated. "You must admit you're the most adventurous member of the family, even a bit reckless at times."

Nadia pulled in a steadying breath. "In what way?"

Samira looked flustered. "Going out on your own for hours at a time on those painting expeditions. Father may believe you're indulging in your hobby, but I'm sure there's more to it. I've been dying to ask, do you have a lover?''

Nadia almost laughed. Trust her younger sister to suspect such a thing. ''No, I don't have a lover. I'm an engaged woman. I was going to ask you the same thing.''

She had turned the question on Samira as much to deflect her sister's attention as learn if it was true. Now she was intrigued to see color flood Samira's cheeks. ''What if I do?''

''You...you do?''

Samira wrung her hands. ''You wretch, Nadia. You didn't know, did you.''

''I do now. Is he anyone I know?''

Samira shook her head, her lovely black hair flowing around her shoulders in shimmering waves—the way their father would like to see her older sister's, Nadia thought ruefully. No such luck. Hair like Samira's took lots of work to keep looking so fabulous, and Nadia hated wasting time on such pursuits.

''He isn't from Tamir,'' Samira confessed. ''That's why I've been keeping my feelings to myself.''

''You think father may not approve?''

''I know he won't. He wants me to marry a Tamir man of noble birth.''

''Like Butrus Dabir,'' Nadia said.

''Butrus is a good catch. Handsome, personable. Maybe a little cold at times, but he's a man. They're all the same.''

Not Gage Weston. The thought sprang to Nadia's mind with disturbing certainty. She had seen his reaction to meeting little Sammy. Butrus would have kept his distance, afraid of catching something. But Gage had stepped forward without hesitation and set out to win the little boy's trust. Sammy had responded just as warmly. No, Gage couldn't be described as cold.

''You've gone away from me,'' Samira said. ''Tell me what's really going on with you.''

In fairness Nadia couldn't involve her sister in her affairs and risk getting her into trouble with their father. ''Nothing's going on,'' she replied. ''What's wrong with wearing national dress if I feel like it?''

''Nothing, if you don't mind looking like an escapee from a harem. Aren't you the one who says we're living in a new millennium and should modernize accordingly?''

Nadia turned to the mirror, inspecting her outfit critically. White trousers ballooned around her legs, the fullness caught at each ankle by gold embroidery. Her narrow waist was cinched with a gold circlet. Above it she wore a gossamer-thin blouse of pale-green silk, threaded with gold, the billowing sleeves captured at the wrists by more embroidery. Beneath the translucent blouse, she wore a modest shift of midnight blue. The costume had been passed down to her by her grandmother, and Samira was right; it was rarely worn outside tourist venues or on the most ceremonial occasions and could hardly be called modern.

''Tradition has its place,'' she murmured, turning to check the back. She frowned. ''I don't really look as if I belong in a harem, do I?''

''Actually, no,'' Samira said. ''You look amazing. I wish I were as tall as you and could wear anything I wanted to— although you still haven't told me what you're up to.''

''What makes you think I'm up to anything?''

''I know you too well. The last time father conscripted you to act as his hostess, you wore a low-cut, western evening gown to annoy him. That's it, isn't it? You're hoping to deter him from imposing on you again.''

Relieved that her sister had arrived at a satisfactory explanation for her choice of dress, Nadia nodded. She had really chosen the costume for the diaphanous veil, the only way she could think to hide her features when she met Gage Weston. Her choice, fueled by desperation, was bound to cause comment, as it had done with Samira. Few women in Tamir wore the veil nowadays. Those who did usually let it hang to one side of the face rather than fastening it across their features as Nadia intended to do.

She slipped the veil into place across the lower half of her face, amazed at how mysterious and feminine she suddenly looked. Her eyes, highlighted with kohl, seemed huge and intriguing. She looked downright seductive, she thought in amazement.

She had never thought of herself as especially feminine, and she didn't approve of using womanly wiles to get her own way. She preferred the direct approach, much to her father's horror. But dressed like this, veiled and perfumed with her favorite jasmine scent, she not only looked as if she could seduce a man, she *felt* as if she could.

Tempted to tear the veil from her face before she got any more crazy ideas, she kept her hands at her sides. This wasn't for her, but for the children at the orphanage. The thought of them waiting in vain for her to return lent her the strength to move toward the door. "I'd better go. Duty calls."

"Have fun," Samira said to her sister's departing back.

Fun? thought Nadia derisively. She would rather be boiled in oil. Making polite conversation with the wives of the trade delegates was hardly her idea of a stimulating evening. Her father would be shocked if she followed her inclinations and conversed with the men, because they would be talking about the really interesting matters, like international trade and diplomacy.

She wondered what Sheik Ahmed would think if he knew how keenly she followed her country's affairs, resulting in her being as well-informed as any of his advisers. He would probably remind her that she would have little need of such interests once she was married, when children and domesticity would be sufficient to occupy her mind.

Children she didn't mind. Obviously, or she wouldn't be so anxious to help the orphans. There were times when she could hardly bear to be around the younger ones because her longing for a child was so overwhelming. The rest of the package was what alarmed her. Being restricted to domestic concerns terrified her. Why couldn't she marry, have children *and* be involved in world affairs?

She knew she was focusing on these matters to avoid her

real worry—Gage Weston's reaction when they were introduced. Perhaps he would be like the men of her own country, greeting her politely while glancing around for someone more interesting to talk to.

Somehow she knew he wouldn't be.

First she had to deal with her father's reaction. In deference to his guests, Sheik Ahmed was dressed in an impeccably tailored business suit, the only mark of his rank, his flowing headdress fastened by a coiled gold *'iqual.* The other Tamir men wore similar attire, but minus the *'iqual,* which was worn only by men of royal blood.

Nadia breathed a sigh of relief when she noticed a couple of other women guests wearing traditional dress, although they hadn't veiled their faces.

Butrus Dabir, who regarded himself as a man of the world, had dispensed with the headdress. In a western-style business suit, she had to concede that he looked impressive, more like a sheik himself than an attorney. Of course, he would be a sheik once they were married. Her father would confer titles and land on Butrus, as befitted the ruler's son-in-law. Not that he was penniless now. Coming from a noble family, Butrus was wealthy in his own right. Married to a princess, he would be one of the most powerful men in Tamir.

As she made her entrance, she saw an expression of thunder settle on the sheik's features. He said a few curt words to Butrus, who immediately came and took her arm. "What do you think you're doing?"

"Acting as hostess at my father's request," she said smoothly, struggling to keep the tremor out of her voice. "I thought you'd appreciate my effort."

"If I knew this get-up was a genuine attempt at womanly modesty, I might."

"How do you know it isn't?"

His eyes narrowed with suspicion. "You're telling me that your status as my bride-to-be has persuaded you to moderate your wilfulness?"

She nodded, casting her gaze down, glad that Butrus

couldn't see the twitch of her mouth behind her veil. "Father told me yesterday that you have set our wedding date. Preparing myself seemed like a good idea."

Butrus looked pleased. "Very well. I shall accept your gesture in good faith and look forward to seeing more of this new Nadia." He leaned closer. "I should tell you that I find the veil extremely provocative."

A shudder rippled through her. In the mirror she had seen for herself the effect the veil created. Butrus's reaction confirmed it. She could only hope that Gage Weston wasn't similarly intrigued. That was the last thing she needed.

She hadn't been able to stop herself from scanning the assembly for signs of him. Tamir was a country of tall imposing men, but Gage was even more prepossessing. A man among men, he might be described as. She quickly recognized the British ambassador, Sir Brian Theodore, and his beautiful wife, Lady Lillian. Nadia's father had said that Sir Brian was Gage's godfather, but he wasn't with them.

Butrus introduced her to the wife of a trade delegate and returned to the sheik's side. Nadia concentrated on conversing politely, containing herself with an effort her father would have found commendable, if unusual.

Without removing her veil, she couldn't eat or drink anything, and her throat began to burn as the others around her enjoyed refreshments. She distracted herself by listening to the music being played by the palace quartet from a low dais at one end of the courtyard.

Explaining the significance of her costume to the curious western women for the umpteenth time was starting to become tiresome—when she spotted him.

Gage stood at the top of the sandstone steps leading to the courtyard where the reception was being held, his green eyes taking in everything.

Amazing how twenty-four hours could distort a memory, she thought, feeling her limbs go weak. She had convinced herself that he couldn't possibly be as compelling as she had first imagined.

He was more!

The authority in his pose took her breath away. He was only a leader of a trade delegation, not even an ambassador, yet he carried himself as if he was accustomed to giving orders, not taking them.

She ducked her head, feeling conspicuous. Wearing the costume had been a mad idea from the start, but changing was hardly an option now.

She could swear she felt a burning sensation as his gaze settled on her. Tilting her head slightly to monitor him through her lashes, she felt her gaze collide with his and almost gasped in shock. He knew, she thought, seeing his expression change swiftly from cool indifference to a searing and blatantly sensuous assessment.

Somehow, she couldn't imagine how, he already knew who she was under the veil, and his challenging look was a gauntlet thrown down. He probably thought because he knew her secret, he could stare at her as he wished, without fear of retribution from her father or fiancé.

Guilty conscience was leading her to imagine his predatory focus on her, she told herself. As a foreigner, he was probably curious about her attire, that was all. But she hadn't imagined what she saw in his gaze. She had only to remember how Gordon used to look at her to be sure that a man only looked at a woman that way when he desired her.

Defiance surged through her. If she kept her head, whatever advantage Gage thought he had over her would be useless. Her word as a princess was worth more than his as a minor foreign diplomat.

Over the head of the woman chattering to her about how much hotter it was in Tamir then back home in wherever, Nadia saw Gage break his stride in her direction and veer to the sheik's side. She waited for her father to greet him politely, then dismiss him in favor of more important guests, but to her dismay, the sheik seemed to welcome Gage's company. Merciful stars, he wasn't reporting her to her father, was he?

Her heart pumped as the sheik turned his head in her direction. He was smiling. Surely he wouldn't smile if Gage had just told him that his daughter made a habit of eluding her bodyguard to behave in ways the sheik would regard as unbefitting a princess.

Her breath caught as the sheik moved toward her, Gage at his side. Her mind raced. She would deny everything. No, she wouldn't. She would confess to her father before Gage could betray her. Then she would hold her head high and face whatever music her unconventional behavior had invited.

The sea of dignitaries parted for the sheik and his companion. By the time they reached her, Nadia's veil fluttered with the effort of controlling her breathing. "Father, I need to tell you…"

The sheik gestured her to silence. "In time, my daughter. I wish to present the emissary from England, Mr. Gage Weston. Mr. Weston, Her Highness Princess Nadia Kamal."

Gage executed a skillful bow that managed to mock her at the same time. "Your Highness."

Her dry throat made her voice husky. "Welcome to Tamir, Mr. Weston."

"Mr. Weston has expressed an interest in our customs, in particular the dress you have chosen to wear in his honor," the sheik continued.

Hardly in his honor. He *was* the driving force behind the choice, but not for the reason her father evidently believed. "I'm glad Mr. Weston appreciates it," she said through clenched teeth.

"Oh, he does, my dear, as do I."

Her father sounded amused, she thought in confusion. For once, she was glad to keep her gaze properly downcast to avoid having to meet Gage's blatant appraisal. She was utterly convinced that he had recognized her. Her glimpse of his determined expression as he approached was enough to warn her that he intended to use his knowledge, although to what end, she didn't want to think.

Her palms grew moist as she waited for Gage to betray her to her father, but he only stood rock still beside the sheik as if he had all the time in the world. She decided two could play this game, and willed herself to silence and stillness, although every nerve in her body tingled with awareness.

"I informed Mr. Weston that your costume is traditionally worn for the performance of the Water Dance," the sheik went on.

"Yes, Father." Volunteer nothing, she instructed herself. Never had she found being silent more difficult.

"Then you *do* intend to perform the dance for us, daughter?"

Startled, she lifted her head to find the sheik pinning her with a hard glare that belied the amusement in his expression. Gage Weston merely looked interested, as befitted a visitor of his status. But in *his* eyes, she saw a sensual challenge that shook her to the core.

Gage was waiting for her to refuse and get herself into deeper trouble with her father, she thought, again disturbed by the almost telepathic communication between them.

Her father had suggested the dance to punish her for making an exhibition of herself. Knowing how much she would hate being forced to perform for the assembled businessmen and their wives, the sheik had chosen a devastating way to exact his penance.

Her father probably expected her to slink away in disgrace and apologize later for her behavior. She saw a similar expectation in Gage's expression. Was that why he hadn't unmasked her? Was he waiting to see the sheik bring her to heel so he could have the last laugh?

Over her dead body.

If her father wanted her to dance, then dance she would, she thought defiantly. Not humbly or reluctantly, but with style. Let Gage see that she wasn't afraid of him or any man. She felt his gaze following her as she mounted the dais and heard her father announce the entertainment to his guests.

* * *

Gage watched the princess in reluctant admiration. Arriving with Sir Brian and Lady Lillian, he had waited outside the courtyard, ostensibly to renew an old acquaintance, but really so he could observe the later arrivals. He had slipped into the shadow of a statue when Nadia walked in. Her choice of national costume had startled him, too. She looked like a butterfly among a collection of moths.

He had seen her fiancé lecturing her and hadn't been fooled by her downcast eyes, although Dabir evidently had been. Why had she risked his anger and her father's wrath by dressing so outlandishly? Of course, the veil. She didn't know Gage had seen her exchange clothes with her maid and had no doubt thought to prevent him from recognizing her. Even if he hadn't already known her secret, his first breath of her distinctive jasmine perfume would have given her away.

He didn't need intelligence skills to work out that ordering her to dance was the sheik's way of teaching her a lesson, and Gage's conscience was troubled. Outwardly Nadia seemed comfortable at the center of attention. But he'd noticed the lines around her eyes. Gage didn't like witnessing her distress and wished there was something he could do about it. Telling himself that she had started this with her deception didn't help. He had no option but to watch her dance.

The story was a simple creation myth such as existed in many cultures. In Tamir's version, the original humans were Ishara, the giver of water, and Ranif, the giver of light and life. Nadia danced a wonderful Ishara, managing to conjure up the invisible Ranif with her poetic gestures and lissome movements.

In the myth, Ranif readily released his gifts over the land, bringing light and life, but couldn't persuade Ishara to offer her gift of water. So he decided to leave, forcing her to admit her love for him. Her tears of sorrow released water into the land as the precious gift it remained to this day. Ranif returned and married Ishara.

Gage knew that countless films had distorted the concept of veil dancing. The Mata Hari idea of peeling back layers of veils to tantalize onlookers was as much a myth as the Ishara story. Using a veil in such a way would amount to a striptease, unacceptable in Tamir culture. So Nadia's dancing had none of the seductive mockery of the western version. Yet seductive she was, in subtle ways that were many times more effective. Gage had never felt so aroused by a dancer in his life.

Was it the lure of the unattainable? Veiled and moving so fluidly, she projected a mystique that spoke to his soul, making him want to rip away the covering and possess her utterly.

Looking around at the attentive audience, Gage was astonished to feel anger snarling through him. He didn't like Nadia's being the cynosure of all eyes. Suddenly he understood why the men of some cultures insisted on women being veiled. Keeping Nadia to himself, her beauty for his eyes alone, had a powerful appeal.

The dance ended and he shook off the thought. She was engaged to Butrus Dabir, Gage's number-one suspect, for goodness' sake. She could well be in league with Dabir, or herself be the traitor Gage sought. Letting her get to him was playing with fire.

Letting a woman like Nadia get to him at any time was playing with fire.

She acknowledged the rapturous applause gracefully enough, but her eyes shone with moisture as she came down off the stage. She kept her head down and almost ran into Gage in her haste to escape.

He parked himself in her way. "You were wonderful, Your Highness. Or should I say, Addie."

Anger and humiliation swirled in her expressive eyes. "Are you pleased you've had your revenge, Mr. Weston?"

Gage would never have put her through such an ordeal, and he didn't like being lumped in with the man who had. "The dance was your father's idea, not mine," he protested.

"When did you first recognize me?"

Telling her he'd seen her change clothes with her maid would blow his cover, so he said, "Since you found me on the side of the road."

"So this was for nothing."

"I wouldn't call it nothing. Your dance was magnificent."

She tore the veil off her face, letting the gossamer fabric hang down one side. "There's nothing magnificent about being looked upon as an amusement, a plaything. My father would never humiliate one of his sons this way."

Gage started to wonder if he was on the right track. Nadia was such a bewildering mixture of innocence and worldliness that he found it increasingly hard to believe she could be a traitor to her family and her country. A worry, yes, but a traitor?

You're getting soft, Weston, he told himself. The best spies were invariably the last people anyone suspected. The thought made him remember that he had a job to do. "I want to see you again," he said in an undertone.

The panic in her expressive eyes was quickly masked by resolve. "If you think you can blackmail me with what you know…"

"This isn't blackmail," he said quickly. "I only want to visit the orphanage again. I know someone who may be able to help the children find homes. Will you take me with you when next you visit?"

Her long lashes fluttered acceptance of her lack of choice. "Very well. I'll be going again on Thursday morning. You can meet me there."

Gage saw Dabir making his way to them through the throng, a frown on his face. So the attorney didn't like another man chatting to his fiancée. Gage could understand that. "I'll be there," he said quickly, and she nodded.

She moved to intercept Dabir. Gage lifted a glass of chilled juice off the tray of a passing waiter, but didn't drink. His thoughts were too busy. He did know someone who could help the orphans—his sister, Alexandra, who was married to a British duke. But Gage's main reason for revisiting the orphanage was to investigate whether it could be a front for the Brothers of Darkness. He hoped not, but in his business, it didn't pay to discount any possibility until he had checked it out thoroughly.

The princess didn't have to be with him for that, so why take the risk of arranging a meeting? Instinct, he told himself, and almost laughed aloud. Hormones, more likely. Although she hadn't danced to seduce, she had aroused him in a way no woman had done for a long time. The need to see her again was like a fire in his blood. He caught her watching him over her fiancé's shoulder and lifted his glass in a silent tribute to their next encounter.

Chapter 4

Long accustomed to the ritual, Nadia stood impassively as her sleeping robe was lifted from her body and she was helped into her morning bath. As the silken waters closed around her, she wondered how it would feel to bathe herself and wash her own hair.

She knew better than to suggest such a thing to her personal attendants. Not only would they be scandalized that a royal princess should wish to do such menial tasks for herself, but they would also fear for their futures. If she denied them the honor of serving her, what else would they do?

As she knew from bitter experience, meaningful work was at a premium for females in her society. Mostly they were expected to occupy themselves with their husbands and children. If the Almighty didn't grant them such blessings, they had two choices—inflict themselves upon their relatives or go into the service of some more fortunate woman.

Nadia sighed. She was that woman, so why didn't she feel fortunate? Because but for an accident of royal birth, she would have been one of society's misfits, she knew. Unmarried for all this time and preoccupied with her art, she was hardly an example of the ideal Tamiri woman.

She moved her limbs restlessly in the delicately scented bath, which was as big as a child's pool. Closing her eyes, she tilted her head back as her hair was lathered with sweetly perfumed lotion. The massaging action soothed her in spite of the faint guilt she always felt at being so pampered.

With only her thoughts to occupy her, she took an inventory of her attendants. Nargis was the one doing her hair. Although no older than Nadia, she regarded herself as Nadia's second mother, always ready with advice whether Nadia wanted to hear it or not. Nargis had the advantage, depending on how one looked at it, of knowing almost everything that went on around the palace and being almost unable to resist sharing her knowledge. While Nadia didn't like to encourage gossip, she knew there were times when Nargis's information had its uses.

On both sides, the princess's hands had been captured for attention by Thea and Ramana. They were twins, raven-haired and also close to Nadia in age. The only reason they hadn't married was their insistence on staying together. Should a man show interest in one of them, he invariably learned that a permanent house guest—the other twin—came as part of the package. Not surprisingly most men found the prospect daunting.

Then there was dear Tahani, Nadia's partner in crime, who was at this moment restoring order to Nadia's bedchamber. Tahani could well have her own family by now, Nadia thought with a twinge of remorse, but her loyalty to the princess was too strong. Somehow Nadia would have to persuade Tahani to think of her own future. She should have done so already, she knew, but without Tahani's willing assistance, how was she to escape the confines of her royal life?

Nargis, Thea and Ramana were devoted to her, but she suspected they would balk at disobeying the sheik so flagrantly. Only Tahani shared Nadia's adventurous spirit. In a more equal society, she would have been a success in some creative field, Nadia knew. They often made a game of imagining their lives differently. In the game, Tahani was an interior decorator, or a set designer for the movies. Nadia imagined herself as a great painter, her works hung in the world's most respected galleries and sold to discerning buyers, not only out of charity, but because they spoke to the buyer's soul.

Buyers like Gage Weston, she thought dreamily. She would see him again this morning when she kept their appointment at the orphanage.

The thought of the meeting made her eyes flutter open, letting a trace of shampoo trickle into them, stinging horribly. With a cry of alarm, Nargis dipped a fresh towel in clean water and dabbed at Nadia's eyes until she could see again.

"My princess, my carelessness has harmed you. How can I make amends?"

The effusiveness of the apology only made Nadia feel worse about her errant thoughts. "It wasn't your fault, Nargis, so you can stop acting as if you're about to be beaten." The servant knew as well as Nadia that such a thing had no part in Tamir culture. "We both know I should have kept my eyes closed."

The remorse fled from the attendant's expression. "I'm more interested in what shocking thought made them fly open."

Nadia pretended innocence. "Why should my thoughts be shocking?"

Nargis had served Nadia's family for a long time and knew her as well as anyone. "They invariably are. Let me guess, you were thinking of a man."

Was she so transparent? "If I was, why would that be shocking?"

"As long as the man was Butrus Dabir, it wouldn't be. Were you thinking of your husband-to-be?"

In the privacy of the boudoir, Nadia felt no need to dissemble. "No," she said on a heavy out-rush of breath. She decided to change the subject. "Did you know Butrus has petitioned my father to set our wedding date?"

Nargis held out a huge velour towel, a sign for Nadia to step out of the bath and be swathed in the folds. As she did so, her attendant said, "Palace gossip speaks of a wedding day, not that I pay any attention to gossip."

Nadia kept a straight face. "Of course not."

"You are blessed to have such a distinguished man as Butrus Dabir, my princess."

Nadia nodded, wishing she felt more blessed. "You're right of course."

She was aware of Nargis's giving her an assessing look as Ramana tucked the towel around Nadia like a sarong. Thea wound another around her hair, then she was steered to a chair so Ramana could massage perfumed lotion into her arms and legs, making her skin silky smooth. Not that anyone would get to appreciate the results, Nadia thought with an inward sigh. Not for her, the freedom to wear skirts that showed off her long legs, or a bikini on the beach to allow the sun to kiss her body.

As a result, her skin was milky and unblemished. At least she didn't have to worry about turning into a dried-up prune in her older years, she consoled herself, trying to think positively. Nor did she ever have to deal with unwanted male attention. Her way of life had some benefits.

"You're thinking of him again," Nargis said with bothersome insight.

Nadia swung her head up, almost dislodging the towel swathing her hair. "Who?"

"This man who isn't Butrus, who makes your cheeks glow and your eyes shine."

"He doesn't. I mean, you're imagining things, Nargis. Get on with your work and stop being so fanciful."

"Humph. I doubt I'm the one being fanciful."

Nadia knew she had earned the other woman's disdain. Complaining about the strictures of royal life, but pulling rank when it suited her was hardly fair. It didn't help that

Nargis was right. Nadia was preoccupied with thoughts of a man.

Gage Weston.

His name sent a shiver through her. She hadn't seen him since the sheik's reception three days before, but he had appeared in her thoughts more often than she wanted. She told herself it was because he had insisted on today's meeting, but knew there was more to her preoccupation.

The prospect of seeing him again made her feel more elated than she had any business being.

She remembered the expression she had seen on his face when her father insisted she perform the Water Dance for his guests. Gage had understood that her father intended to punish her, and the sympathy she had glimpsed had almost been her undoing.

During the dance she had seen a look of black anger descend on Gage's features, and at first thought he was as annoyed with her as her father was, until gradually she realized that Gage's anger was on her account. He hadn't liked the way the other guests were looking at her, she had noticed, unwillingly gratified. In fact, he had looked as if he wanted to slug someone, possibly her father, for putting her through the ordeal.

Nargis had said she was being fanciful, and no doubt she was. But she couldn't shake the belief that Gage had been on her side. In desperation, she had looked to Butrus for some sign of leniency, finding none. Throughout the dance her fiancé had glowered at her from under lowered brows, as if to say he hoped she was learning her lesson. He and her father were a pair, she thought, both making their disapproval painfully evident.

The other male guests had watched her with enough interest to make her squirm inwardly, unaccustomed as she was to disporting herself for the eyes of men. Like all Tamiri women, her training in dance had been to develop graceful movements, not to entertain others.

Only in Gage's face had she seen concern for her as an

individual. Inspired, she had danced to the limit of her skill. As she interpreted the romantic legend, she had felt herself transported beyond the disapproval of her father and fiancé, even beyond the cupidity of their male guests, until she felt as if she danced for Gage's eyes alone.

Afterward when he complimented her on her dancing, she had seen nothing but compassion and—dare she think it?—admiration in his eyes. Until he spoiled everything by insisting on another meeting. With her secret in his keeping, he must have known she couldn't refuse. Why hadn't he betrayed her to her father? Was he hoping to use what he knew for his own benefit? In Nadia's experience, it was what most men would do. She found herself hoping he wasn't like most men.

Ramana held out a silky robe and Nadia slipped out of the towel and into the robe, belting the sash around her slender waist. In her bedroom, Tahani had set out her mistress's clothing for the day. Nadia surveyed the choices. A long skirt in tones of sea-green and blue threaded with gold, a matching silk shirt, a wide blue sash and silk-covered pumps in the same iridescent blue. Nadia suspected that Tahani herself coveted the outfit. Since the maid would be the one wearing it for most of the day, why not?

"Excellent choices for a day of painting," she told Tahani as the maid helped her to dress. She regarded Tahani's own outfit with approval. "I'm glad you're wearing the blue *galabiya.*"

Tahani's dark eyes sparkled. "It is one of your favorites, Your Highness."

"Blue has always been my favorite color." It also lent a sparkle to her dark eyes, she knew, wondering at the same time why she cared what she looked like when she was only going to visit the orphanage. The children certainly didn't care what she wore.

Annoyed with herself, she shifted impatiently as Tahani fluffed her hair into a becoming halo around her head. Her father might not approve of the style, but Nadia appreciated the sense of freedom it gave her. Considering how little freedom she did have in her life, she savored what she had.

At long last, Tahani stood back to admire her handiwork. "You look breathtaking, my princess. Were I Butrus Dabir, I would walk over hot coals to win the heart of such beauty."

What would Gage Weston do to win the heart of the woman he loved? Nadia found herself thinking. She made a dismissive gesture. "Butrus has no need to make sacrifices on my account. He has already won my hand."

If Tahani noticed that Nadia didn't include her heart, she refrained from commenting. Instead, she said, "Perhaps."

Nadia felt a prickle of unease. As well as having an artistic eye, Tahani was known for her prescience. Since joining Nadia's service a few years before, Tahani had made many predictions, and Nadia hated to think how many of them had proved accurate.

"There's no 'perhaps' about it. I'm to marry Butrus and that's that."

Again her maid gave a maddening half smile. "Perhaps."

Unsettled, Nadia brushed a nonexistent speck off her blouse. "You drive me crazy when you do that."

Returning brushes and cosmetics to their places, Tahani paused, looking genuinely puzzled. "Do what, Your Highness?"

"Hint at a future only you can see."

Tahani capped a tube of eye shadow and replaced it on Nadia's dresser. "You must know by now that I can't see the future, Your Highness. Sometimes an insight just comes, like a whisper in my ear."

Nadia kept her hands at her sides, although she wanted to twist them together. "Does your whisper tell you any more than 'perhaps' where Butrus and I are concerned?"

Tahani gave an apologetic shake of her head. "When you stated so emphatically that you were to marry him, the word popped into my head. I don't even know what it means. Probably no more than a woman's foolishness."

Nadia tried to ignore the sudden hope welling inside her

like the flickering of a candle flame. No amount of soothsaying was going to show her a way out of marrying Butrus, nor was she looking for one. She would meet Gage today as agreed, but make it clear to him that it must be for the last time. Then she would do her duty.

Astonished at the regret accompanying this thought, she said, "We all have our moments of foolishness. Gather my painting materials and have Mahir bring the car around. It's time we were on our way."

Tahani brought her palms together at breast height and bowed over them before hurrying away to do Nadia's bidding.

Nadia sat for a few moments, barely aware of her reflection in the mirror in front of her. What was going on here? She had believed herself resigned to marrying Butrus. Yet one word from Tahani, suggesting that a different fate might lie in store for her, had set Nadia's hopes soaring.

She quashed them with a determined shake of her head. Nothing was going to change, so she might as well accept it. She would be Butrus's wife and that was that.

Still, she was aware of the hope flickering persistently inside her like a flame that refused to be extinguished as she made her way out to the courtyard where her driver, Mahir, would be waiting with Tahani and the car.

The courtyard was deserted.

She schooled herself to patience. Something was probably amiss with the car, and they were changing to another. She gave a start when a hand dropped on to her shoulder. "I told Tahani to tell Mahir you won't need him until later today."

She swung around to find Butrus looming over her, and she felt her heart beating ridiculously fast. "Butrus. I didn't expect to see you this morning."

"I rearranged my schedule so we could talk."

She glanced around the courtyard as if doing so would conjure up her car. "Now?"

Butrus frowned. "From your maid, I understood you were

only going out painting. What difference can it make if you go in the afternoon, instead?''

She let her hands flutter at her sides. ''The morning light is better.''

He frowned. ''The light is the light. I have appointments this afternoon.''

His message was clear. He wanted her attention now, and her own plans would just have to wait. Thinking of Gage waiting for her, she debated whether to argue, but knew she would only arouse Butrus's suspicion. ''You're right, I can paint this afternoon,'' she conceded. She would have to send a message to Gage, telling him she had been detained.

Butrus let his hand trail down her arm. ''You'll have little time for hobbies after we're married, little one.''

She drew herself straighter. They were almost of a height and his use of the endearment rankled almost as much as his dismissal of her work. ''My art is hardly a hobby.''

He smiled indulgently. ''Your passion, then. As your husband I shall provide more womanly outlets for your passion, so you'll have no need of art.'' The gleam in his gaze told her what kind of outlet he had in mind.

She would always need her art. It was as natural to her as breathing, but she could see that Butrus would never agree. Her heart ached. How could she commit her life to a man who refused to understand the simplest thing about her? ''Surely there's room in life for more than one kind of passion?'' she asked.

He took her hand, leading her back inside to where servants had set out tea and exquisite pastries for them.

After they were served and the servants withdrew to a discreet distance, Butrus said, ''Your experience of the world of men has necessarily been limited. But I promise, when you are awakened to the passion that can exist between a man and a woman, you will desire no other.''

His conceit almost made her laugh out loud. She might have been raised in the cloistered environment of the royal palace, but she had known true love. She doubted that Butrus could transport her to more-earthly delights than she had known with Gordon while they were together.

"I'm not a child," she insisted, stirring against the bank of cushions at her back. "My education was quite thorough."

He chuckled softly. "I don't doubt it, but theory and experience are very different things, my princess, as you will discover in time."

She restrained a heavy sigh. He was determined to regard her as a hothouse flower, virginal and innocent of the ways of the world. "I'm sure I will, with you to guide me."

Her reply gratified him, she saw as his expression softened. Butrus was right. Theory and experience were very different. From her mother and attendants, Nadia had learned what to say and do to please a man. She hadn't expected the words to stick in her throat like insufficiently cooked meat.

How did her mother endure such a proscribed existence? Why couldn't she say what she meant and have her opinions respected? Nadia despised the idea of getting her own way through flattery and manipulation, however effective.

She set her cup down, shaking the empty cup to signal to the servant rushing to refill it that she had had enough. Facing Butrus, she said. "There's something you need to know about me."

Leaning closer, he silenced her with a finger pressed to her lips. "I know all that I need to know, little one. You are beautiful, innocent, a little headstrong perhaps, but marriage and motherhood will soon tame your wilder instincts."

She reared away from his touch. "I'm not a horse in need of taming."

He frowned as if unaware he'd said anything wrong. "Gentling, then. I will be gentle with you, Nadia, even as you submit to my dominion."

She had to struggle not to raise her voice. "Taming, dominion, can you hear yourself? I understand marriage to be a partnership."

"It is a partnership," he agreed somberly, then ruined the

effect by adding, "In every partnership, there can be only one leader."

"You, I suppose," she said.

Butrus looked pleased. "See? We are close to an understanding already."

This understanding was keeping her from her meeting with Gage, she thought, striving to conceal her restlessness. She stood up. "I'm glad we had this talk. Now I really must go."

Snagging her wrist, he pulled her down beside him, his fingers tracing a line along her arm before he pulled away with obvious reluctance. "I can see I've upset you by talking of the passion within marriage. Forgive me, Nadia. Your beauty fills my mind with little else, but I am a man and men's needs are different. Let me make amends by speaking, instead, of our wedding date."

She felt color flood her cheeks and was guiltily glad Butrus blamed it on embarrassment at his choice of subject matter. "Father told me you'd petitioned him to set the date," she said, hoping to end this quickly.

He nodded. "Three months will seem like an eternity."

She wished she could say, "For me, too," but couldn't bring herself to lie. She settled for, "I'm sure my father knows what's best."

"No doubt. He has offered us the royal yacht for our honeymoon cruise."

Her heart sank at the prospect of being confined to the yacht, playing the part of the dutiful wife. "Can you spare the time from your business?" she asked.

"I thought of combining the two. A few meetings aboard ship won't get in the way of our truly getting to know one another," he promised.

"Sounds wonderful," she said weakly, aware that the heirloom clock on the wall was ticking away the minutes. Gage must be wondering where she was. Butrus hadn't given her the chance to send a message.

"Then it's settled. Now all we need to discuss are a few formalities. As his wedding gift to us, your father intends to build a private apartment for us within the palace grounds, so your family can provide company for you when I have to go away."

She almost groaned out loud. Living within the palace was the last thing she wanted. "I understood we would live at your estate at Zabara."

"You flatter me, but my home is hardly suitable for a princess and her consort. As his son-in-law, I'll be more useful to your father if I am nearby."

And more privy to the workings of the court, she thought. "You've thought of everything," she said, knowing the irony would be lost on Butrus.

"I'm pleased you agree," he said, unwittingly proving her point. He held out his hand to help her to her feet. "I wish we could spend more of the morning together, but I'm afraid I have business I must attend to."

"Of course." She kept her expression bland, but inwardly, she despaired. More than an hour had passed. By now Gage would know she wasn't coming, and it was too late to get a message to him. She shivered, wondering what he would do now.

Chapter 5

Gage had half expected the princess to stand him up, but still, he felt disappointed. Not because he wanted to see her again, he assured himself, but because he needed answers.

In his line of work it was prudent to suspect everyone's motives, even women as beautiful and apparently innocent as Nadia Kamal. Especially women as beautiful as Nadia.

When he'd decided he'd waited long enough, he set about investigating the orphanage on his own. Probably better that way. He could look where he wasn't supposed to, go where she wouldn't have taken him.

It was late morning by the time he'd investigated the buildings and immediate surroundings, careful not to be seen by the children or their caregivers. The noise level of the children playing in the courtyard provided a welcome cover for his movements.

When the doctor, Warren, emerged from his dispensary, Gage ducked under a stairwell that was cloaked in shadow. Waiting there, he was startled to feel a tug at his sleeve. He looked down to find Sammy crouching farther back in the same space.

"Sammy hiding, too," the child whispered solemnly, his large dark eyes luminous.

Steadying his unsettled nerves, Gage smiled. "I won't tell on you, if you won't tell on me."

Sammy nodded and patted his ear. Gage took a minute to work out what he wanted, then remembered. Keeping a wary eye on the doctor talking to some of the other children in the courtyard, he pulled a coin out of his pocket, showed it to Sammy, then made it disappear, only to reappear magically behind the little boy's ear.

The child's giggles caught the doctor's attention. He squinted toward the shadows. "Sammy, are you under there?"

Gage gave the boy a gentle push and whispered, "Sorry, son, you've been found. Off you go."

Sammy tried to tug his new friend out with him, but Gage shook his head. "They haven't found me yet." With any luck they wouldn't. He was relieved when the little boy trotted out into the sunlight and soon became absorbed in a new game.

Deliveries of what looked like groceries and other supplies were made, but as far as Gage could tell, nothing untoward took place. Of course, nighttime might tell a different story, and he resolved to return under cover of darkness to test that theory.

Until then, he felt safe taking the orphanage at face value.

He wasn't so confident about the princess's involvement. The orphanage itself might be clean, but could still be a drop for information or a meeting place for the Brothers of Darkness. With only his own finely honed suspicion that Butrus Dabir was involved with the Brothers, speculation was all Gage had for the moment. As Dabir's fiancée, Nadia could well be part of the organization, too, which meant there was probably a connection with the orphanage somewhere along the line.

Gage decided it was time to pay the lady a visit. He waited until the children were shepherded inside out of the sun, then made his way safely back to where he had hidden his car.

Getting into the palace without an invitation was more of a challenge than infiltrating the orphanage. He was used to slipping in and out of places uninvited, but most of them didn't have watchful guards at every entrance and hordes of twittering females between Gage and his target.

It took him an hour of careful reconnaissance before he found a way in. A private stretch of beach had been reserved for use by the women of the royal family and their attendants. The pristine sands held a number of bathing pavilions, where the women could change or rest out of the hot sun. Substantial grilles at both ends deterred strangers from wandering onto the sand. The beach was, at present, unguarded, although Gage presumed that a guard would be posted when the beach was in use.

When he tested the grilles, he found them strongly embedded into rock; they wouldn't give at all. From their appearance, they had been in place for a long while, allowing time for the tides to alter their pattern. At low tide, he was able to slip around one of the grilles, soaking only his shoes and the cuffs of his pants.

Sticking to the rocky areas to avoid leaving footprints, he crossed the beach swiftly, clambering up a cliff path that led, as he had hoped, straight to the women's quarters. Locating the princess among the rabbit warren of rooms was almost as big a challenge as avoiding the twittering hordes. Twice he was nearly caught.

Slipping into a side room to avoid yet another pair of chattering females, he got his break when a familiar voice said from behind him, "What on earth are you doing here?"

His heart pounded with shock, awareness following a split second later. He turned and sketched a mocking salaam. "Princess Nadia. I'm merely keeping our appointment."

"How did you get in? You shouldn't be here."

He grinned. "As I recall, neither should you."

She blushed. "I was prevented from keeping our appointment by my fiancé."

"Did he know you were supposed to be meeting me?"

She looked startled. "Of course not. And I wasn't meeting you, as you put it. I was merely going to guide you around the orphanage."

"I managed to guide myself," he said, not enlightening her as to his method or reasons.

"The children—were they all right?"

"Judging by the noise level, having a great time," he said.

She subsided against her cushioned banquet with a look of relief. "I'm glad."

He paused long enough to lock the door, then moved closer to her. In one hand she held a sketchbook and in the other a stick of charcoal. Her fingertips were smudged, he noticed. He looked over her shoulder. She had captured one of the little orphans in a cheeky pose that was so lifelike, Gage half expected the drawing to speak. "You have a lot of talent."

"I believe you already own one of my paintings, Mr. Weston."

"I told you to call me Gage. And yes, I do. A study of a sea eagle on a clifftop somewhere near here. You captured the bird in the split second before takeoff, so you can practically see the muscles bunching under the feathers. Impressive stuff."

Nadia felt color seep into her cheeks. The sea-eagle series was among her favorites. She was inordinately pleased to hear that one of the pictures was in the hands of someone who appreciated it, not for the pedigree of the artist, but for its own sake. "I'm glad you like it," she said.

Irritation darkened his eyes. "'Like' is too tame a word for what the painting makes me feel. There's a sense of freedom about to be regained, as if the artist knows a thing or two about breaking free from limitations."

She looked away. "All worthwhile art contains an element of the personal, Gage."

He studied the sketch of the child. "You really care about the orphans, don't you."

"Why do you think I go to such lengths to spend time with them?"

"In your position, writing a substantial check would be easier."

She tightened her grip on the charcoal. "You think it's that simple?"

His gesture encompassed the opulence of the room around them, and by implication, the palace beyond. "Why not? You're obviously not poor."

"My father isn't poor."

She saw a shadow flit across Gage's strong features and wondered at the reason for it. Did he doubt that she had access to her family's fortune only through her father? If so, he was no different from the other men she'd known, who were more interested in her position than in the woman who occupied it. Gordon had been the single exception and had assured her he would love her if she had only the clothes she stood up in, as long as they could be together.

"I have limited resources of my own," she went on coldly, chilled by the doubt she'd glimpsed in Gage's expression, and more hurt than she wanted him to see. "I do what I can with what I have, but there is always more that needs to be done."

"Why not ask the sheik for help?"

"You must know why I can't."

"Because your father would question how you know so much about the orphanage, and the nature of your involvement would come out," Gage said, supplying his own answer.

She set the drawing materials to one side and folded her hands in her lap, pretending a composure she was far from feeling. "He would forbid me to go to the orphanage unescorted. As for working side by side with a single man, even a doctor..." She let her shoulders lift and fall.

"'Get thee to a nunnery,'" Gage quoted. "I assume being

found talking with me in your apartment won't win you any prizes?''

''I can always scream for help and tell the guards you forced your way in here,'' she pointed out. ''It isn't too far from the truth.''

''But you won't,'' he guessed with maddening assurance. ''Because then I'd have to blow the whistle on your extra-curricular activities.''

She kept her expression carefully impassive, although her heart was racing and her palms felt clammy. ''Why haven't you done so already?''

He massaged his chin between thumb and finger. ''I honestly don't know.''

She felt the first stirring of expectancy. ''Then you didn't come here to blackmail me with what you know?''

''I came here because you intrigue me,'' he said flatly, not sounding particularly pleased about the admission.

As an engaged woman, she shouldn't have been pleased, either, but a totally inappropriate frisson of satisfaction rippled through her. Gordon had been the last man in her life to admit to being intrigued by her, moments before he took her in his arms and kissed her for the first, although not the last, time.

How would it feel to be taken in this man's arms and feel his mouth claiming hers? The shocking thought rocketed through Nadia's mind before she could arrest it. ''If I'm supposed to be flattered...'' she began, disturbed by how much she was.

''Don't be,'' Gage said, dispelling any hint of pleasure. ''I don't believe in flattery. If I pay a compliment, it's because it's earned, not to gain favor.''

''Then you are an unusual man,'' she observed. ''In my experience, compliments are common currency between men and women.''

''A currency soon devalued if used to excess.''

''And you are not given to excess?''

Why had she asked such a stupid question, she wondered

as soon as she saw his gaze flash in response to her comment. What was it about Gage Weston that made her want to provoke him so? It wasn't as if she liked him or had any wish to know him better.

She would do better to pretend agreement, as her mother had taught her to do, giving him no excuse to continue the discussion. She still didn't know why he was here, and he seemed in no hurry to enlighten her.

"I prefer my own kinds of excess," he said.

She stood up, feeling the urge to meet him eye to eye. His greater height made that impossible, but at least she could face him directly. The energy radiating from him almost made her step back, but she held her ground. "This is not an appropriate conversation for us to be having."

He slanted an amused look at her. "For a princess and a commoner, or a man and a woman?"

She became vividly aware of the lock she had heard him turn when he came in. They were alone in the room, unlikely to be disturbed for some time, as her attendants were getting ready for the noonday meal. Nadia licked her lips, finding them annoyingly dry. "Either will do."

They became drier still as his gaze fastened on her mouth. He wanted to kiss her, she knew. To her horror, she actually felt herself lean toward him, as if to meet him halfway. The unusual fragrance he wore reached out to her. Not something from Tamir, and probably not English, either. Something tantalizingly wild, and alarmingly erotic.

She almost moaned as his hands slid up her arms, coming to rest on her shoulders. His touch felt like fire through the silk of her blouse. Her lashes began to flutter closed, but she held them open with an effort of will.

"No," she managed to force out.

He gave a sigh that was part regret, part promise, and released her with obvious reluctance. Moving stiffly, he crossed the room and began to pick up a collection of brass trinkets, one after the other. She could swear he hardly looked at them before setting them down.

"Why did you come?" she asked belatedly, wondering if he had just given her the answer.

He kept his back to her. "When you didn't keep our appointment, I wanted to be sure you were all right."

She recognized the lie as soon as he uttered it, but suspected she wouldn't learn the truth unless he wanted her to. Who was he? What was he? She couldn't accept that he was merely a minor diplomat. No minor diplomat of her acquaintance made himself so much at home in royal surroundings or dealt so familiarly with a member of the royal family.

Not for Gage, the deference accorded to his betters, she thought. He was definitely more than he seemed, but how much more?

"Now that you've satisfied yourself, you should leave," she said shortly.

He swung around. "If I had satisfied myself, you wouldn't want me to leave."

She pretended ignorance, fighting the riot of unwelcome sensations tearing through her. "I have no idea what you mean."

His dark eyebrows canted upward, his gaze reading her like a book. "Oh, no? I wasn't the only one wondering what it would be like if we kissed."

"Wondering is not the same as finding out," she said shakily.

He shot her a look of unmistakable regret. "Unfortunately it isn't. And you're a princess and engaged to be married, so we'll have to go on wondering."

Fine with her, until he added softly, "For the moment."

She lifted her head, fixing him with a regal glare that refused to acknowledge how shaken she was by his words and the promise underlying them. "You presume a great deal for someone I could have thrown into jail at the snap of a finger."

He stalked to the door and unlocked it. "The ball's in your court, Princess."

"You'd like me to call someone, so you could throw me to the wolves."

He crossed his arms over his chest, a smile curving his mouth. "As I said, your call, Princess."

She wasn't going to turn him in, and it galled her that he knew it. "How did you get past the guards, anyway?"

"The grille fencing off the beach doesn't reach all the way down at low tide."

Her gaze went to the telltale dampness around his ankles. "How do you plan to get out? You won't be able to use the same route now that the tide is in."

"I was hoping you'd help me."

"What can I possibly do? I can't be seen with you."

"Unless you were to come across me wandering lost in the palace grounds and help me to find my way."

He composed his features into such an expression of foppishness that she was forced to smile. "It might work, although you could have trouble explaining your wet footwear."

He looked down, then back at her. "I stumbled into one of the ornamental ponds on the palace grounds."

How easily the lies sprang to his lips, she thought with a twinge of unease. She would do well to bear that in mind if he complimented her again. Not that such a thing was likely. By trespassing on royal property, he had evened the score between them. If he betrayed her, she could equally betray him, having him removed from Tamir and almost certainly ending his diplomatic career. If he realized that, he didn't seem troubled by the possibility, she noted.

She went to the window and looked out. At this hour, many of the palace staff were indoors avoiding the heat of the day. Her attendants would be looking for her soon to escort her to her noonday meal. "If we're going, we'd better hurry while the grounds are quiet," she urged.

Tension coiled through her as she led the way along a maze of corridors to an open pavilion with a lily-covered pond at its center. She skirted around it, the heels of her shoes clicking on the ancient tiles.

"This walkway leads to the public rooms," she explained, her voice husky with anxiety. Until they were clear of the women's apartments, she had no way of explaining his presence that wouldn't cause a scandal.

When they emerged, unchallenged, in the area of the palace reserved for offices and meeting places, she began to breathe a little easier. At least here Gage's story of becoming lost would seem plausible, if not likely. Visitors were usually escorted while within the palace, but it wasn't unheard of for someone to take a wrong turn and lose sight of his guide.

She saw Gage looking around with interest. "I think I know where I am now. Isn't that the pavilion where the reception was held the other night?"

She wished he hadn't reminded her. "These rooms are often used to receive visitors," she said, her tone reflecting her acute discomfort.

He caught her elbow and pulled her into the shadow of a pillar. "There's no need to feel anything but pride about the way you danced that night."

She shrank away from him, daunted as much by her response to his nearness, as by his words. "You don't understand anything about our culture, do you."

"I understand that you were a vision of grace and beauty up on that stage."

"I was a laughingstock," she said bitterly.

His grip tightened. "You were admired by everyone who saw you. You are only a laughingstock if you decide to be. Addie wouldn't allow anyone to touch the core of who she is, no matter what happened to her."

Her eyes blurred and she blinked hard. "Addie lives in a different world from mine."

"I think if you look closely, you'll find they're not so different. There's a way out of any box, provided you want it badly enough."

How she wished he was right, but he wasn't allowing for

her country's traditions, forged over thousands of years. No amount of wishing could change things that easily, as she well knew. "There's no time for this," she said.

He stepped out into the sunlight, towing her with him. "Think about what I've said."

Suddenly he let her arm drop and came to a kind of attention. She understood why when Butrus emerged from behind a pillar. How long had he been standing there, and how much had he heard?

Her fiancé's smile revealed nothing, but his tone was equable as he said, "Nadia. Mr. Weston. Is there something I can do for you?"

"I lost my bearings on the way out. Her Highness was kind enough to give me directions," Gage said smoothly.

Butrus's eyes narrowed. "Were there no guards you could ask to escort you?"

"None he could find," Nadia slipped in. "I'm so glad you're here, Butrus, because Mr. Weston was just telling me how much he admires your work."

Her mother's lessons had their uses, she thought, as she saw Butrus's hard expression soften slightly.

"How is it that you know of my work when you are new to Tamir?" he asked Gage.

"Before joining the diplomatic corps, I studied economics, then took a second degree in law," Gage explained. "At university, your redrafting of the constitution of Tamir was regarded as exemplary in the field."

Butrus looked pleased. "Constitutional law is an interest of yours, then?"

Gage nodded. "One of many."

"Perhaps you'd be interested in seeing how I conceived some of the elements of the document," Butrus suggested. "The new preamble is still to be written, so I am assembling some business associates at my estate in a few days' time to arrive at a suitable draft. You would be welcome as an observer. Much of my work on the new constitution was done at the estate, and I have retained my notes there. If you would like to join the party, I'll be happy to discuss them with you.''

Gage inclined his head. ''Are you sure I won't be intruding between you and your fiancée?''

Belatedly Butrus seemed to remember her existence. ''Her Highness will accompany the party, naturally, but we do not put the same store on spending time alone as you British do. In our culture, it is regarded as unseemly.''

''I shall be chaperoned by my attendants,'' Nadia explained. ''My role is to provide cultural enlightenment and diverting small talk.'' She let her tone convey how unappealing she found the prospect.

Butrus didn't seem to notice, but Gage flashed her a wry look. ''Then I accept with thanks. Naturally I shall have to approach our ambassador for his approval.''

Butrus gave a knowing smile. ''Since Ambassador Theodore is your godfather, I am sure he will be delighted. The ambassador was invited to participate in our deliberations but had to decline, due to pressure of other commitments. He will be gratified that you are able to attend in his stead.''

The tightening muscles around Gage's eyes told Nadia that he wasn't sure he liked Butrus's being so well-informed. Didn't he realize that this was Tamir? Information was a kind of currency, and the best-informed people were invariably the most successful. Butrus made it his business to be well-informed.

She felt excitement quiver through her. The house party, which had seemed dull in the extreme, held far more promise now that Gage was going to be there. She resisted asking herself why. Her duty was to Butrus, and she would give him no cause to find fault with her behavior. But she saw no reason she couldn't enjoy Gage's presence, like a touch of spice in an otherwise bland dish.

Gage's gaze remained on Nadia as he added, ''I shall look forward to the occasion.''

''I shall escort Mr. Weston from here, Nadia,'' Butrus said.

He didn't add, "Run along," but his tone conveyed the dismissal equally well.

Concealing her annoyance, she nodded agreement. "As you wish, Butrus. We'll meet again at my fiancé's estate, Mr. Weston."

As Gage returned her salaam with a practiced one of his own, not by a flicker of an eyelash did she let him see how eagerly she found herself anticipating the experience.

Chapter 6

So much for anticipation, she thought a week later as she fed bread to the swans craning their graceful necks toward her on the ornamental lake at Butrus's estate.

Their party had arrived at Zabara two days ago, and the only people she had spoken to were Butrus, his servants, her sisters on the telephone and the women who would have attended her at the royal palace, anyway.

She might as well have remained at home. Then at least she could go to her studio to paint or sculpt. Her hands ached with the need for something to occupy them, and her brain felt as if it was turning into humus.

Her sketching materials lay on a table in the shelter of a filigreed-metal pavilion. Seated on cushioned banquets in the comfortable structure, she had made several sketches of the swans this morning, but they weren't nearly enough to satisfy her. She yearned for the tactile excitement of fresh clay under her fingers, a piece of marble to chisel or a blank canvas driving her to cover it with paint.

She also missed her visit to the orphanage. Were the children missing her as much as she missed them? On her last visit, she had explained to them that she wouldn't see them for a week because she had to go away. She had almost changed her mind when she saw little Sammy bite his lower lip to stop himself from crying.

He had become used to people disappearing from his life and probably thought she was going to do the same. She had assured the child she would be back, but he had looked at her with tragically round eyes, as if she was already lost to him. She made up her mind to buy the children special presents to take with her when she returned.

Frustration continued to gnaw at her. She had asked her fiancé if she might sit in on the discussions about constitutional law with Gage and the other businessmen, but Butrus had assumed that her reason for asking was because she wanted to watch him at work. It had never occurred to him that she might have something to contribute.

"I appreciate your wish to support me, little one, but I don't want you to be bored," he had said. "The estate is at your disposal. Go where you will within the boundaries and enjoy yourself."

Always the qualification "within the boundaries," she thought, crumpling a piece of bread savagely. She wished she could swallow her anger as easily as the swan swallowed the bread she threw to it. At least her father permitted her mother to join him in his office and be a party, however passive, to the affairs of state. It seemed Butrus didn't intend to allow Nadia even that much involvement in his activities.

A masculine voice behind her startled her. "I know swans can be savage when they have young to protect, but the look on your face makes you seem far more fierce than these beautiful birds."

She swung around to find Gage leaning against a tree, watching her. For some reason, she was troubled that he had seen the anger she went to such lengths to conceal from her fiancé. She gathered her royal dignity around her like a cloak. "You shouldn't be speaking with me. Tahani has only gone inside to fetch a cool drink for me. She'll be back at any moment.''

''And you'll be the one getting into trouble for talking to a man alone,'' he guessed. ''How do you stand it?''

She threw more bread to the swans, pretending ignorance. ''Stand what?''

''Being kept at arm's length from anything remotely important and treated as if you don't have a brain in your head.''

The keenness of his observation rankled. Bad enough to be excluded from the discussions, without Gage being so aware of it. His opinion shouldn't matter, but it did. ''What makes you think I have brains?'' she asked, lacing her tone with irony.

He came to her so quickly and silently that he was behind her before she knew it. His hands on her shoulders were rough as he spun her around. ''The woman who painted the eagle hanging on the wall of my study back home isn't stupid. To represent nature so accurately, she needs to have studied anatomy, aviculture, botany, and have a sharp eye for observation, before we even get to artistic ability.''

No one except her attendants touched a member of the royal family, much less as roughly as Gage had. Nadia knew she should be shocked, but instead, she felt a disturbing thread of excitement wend its way through her.

He was so close that she felt the curl of his breath against her cheeks. The sun glinting off his features chiseled them to almost sculptural sharpness. The fine lines radiating from eyes and mouth suggested a life far removed from diplomatic ease and comfort. Not an indoor man. A man of action, she concluded, the impression at odds with the little she knew about him. Perhaps he had been a soldier before becoming a diplomat.

The compulsion to touch his face to see if he was as hard as he looked was almost irresistible. His green gaze flashed a challenge at her, as if he sensed what she barely restrained herself from doing.

Only years of royal practice kept her hands at her sides and the reaction from reaching her face. Afraid that her gaze might betray her, she lowered her lashes. "Take your hands off me," she said in a commanding tone that any Tamiri would have obeyed without question.

As troubled by her response as by his touch, she wasn't surprised when he made no move to release her.

"When you admit I'm right about you," he insisted.

She opened her eyes, almost closing them again as his masculine aura slammed into her anew. "You're a man. It goes without saying," she said, striving to sound matter-of-fact. She suspected she failed miserably.

He continued to study her with unsettling intensity. "Not in my country."

"You are not in England now," she pointed out, struggling to keep her breathing even. She was torn between wishing that Tahani would return and interrupt them, and desperately hoping she wouldn't.

"I'm not…" he began. She saw him visibly check himself before saying, "I'm not talking about any particular country, but about basic human rights. You're a grown woman." His voice softened, and now it sounded like a caress. "You're a beautiful intelligent woman, and you have a right to your opinions."

What had he been about to say before he so obviously stopped himself? That he wasn't from England originally? She had worked that out for herself. He was right about the artist in her having well-developed powers of observation. They functioned even when she didn't want them to. Now they told her that his cultured English accent overlaid another, more musical accent, the language of his birth, perhaps. She found herself speculating on where that might be.

He thought her beautiful and intelligent, a traitorous inner voice said. The men of her own country appreciated beauty, but rarely endorsed her gender with intelligence. She had to fight the glow of pleasure that enveloped her at Gage's words. "You're not from Tamir," she said tiredly. "When you've been here a little longer, you'll see that our way is different, but not necessarily wrong.''

He seemed to have forgotten that his hands still rested on her shoulders. The bite of his fingers had eased to a comfortable weight, his palms sliding down to her upper arms in the suggestion of an embrace. She knew she should move away or insist that he move away. She did neither, finding the touch far more enjoyable than was wise.

''Stopping people from reaching their full potential is always wrong,'' he persisted. His voice sounded husky, as if the closeness was affecting him, too, finally.

She felt her eyes start to swim as she stated the obvious. ''My potential lies with my husband and the children we shall have. The only one stopping me from achieving that potential is me.''

''Why?''

The question caught her off guard. With Tahani she had often discussed the paths their lives might have taken had things been different. But never with a man, not even Butrus. He had never been interested enough to ask, she thought with a touch of bitterness.

''Perhaps I was waiting for change,'' she whispered, recognizing the truth in her heart. Gordon had represented change, and he was gone. Now she had finally accepted that waiting was getting her nowhere.

''Change doesn't come to you. You make it happen.''

Gage would make change happen, she thought, hearing his voice ring with conviction. He seemed like a man who took life by the scruff of the neck and shook it until it did his bidding.

The belief struck her as being at odds with his role as a minor official in the British Embassy. ''Considering who you are, you're hardly in a position to talk,'' she challenged.

His hold on her arms tightened and his eyes narrowed. ''What do you mean?''

She sensed his attention sharpening and wondered what she had said to provoke the change. ''You speak like a man of action, yet you occupy yourself with trade and diplomacy," she explained.

He let his hands drop. She felt a rush of disappointment, as if she had wanted the touch to turn into something more. Such a thought was so morally wrong that she shuddered inwardly.

"You're right of course." But he sounded amused rather than angered by her accusation. She waited for him to justify his choice of career in light of his provocative talk, but instead, he gestured toward the ornamental lake. Tired of waiting for more largesse from her, the swans had glided gracefully away, heading for the reed beds on the far side of the lake. "This fantasy setting tends to make one idealistic."

She should be pleased that the conversation had shifted to safer ground, but she felt regretful that the verbal sparring was at an end. It had made a refreshing change from her usual experience. She told herself she didn't rue the loss of Gage's touch, almost making herself believe it. "The estate is remarkable, isn't it?" she observed.

His gaze took in the acres of manicured gardens, leading down to a private, white-sand beach, overlooked by a turreted mansion furnished with antiques and priceless works of art. "Your fiancé must come from a wealthy family."

In Gage's expression she saw mirrored her own curiosity about how Butrus had amassed the fortune this place must cost him to maintain. His family, though wellborn, were not as wealthy as the estate implied. Loyalty to Butrus made her say, "Reasonably so. He has also done well in my father's service."

"Your father is obviously a generous man and will be even more generous, no doubt, once Butrus becomes his son-in-law."

Anger coursed through her, as much at herself for letting this insolent man touch her as at his outrageous comments. That he might be echoing her own deepest concerns, she didn't like to think. "That's hardly any of your concern, Mr. Weston."

A smile curved the corners of his generous mouth, taunting her. "So it's Mr. Weston again, is it? Am I to be punished for speaking the truth?"

"Your kind of truth."

"Surely there can be only one truth."

She dragged in a steadying breath. "Are you a man of honor, Mr. Weston?"

Something indefinable flickered across his features, making her suspect that she had touched on a truth he didn't wish her to know. She would give a lot to know what it was.

"Most men like to think of themselves as honorable," he said.

She recognized his evasion and wondered again what he was keeping from her, but decided she would gain nothing by taking the direct approach. Better to watch and wait, see what he revealed in time. Another feminine skill her mother had imparted. "If you are truly a man of honor, you will keep a respectful distance from me in future, instead of trying to make me think less of the man I am to marry," she said.

Gage crossed his arms over his broad chest. "Is that an order, Your Highness?"

She inclined her head with regal grace. "You may consider it so."

"Then I must refuse."

Her head came up and she made no attempt to conceal her shock this time. No one refused to obey a royal command. "I can have you thrown in jail or deported from Tamir for such insolence."

He gave a careless shrug. "It's hardly insolent to tell you what you already suspect."

She turned away, wishing she had more bread to attract the swans, anything to occupy her hands and whirling thoughts. But she had nothing, so she pretended interest in inspecting a rare orchid just coming into bloom beside the lake. Cupping her hands around the bloom, she said, "You presume a great deal."

He placed his hand under hers so that they shared the or-

chid. "Bad habit of mine, I'm afraid." He didn't sound in
the least regretful. "How well do you know Butrus Dabir?"

As Gage's palm grazed the backs of her hands, she sup-
pressed a shiver of reaction. Such a light touch, but it reso-
nated through her like the most passionate embrace. Taking
her hands away would be far too revealing, so she stayed
where she was, the sound of the blood pounding in her ears
making it hard to concentrate.

"I've known Butrus most of my life. He is my father's
closest adviser and a respected emissary for Tamir abroad."

"But how well do you really know him?"

Absently Gage's fingers twined with hers, making the orchid shiver against Nadia's palm. The sensation was unbe-
lievably erotic, and she almost closed her hand around the
delicate flower in shocked response, stopping herself barely
in time.

"I'm not sure what you're implying, Gage."

She hadn't meant to use his first name but it slipped out,
and she saw the gleam of gratification in his eyes. "This
estate and everything in it didn't come from nowhere. Have
you considered that your fiancé may be involved in something more than royal affairs?"

She had considered it, dismissing the possibility as far-
fetched. No one in her father's service would be involved in
anything underhand, and certainly not criminal. She had accepted Butrus's refusal to involve her in his business matters
as male chauvinism. She resented Gage for attempting to
make her think there could be a more sinister reason.

She shook her head, forcibly driving away the suspicion.
"I don't know what advantage you hope to gain by under-
mining my faith in Butrus, but it isn't going to work. I command you to refrain from making such heinous remarks about
him. Is that understood?"

He took his time removing his hands, letting them slide
under hers slowly, provocatively, until she felt dizzy with the
need for more of his touch. She wanted to find out what it
would be like to be held in his arms completely, kissed by

him, drowning in the desire that tantalized her at so slight a contact.

What was she thinking? Hadn't she just lectured him on showing respect for Butrus? What was she doing, if not dishonoring the man she was to marry by her very thoughts?

"I understand completely, Your Highness," Gage said softly. "From now on, if I speak of Butrus at all to you, I shall only speak in the most glowing terms."

She tried to feel mollified but was too shaken by Gage's effect on her. "Thank you," she said, hearing her voice come out infuriatingly husky.

Unexpectedly he caught her hands and lifted them to his lips, kissing her fingertips. "You're welcome, Princess."

Pleasure coiled through her, hot, sharp and totally inappropriate. She pulled her hands away as if burned. "It would be best if you rejoined the other men." Best for whom, she wasn't sure and was glad he didn't ask.

He gave the mocking salaam she had begun to expect from him. "Your wish is my command, Princess. I shall see you at dinner."

Anxiety gripped her as she watched him walk away. She had forgotten that she was to dine with the other guests and their wives that evening. She recoiled from the prospect. How could she sit at Butrus's right hand and act as if nothing had happened between her and Gage this afternoon?

Nothing *had* happened. A few looks, a casual touch or two, hardly amounted to disloyalty to Butrus, did they? Only if she accepted that they had meant more to her than they should have done. They hadn't, had they?

She was probably reading more into the encounter with Gage than was warranted because of the novelty of being touched by a man, she told herself.

She had allowed Gordon to touch her, and look where that had led. Afterward she had promised never to leave herself open to such heartache again. Agreeing to marry Butrus was a way of keeping that promise.

She told herself she was happy for her world to remain a

sheltered one where her attendants and female doctors were the only people permitted to touch her. Even Butrus had done little more than take her hand in greeting or when they parted. By custom, he would do no more until they were man and wife.

Gage wasn't of their culture. To him, kissing Nadia's fingertips was probably no more than a gallant gesture, forgotten moments later. She wished she could forget it as swiftly.

She had lifted her hand to her mouth in imitation of his touch before she became aware of the movement and let her hand drop to her side. A rustling along the path brought her head up, expectancy coursing through her, try as she might to subdue it. Had Gage forgotten something and returned?

But it was only Tahani, bearing a tray. "I'm sorry to take so long, my princess. The foolish kitchen maid dropped the first pitcher of lemonade and I had to wait while she prepared another."

Lemonade was the furthest thing from Nadia's mind right now. She felt as if champagne was the only drink capable of matching the tumult inside her, and she had never craved such a drink in her life. What was it about Gage Weston that put such thoughts in her head?

"I don't mind," she said, wondering exactly to what she was referring. "I'm no longer thirsty, anyway. But I'll drink a little of the lemonade," she added, seeing Tahani look distressed.

The attendant placed the tray on a wrought-iron table in the shade of the pavilion and poured a drink for Nadia, who insisted Tahani have some, too. When they were seated out of the sun, Tahani said, "I saw Gage Weston coming from this direction, Princess. I hope he didn't intrude on your privacy."

If she only knew. "No, no. I was busy feeding the swans. They are lovely creatures, aren't they?"

As she'd hoped, the comment diverted Tahani from thoughts of Gage, and they began to discuss the many birds inhabiting the grounds of the estate. Despite Tahani being her closest confidante, Nadia was glad that the maid didn't know that talk about the swans and the hummingbirds only occupied part of the princess's mind.

Another part insisted on replaying a scene where she held an orchid in her hands, and Gage held both of them in his.

Why didn't he simply carry a placard advertising his suspicion of Butrus Dabir? Gage thought, angry with himself as he strode along the mosaic path back to the mansion. He had all but announced his concern to Princess Nadia just now. How much more unprofessional could he be?

He told himself he had wanted to find out how much she knew, but honesty made him accept that there was an element of jealousy, as well. She had thought herself unobserved, but Gage had seen her dancing attendance on Dabir since this gathering began, acceding to the man's every whim, never speaking up for herself. Couldn't Dabir see the strain around her lovely dark eyes every time she was treated like an empty-headed decoration?

Evidently not. Dabir had looked insufferably pleased with himself. Gage could swear the man heaped indignities upon Nadia for the sheer satisfaction of lording it over a member of royalty. Not that their relationship was any of Gage's affair, but he couldn't help pitying Nadia once she married Dabir, if the man was this dictatorial toward her now.

Gage's investigation into Dabir's past showed that he wasn't as high-born as was generally believed. He had been raised in a family of bluebloods, but Dabir himself was only the nephew of the man usually taken to be his father. His origins were far more modest, his real father having been killed in an accident in the oil fields while serving the Dabir interests. His mother had died in childbirth, so conscience probably drove the Dabirs to take Butrus in and raise him as their own, Gage concluded. Had the young Butrus resented being an object of charity? It would explain his driving ambition, which extended to marrying a princess.

Looking around at the lavish estate and thinking of his

assigned quarters with their antique furnishings, ancient mosaic floors and valuable artworks, Gage had to admit that
Butrus had succeeded spectacularly. A royal marriage would
seal his emancipation from charity case to second-most powerful man in the country.

Knowing the man's unbridled ambition and the unsavory
types he associated with, Gage had had to restrain himself
from hauling Nadia away whenever he saw her with Dabir.

Gage froze in his tracks. When had he stopped thinking
of her as a potential accomplice of Dabir's? He had no more
proof of her innocence than he did of Dabir's guilt, although
he still hoped to find evidence during the house party.

He had established that none of the guests he'd met up to
now were linked to the Brothers of Darkness, although Gage
was so convinced this party was a front for a meeting of that
group that he could smell it.

The sessions he'd attended had been exactly what they
seemed—tedious discussions aimed at drafting a modern preamble for the Tamir constitution. Dabir had even sought
Gage's opinion once or twice. But Gage was sure this was
only a cover for more sinister activities. Did the princess
know what they were, or was she as much in the dark as
Gage himself?

In his experience, suspects were guilty until proved innocent. He would have to beware that Nadia's hypnotic attractiveness didn't blind him to reality. Once was enough to be
taken in by a woman's beauty and charm.

He stepped out of the way of a maid carrying a tray of
drinks and sweetmeats along the path. She smiled shyly at
him before continuing on her way, as did he.

Tahani—his mind supplied the name automatically. Taking refreshments to her mistress at the ornamental lake.

One of the glasses on the tray would soon be cupped in
Princess Nadia's fine-boned hands, he thought. Jealousy
flashed through him, white-hot and searing in its intensity.
He wanted to be that glass. Hell, he wanted to hold her more
than he had wanted anything in a long time.

He almost laughed out loud at the foolishness of his thought. A glass held in her hands, indeed. What if she was in league with Dabir? She would also share responsibility for Conrad's death. Would Gage want to hold her then?

Yes, he would, he thought, mortified. He would hate her and probably himself, as well, but he would want her no matter who she was or what he discovered she'd done. Why else seek her out so persistently?

Telling himself the contact was part of his investigation didn't make it the truth. Finding evidence of Dabir's culpability was likely to indict her or clear her, as well. Spending time with her wouldn't make any difference to Gage's report to King Marcus.

Gage wished he could promise himself that he would stop seeing her, but knew he couldn't. Something about the princess attracted him like iron filings to a magnet. Pity that a princess of Tamir couldn't just have an affair and be done with it. Making love to her might be one way to get her out of his system.

The heat pouring through him at this idea made it seem unlikely. In any case, being who and what she was, a love affair was out of the question. Talking to her alone was difficult enough. Taking her to bed without benefit of a wedding ceremony would probably get him beheaded.

He massaged the back of his neck as if feeling the kiss of cold steel. Conrad used to joke about men losing their heads over women. Gage knew he would have to watch himself if he didn't want it to become a literal truth.

Chapter 7

The dinner was a dignified affair, held in the Great Hall, which was lit by torches, their stuttering flames creating giant dancing shadows that made Nadia feel distinctly uneasy.

Her traditional costume would have looked more at home in such a setting than the Grecian-style gown she had chosen to wear. The flowing dress of opalescent blue silk had long sleeves that ended in peaks over her hands. Seed pearls embellished the high collar and were sewn around the hem of the long skirt, the precious pearls having been Tamir's wealth before the discovery of oil.

Like the other guests, her feet were bare and sank into the sumptuous Shirazi carpets piled one on top of the other as carelessly as if each one wasn't worth a king's ransom.

Nargis had dressed her black hair into a shining cap of curls threaded with more pearls and miniature gold coins, which tinkled as she glided across the room to where Butrus waited for her.

He wore a superbly cut white dinner jacket, its snowy perfection suggesting that this was the first time he'd worn it.

She knew that wasn't unusual for Butrus. He frequently wore garments only once before passing them on to his servants. One of them had told Nargis, who had inevitably shared the information with her mistress.

Nargis had thought Butrus's behavior splendidly magnanimous. To the princess, it seemed more as if her fiancé needed to prove to himself that he could always have more of whatever he wanted. Was marrying her a further expression of this need?

So what if it was, she reproved herself. She had her own agenda for agreeing to marry him. Wasn't she trying to finally win her father's approval by accepting his choice of husband for her? If she also gained more freedom as mistress of her own domain, so much the better. It was only proper that they both gained something from the match.

As she reached him, Butrus stood and held out his hand to help her to a seat beside him on one of the cushion-strewn divans at the head of the long low table. "You look enchanting tonight, little one," he said, adding close to her ear, "However, I miss the veil. So mysterious, so provocative."

"So medieval," she murmured under her breath.

"Excuse me?"

"I said the hall looks so medieval tonight. I feel as if I've been transported back to ancient Arabia."

He gave her a gratified smile. "Exactly the impression I wanted to create. I've arranged a banquet fit for the sheiks and sheikas of old."

Butrus would favor the old traditions, she thought, suddenly glad that he wasn't in line to the throne. If he were ruler of Tamir, he would probably insist on every woman being veiled from head to toe. She gave a slight shudder at the thought.

Butrus probably thought he was being astonishingly liberal by allowing the women to share the same table as the men. Not so long ago, they would have been sequestered behind rugs and hangings. In many countries, they still were, she thought with another shudder.

She watched with interest as the guests took their places at the long banquet table. She had seen some of them going to the meetings Butrus had dissuaded her from attending. One group of men, wearing western dress, was unfamiliar to her. They looked foreign, possibly American, she thought, her curiosity piquing.

"Who are those people?" she asked Butrus, who had turned to speak to the man on his left.

Turning back to her, he gave a dismissive wave of his hand. "No one you need concern yourself about, little one. Foreign business associates I deemed it politic to invite."

To Nadia, they looked more like the shady types she'd seen in the souks, watching warily from the narrow doorways of shops or talking furtively with others of their ilk in back alleys. Hardly the kind of men she would have expected Butrus to welcome to his estate.

Still, as he'd said, they were not her concern and for once she was glad. None of them looked like the sort of person she wanted to associate with.

Then there was Gage Weston.

She realized she'd been studying the unsavory-looking group to avoid letting her gaze come to rest on Gage, but he was impossible to ignore for long. Almost a head taller than most of the other men, he radiated an air of assurance that had her wondering about his true nature yet again.

He was seated between two of Butrus's associates, and was deep in conversation with one of them, so she could look her fill for the moment. She was troubled by how much she wanted to.

Unlike many of the foreigners, including the unsavory-looking ones she saw squirming in obvious discomfort, Gage had no difficulty relaxing on the low divan. He had one knee raised, the other tucked under him, one arm resting easily atop the raised knee. He had also pulled up his right sleeve, evidently aware of the local custom of using only the right hand for eating.

How easily she could imagine him in the flowing robe and

headdress of the desert, enjoying the same meal on rugs spread on the sand as he leaned against a camel saddle, the smell of brushwood and cardamom coffee tangy in the night air.

He looked up and caught her studying him. In a gesture that brought color rushing to her face, he lifted his hand and touched the fingertips to his lips, the message unmistakable. He was reminding her of how he had kissed her hand beside the lake this afternoon.

As if she could forget. Maybe there was some merit in being segregated behind rugs and hangings, she thought as she felt warmth suffuse her. She refused to look away, which would reveal how much his gesture had discomfited her.

Picking at her food was not an option, lest she give Butrus the impression his hospitality was lacking, but the sight of so much food being served made her sigh inwardly. To a Tamiri, hospitality was not a favor to a guest, but an obligation. Providing only enough food for the invited number would be shameful. What if one of them brought friends, or travelers arrived unannounced?

No one could accuse Butrus of neglecting custom, she thought as the servants carried in immense silver trays piled high with everything one could possibly want. The centerpiece was a bed of rice topped with a whole roast lamb. Around this radiated dishes of tomatoes, pigeons in wine sauce, a stew of chicken, figs and honey, the finely ground wheat dish called couscous royale with more stew, this one of lamb with vegetables, chick peas and raisins. There were also pastries of meat, onions and eggs, and stuffed vine leaves, many of the recipes originating in the elegant days of the Caliphates.

The guests murmured a prayer of thanks and soft-voiced compliments to Butrus on the size and appetizing look of the feast, then deftly began to dip pieces of flat bread into the stews and sauces, tearing loose portions of the roast lamb and kneading helpings of rice into neat balls with their fingers.

She tried not to watch Gage, but found herself drawn to him, mesmerized by the skillful way he handled the food, unlike many of the foreigners who looked frustrated as rice cascaded from their inexperienced hands.

There was little conversation; it was mostly reserved for the leisurely drinking of coffee and mint tea before and after the meal. Occasionally a guest spoke to a servant standing behind the diners to request a glass of water, which was quickly brought from outside the hall. But otherwise, the only sounds were soft music and of the enjoyment of the food.

For a moment Nadia found herself wishing her people practiced the dinner-table conversation she had encountered during her studies abroad. Anything to distract herself from her awareness of the man seated halfway down the table, where she couldn't avoid seeing him every time she looked up.

She solved the problem by simply not looking up. When she couldn't restrain herself any longer, she found Gage watching her with a kind of wary interest, as if he suspected her of something and was waiting for her to betray herself.

Nonsense, she told herself. He had no reason to suspect her of anything, unless it was showing unseemly interest in him, a man she shouldn't have exchanged words with, much less allowed a closeness the thought of which made her burn inwardly.

The meal seemed endless and she was relieved when people began to drift from the table to the courtyard, where servants waited with urns of warm water, soap and towels. Stooping over a brass ewer, Nadia washed her hands with the soap as a servant poured warm water for her, then dried her hands on a towel held out by another servant.

"Nice touch," came a soft voice behind her. "You'd never guess this place has more bathrooms than bedrooms."

She steeled herself to ignore Gage, who had followed her out to the courtyard, but his touch on her arm made this impossible. He had also washed his hands in the traditional way and was drying them when she turned. "Do you enjoy playing desert queen?" he asked.

"The theme of the evening was Butrus's choice," she said coldly, hoping her tone would deter Gage.

No such luck. "Your intended provided enough food for an army. What happens to all the leftovers?"

He wasn't giving up, she realized, knowing that at some level, she didn't really want him to. His attention made her feel vibrant and desirable, the responses humming through her like the strings of a sitar plucked by an expert. As an engaged woman, she should be ashamed of such feelings, she reminded herself, but to no avail.

"The members of the household will eat their fill, and what remains will be shared with the poor," she explained, the neutral subject leaving her feeling less safe than it should.

She felt glad that Butrus had already retired to the salon where coffee and mint tea would be served and incense burned for the pleasure of his male guests. He wouldn't appreciate her spending time with Gage, however innocently. And she wasn't sure herself how innocent she could claim to be, given the turbulent state of her thoughts.

Gage nodded. "Good economy, handed down from when food was scarce and couldn't afford to be wasted."

She gave vent to a sigh of frustration. "Mr. Weston, why do you persist in speaking to me when you know it's wrong?"

"Why shouldn't I speak to my hostess?"

Because he wasn't content to speak, she knew. He liked to stand close, to touch. She liked it, too, but didn't want to like it, not from him. "Because you confuse me," she admitted.

"Myself, too," he surprised her by saying. "You're an intriguing woman. A princess, an artist, as well as beautiful and beguiling. A powerful combination."

"Enough," she commanded, more shaken than she wanted him to see. "You should join the other men. Butrus will be wondering where you are."

"Where will you be?"

Where she invariably ended up, she thought in annoyance. With the other women, discussing fashion and shopping, although such subjects held only limited interest for her.

"I shall be where I am supposed to be," she snapped. She muttered the leave-taking, which was half a blessing, and moved determinedly away, somehow aware that he stood where he was for a long time. She steeled herself not to look back.

As she'd expected, she was bored by the conversation within a few minutes and had to work to stop her thoughts from drifting to Gage in the men's salon. She pictured him drinking bitter coffee out of the tiny Spode cups the servants refilled from a brass coffeepot, which mysteriously, never seemed to run dry. Was he holding out his hands to receive a few drops of aromatic attar to perfume his skin? Breathing in the fragrant incense of sandalwood burned in a wooden urn on a four-footed brazier set on the floor in front of him?

Stop this, she commanded herself less than successfully. What Gage did was of no concern to her. She should more properly imagine Butrus doing these things, but couldn't make her thoughts turn to her fiancé. What was the matter with her?

"Your Highness looks feverish. Are you well?" the wife of one of Butrus's guests asked in a tone of concern.

Nadia thought quickly. Iriane was the woman's name, and she was the wife of one of Butrus's lawyer friends. "I am well, thank you, Iriane, just…distracted," she admitted. What an understatement that was!

The woman chattered on about how wonderful the evening had been, what a thrill it was to participate in such a night. Nadia listened with only half her attention, giving what she hoped were appropriate responses, all the while wondering how soon she could gracefully escape.

Her reprieve came soon afterward, when she heard Butrus personally showing out those of his guests who were not staying the night. The process required much hand shaking and compliments on the excellence of the dinner and the occasion in general. As host, Butrus waved these aside as no more than the guests' due and gave the blessing/leave-taking she had earlier offered Gage.

Except that he hadn't left.

Without quite knowing how, she knew he was standing in the shadows when she emerged from the salon to make her way across the colonnaded courtyard to her sleeping quarters. Needing a few minutes to herself, she had sent Nargis and the other attendants ahead to prepare the room.

At first she thought Gage was waiting for her, and her heart did an uncomfortable double beat, until she saw the silver device almost concealed in his palm. He was talking quietly on a cell phone and didn't hear her soft-footed approach.

"Dani, me darlin', you're a wonder to be sure," Nadia heard him say in a teasing imitation of an Irish accent. "If you can get that information to me overnight, I'll love you even more than I usually do."

Nadia felt her heart solidify in her chest like a lump of concrete. Somehow she had thought…she refused to allow the thought to blossom in her mind. Gage had meant nothing by his attention and his effusive compliments. How could he? He already had a woman called Dani waiting at home for him.

An aching sense of longing gripped Nadia. She hated that she had made a complete fool of herself, letting him touch her and whisper sweet nothings to her, for that's all they had been. Nothing.

Just as well the only witness was herself, she thought savagely. She hadn't told Tahani about Gage's tender touch, not because of the shame she should have felt, but because she had wanted to savor the moments she had spent with him, going over and over them in her thoughts like a lovestruck adolescent.

Served her right for mooning over a strange man when she was promised to Butrus, Nadia lectured herself. The pain didn't lessen, but she welcomed it as her just desserts.

''Take care of yourself, darlin'. We'll talk in the morning. Sweet dreams,'' Gage said, retrieving her attention as he flipped the phone closed.

At her slight movement, his head snapped up. The air fairly crackled as he cranked up his energy level to a new level of alertness. ''Fancy meeting you here,'' he said, the softness of his tone belying his tense stance. ''How long were you standing there listening?''

''I wasn't listening,'' she denied, then said, ''All right I was, but only to the last part of your conversation, and not intentionally. Was there a reason I shouldn't?'' Such as remaining in ignorance of the woman in his life? she added to herself, wondering why the thought made her feel so angry.

''No reason,'' he said, his pose still arguing with his denial. He seemed to realize it, and rested one shoulder against a marble pillar. ''I was just…checking on things at my office back home.''

''Your wife works for you?'' Nadia asked, wanting him to know she had heard enough to be aware of the other woman's role in his life.

In the shadows his eyes narrowed with puzzlement. ''My wife? Oh, you mean Dani.''

His lover, then. Nadia subdued a fresh wave of jealousy, finding it annoyingly hard to do. ''I'm surprised she didn't accompany you to this posting,'' she said.

''Unlikely, since rock bands aren't a favorite form of entertainment in Tamir.''

Nadia was confused. ''What has a rock band to do with anything?''

''Dani O'Hare is the lead singer of an up-and-coming group known as DaniO. She'd be the last person to think of joining the diplomatic service. Too conservative. No room for women with six-inch platform shoes and spiky purple hair. She's more like—'' he thought for a moment ''—my protégé, although she'd laugh herself silly if she heard me call her that.'' He sobered. ''I found her sleeping in my office doorway one rainy winter night. She was eleven and her mother had kicked her out because she didn't get along with her new stepfather. The mother refused to accept that the stepfather was an abusive bully to anyone smaller than himself. When I found her, Dani only weighed about seventy pounds wringing wet, and she was covered in bruises.''

''So you took her in.''

''What else could I do?''

''Allowed the appropriate authorities to care for her,'' Nadia said.

He gave a hollow laugh. ''The appropriate authorities were responsible for her fix in the first place. Soon after her mother remarried, Dani ran away. She was returned to the family home because the appropriate authorities thought it was the best place for her.''

His eyes were warm as he spoke about the girl he had rescued, Nadia noticed. She felt slightly ashamed of her earlier thoughts, when it was obvious that Gage looked on Dani almost as a daughter.

She touched a hand to her own raven locks. ''Does she really have purple hair?''

''This month, anyway. Last month it was green, as I recall.''

And her father thought *her* hair style was daring. Nadia's mouth curved into a smile. ''She sounds like an interesting person.''

''Funny, she said the same thing about you, Princess.''

She would not let herself feel pleased, Nadia vowed. Hadn't she learned her lesson yet? Gage's life had nothing to do with her. She would never meet Dani, nor did she need the young woman's approval. Or Gage's, for that matter. ''I'm glad you enjoyed discussing me with her,'' she said stiffly, and made to move past Gage.

He stepped between two pillars, blocking her path. ''I wasn't discussing you, so there's no need to take that regal tone of disapproval. I merely told her I'd met a fascinating member of the royal family, who happened to have painted one of my favorite paintings.''

"What you do is your own affair. It isn't my place to approve or disapprove of your actions."

He gave a low growl of impatience. "Save that submissive stuff for Butrus Dabir, Princess. He may enjoy it, but I don't."

Unable to pass him without stumbling through the garden beds, she had little option but to stand her ground. "I have no idea what you're talking about."

"Don't you? I've seen you with Dabir. You can't tell me all that 'yes sir, no sir, three bags full, sir' is the real Nadia Kamal."

"I don't see—" she began.

"That it's any of my business?" he supplied, then rubbed his hand tiredly across his face as if the long festivities had taken their toll. Or was there another reason? She recalled that he had asked Dani to report to him with some information he needed. What about? Instinct warned her not to ask.

"You're right, I spoke out of turn. My apologies, Princess," he said in a curiously flat tone.

She couldn't resist. "Now who's being submissive?"

He straightened and she could almost hear his mind reject such a notion. "You think so?" he said with dangerous precision, and then moved closer, almost rearing over her.

Her mind reeled. Dear heaven, what had she invited? "I didn't mean…"

He ignored her halting attempt to apologize, continuing his relentless progress until her back met cold, unyielding marble. "What was that about submissive?"

Chapter 8

As her awareness sharpened to almost painful intensity, Nadia knew she had several choices. She could scream to summon one of the guards patrolling the boundaries of the estate, aim her knee where it would do the most damage or force her way past Gage and run to her quarters.

None of the choices was as compelling as letting him kiss her.

She had known it would come to this from the moment she first saw him slumped behind the wheel of his car on the road to Marhaba.

Her country's tradition held that people's fates were often written in the stars. Was Gage's kiss an example, or was she merely trying to excuse her own outrageous behavior by blaming fate?

She had little time to wonder as his mouth pressed against hers, warm, demanding and infinitely exciting.

The faint tang of sandalwood incense clung to his hair, and he tasted of the cardamom coffee he had recently drunk.

His jaw felt rough against the smoothness of her cheek, the touch provoking her to match his ardor with her own.

Without conscious intention and with no idea where the instinct came from, she linked her hands around his neck, pulling his head down. She felt a slight resistance in the muscles of his neck, as if he questioned the wisdom of his actions, then he bent his head and deepened the kiss.

Her breath became shallow and she parted her lips to gain breath, but only succeeded in allowing Gage's teasing tongue entry to her mouth. She gasped as he made the most of the opportunity to explore, making her light-headed.

Or was it the heady touch of skin to skin, so rare in her experience, that made pleasure spiral through her, deliciously close to pain? She fought to silence the inner voice warning her that this was wrong and just clung to him, glorying in being held close and aroused so wantonly.

She had thought herself in love before, but Gordon had been no more experienced in such matters than she was. The blind leading the blind. Gage was far from blind, and where he was leading her didn't bear thinking about. She only knew that she was ready to follow him anywhere, if only this wonderful sensation could be allowed to continue.

It couldn't of course, and she should have been glad that Gage had the strength to end it for both their sakes. She felt a terrible sense of loss when he stepped back, swaying a little as if paying a price for his restraint.

"Dear heaven, Nadia," he said, his voice raspy. "I didn't mean to do that."

It was the first time he had used her name without adding her title, or calling her "Princess" in a mocking tone. Added to the intimacy they had just shared, she felt like a fishing vessel cast adrift by a storm tide and had to steady herself by resting a hand against one of the cool marble columns.

Afraid that she would sound as shaken as she felt, she pressed a finger to his lips. "If there is fault, it is mine, also."

He shaped his mouth around her finger, his tongue moistening the tip until her insides cramped in response. She tore her hand away, shocked that such a slight touch could have such a powerful effect on her. It went against all her common sense.

He dragged his fingers through his hair. "Maybe we are equally to blame. But it doesn't excuse me taking advantage like this."

She allowed herself a slight smile. "I didn't exactly—what would you English say?—put up a fight."

His shaky smile answered hers. "True. Why didn't you?"

"Why did you feel the need to kiss me?"

"Touché. We both did what we wanted. So where do we go from here?"

"To bed," she said simply, then blushed as she realized how he was bound to take that. "Our own beds," she amended. "We must never speak of this moment again."

The command was directed as much at herself as at Gage, and was accompanied by an aching sense of emptiness. She not only wanted to speak of it, but to dream of it and, God help her, to repeat it. But she could not and hope to live with herself. She was a princess with responsibilities and duties, engaged to be married. Her life allowed no room for such self-indulgence.

No room for passion. Or love.

With a cry of despair, she pushed past Gage and fled along the mosaic path to her quarters.

Long after he heard the door close behind her, Gage stood in the colonnade, anchoring himself to the marble pillar as he had seen her do. The cold stone was little comfort after the warmth of holding the princess in his arms. He could still feel her lips pressing against his and hear her gasp of response as he plundered her mouth.

She had acted as if his touch electrified her. With her limited experience, it probably had, although he could hardly take all the credit. He was pretty sure he was the first man to kiss her in such a flagrant fashion. In her society men and women rarely mixed, much less touched, unless they were husband and wife. She probably couldn't conceive of making love purely for pleasure.

Was he the loser for living in a more permissive society? he wondered. In his home country of Penwyck not so many years ago, a look or a touch had been considered as romantically daring as they were in Tamir today. Like so much of the world, his country's morality had moved with the times. Now anything went, and experiences had to become ever more intense to achieve the same level of piquancy.

He indulged himself in a sigh. He wouldn't want to lead a cloistered life, were it even possible. But he did envy Nadia her innocence. His roomy four-poster was going to seem cold and empty tonight, and he wondered if hers would feel the same.

The next morning brought no new information from Dani. As soon as he'd returned to his suite, Gage had e-mailed her photos of the new arrivals, which he'd snapped covertly during the banquet with a camera the size of his thumb, but so far Dani had no news for him regarding the identity of the subjects. She'd promised to keep digging.

He knew they had connections with the American underworld, as Dani had confirmed. What he needed now were clear links between Butrus Dabir and the Brothers of Darkness. All he'd gotten so far were more suspicions.

King Marcus wasn't going to be thrilled when Gage reported in. Well, that made two of them, Gage thought. His need to bring Conrad's killers to account burned like a flame inside him, driving him through this mission, although he wanted nothing more than to be gone from Tamir and its palace intrigues.

And its beautiful princess?

He'd lain awake for a long time pondering that one. After one bad experience, he'd resolved to remain coldly professional and keep his feelings out of his missions. He'd even managed to relegate his need to revenge Conrad's death to a part of his mind where it wouldn't affect his ability to function.

What was it about women in need that touched him so deeply? The last time he'd allowed a woman to reach him, he'd come to regret it. He hated to think he was in danger of doing it again.

Nadia was hardly in need. She had everything a woman could want. Except freedom. She was beautiful, talented, strong. Everything in him rebelled against seeing such a woman under the thumb of a man like Dabir. At least, that was the reason Gage gave himself for caring so much. His concern for Nadia had nothing to do with the way her jasmine scent haunted him and her taste lingered on his mouth, he assured himself.

At breakfast Butrus Dabir was the image of the genial host, inquiring repeatedly after Gage's health and how well he had slept after the lavish banquet. As was expected, Gage repeated his effusive compliments about the food and the presentation, although they risked sticking in his throat along with the honey pancakes he was served.

He didn't know if he was glad or sorry that Nadia preferred to eat breakfast in her quarters. Facing her across the table, not knowing which side she was on, was going to be hellishly difficult when his mind insisted on replaying the sensation of her lips on his and her arms tight around his neck.

He forced the image away and concentrated on what he had learned during the banquet. The group of newcomers he'd noticed the previous night who, he'd managed to learn, had arrived at the estate only the previous afternoon, were nowhere to be seen.

During the conversation he'd carefully orchestrated, his dinner companions hadn't been able to tell him anything about the group other than that the men were American. They were obviously close to Butrus Dabir, judging from the warm welcome they had received upon arrival. Since warm welcomes were a feature of Tamiri life, Gage didn't read too much into that.

He thought back to his conversation with Nadia. Gage hadn't lied to the princess about Dani's role in his life or her involvement with the rock band, but he had carefully omitted mentioning how good she was at tracking down information.

He didn't blame Dani for finding nothing. These people were experts at covering their tracks. Gage decided that his best hope was to keep his eyes and ears open when the newcomers joined Dabir's meetings and try to pick up on something more.

Easier said than done, he discovered as he washed his hands after the morning meal and prepared to join the others.

At the door to the conference chamber, Dabir placed a hand on his shoulder. "I have monopolized your time long enough, my friend. You have been most patient with our deliberations when I know that your main interest in Tamiri affairs is in trade."

Gage felt as if a loathsome spider had crawled onto his shoulder. He barely kept the reaction from showing on his face. "Not at all, old chap," he said, all British bonhomie. "When the new preamble to the constitution is unveiled, I shall feel I have played some infinitesimal part in its development. It is a singular honor to have the privilege of watching a master legal mind at work."

He tried to sidestep Dabir and enter the room, but the burly attorney managed to get in his way, looking smugly pleased, although he said, "You give me far too much credit. My role in our history is a mere footnote. You are the one who struts the world stage, dispensing diplomacy on behalf of your great country."

Gage nodded his thanks, wondering where all this was leading.

He soon found out.

"Only a short drive from Zabara is the Black Rock Souk. Located at the top of the famous Zabara cliffs, it is a beautiful and very active center of day-to-day trade."

Dabir wanted him to go shopping? Gage's skepticism must have shown on his face, because Dabir clapped him on the shoulder again. "There is no better place for a man of your interests to study Tamir trade at its grass roots. Trust me, my friend."

Knowing he wouldn't trust Dabir to count the small change in his pocket, Gage managed a stiff smile. "Sounds splendid. I'll make a point of visiting this souk right after the meeting."

"There's no need to trouble yourself further with our trifling affairs. Today we discuss matters of purely local interest. My dishonor would be great if, as my guest, you should be bored. I would be delighted to place a car and driver at your disposal, so you may avail yourself of a visit to the souk this morning."

In short, the talks were none of Gage's business, but it would be impolite to say so directly, much in the manner that a Tamiri would say he'd think about a deal in which he had no interest, rather than insult his guest by saying so outright. In return, a good guest was expected to take the hint and not press the matter.

Gage decided to be a good guest for the moment. "Splendid idea. I'm sure I'll find the souk educational. But I'll take my own car, thanks."

His host frowned. "You must permit me to provide you with a car and driver. If you were to get lost or suffer any ill effects at all, I would never forgive myself."

"The responsibility is mine alone," Gage insisted, resisting the urge to clench his fists over the excess of politeness. He had no intention of accepting the offer of car and driver and thus placing himself so completely in Dabir's hands. Getting lost was far preferable to ending up dumped over a cliff with his throat cut.

After a few more effusive compliments and not-at-alls were exchanged, Gage was left alone, wondering what he was going to do now. Since trade was his cover story rather than his area of expertise, he felt disinclined to visit this souk, but didn't see how he was going to get out of it.

In the main courtyard two black Bentleys waited, their uniformed drivers energetically polishing imaginary specks off the showroom-bright surface. Gage saw Nadia approach the first car, surrounded by her chattering attendants and obviously bound for the same shopping expedition. Dressed in a buttercup-colored *galabiya* threaded with gold over matching wide-legged pants, with a wisp of white scarf fluttering around her shoulders, she looked as fresh as a spring day.

He felt his interest quicken. Maybe the day wouldn't be a total loss, after all. He strode up to the women and performed a polite salaam, greeting them in deliberately woeful Arabic.

The two younger ones, duplicates of one another, giggled and covered their faces with their hands. Nadia winced, but smiled politely and returned his greeting. Not by a blink of her lovely dark eyes did she show that Gage meant any more to her than any of her fiancé's associates, two of whom were waiting with their wives, obviously intending to join the expedition.

If Gage hadn't caught the fluttering of a pulse at Nadia's throat, he might have convinced himself he'd imagined kissing her last night.

"I trust Your Highness will prevent this foreigner from making too many blunders at the souk today," he said, switching to English.

Nadia's face remained impassive. "Nargis is a capable bargainer. I depend on her utterly. You'll be delighted to assist Mr. Weston, won't you Nargis?"

Looking pleased, the attendant hovering beside the princess stepped forward and threw herself immediately into her assigned task. "The main thing to remember is not to buy anything at the first shop you enter. Go to several, drink the coffee you are offered and get a feel for the value of the item you are interested in, then return to the first place you visited and begin to bargain in earnest."

Gage let his look tell the princess that there was only one item of value to him here, and he wasn't going to find it at the souk. She looked away, pretending not to notice, although he was sure she had.

''Come, we must be on our way,'' she told her attendants. To Gage she said pointedly, ''Your car has been brought around for you, and the rest of the party is ready to go.''

Watching Gage move with obvious reluctance toward his car, Nadia released a breath of relief. For a moment she'd thought he might insist on traveling in their vehicle. It was bad enough to have him stand so close to her that she could smell the lingering traces of the attar he had shared with his host last night, the scent reminding her of how shamefully she had succumbed to the temptation of Gage's kiss.

After leaving him in the colonnade last night, she had slept little, and wondered if he had been as disturbed by their encounter as she was. He did remember it, she gathered from the volatile look he'd given her when he approached. But he hadn't had to endure the pangs of guilt that had plagued her. She deserved every one of them, she had told herself as she tossed and turned. She had wronged her fiancé, and it was only proper that she suffer for it.

Unfortunately most of her regrets were in her head and refused to reach her heart. There, she felt only a soul-deep yearning to know more of Gage's attention, to find herself once more in his arms, his hungry mouth claiming hers.

She looked up to find Nargis regarding her speculatively. Although her attendant said nothing, Nadia could almost hear the other woman's earlier accusation that Nadia was thinking about ''this man who isn't Butrus, who makes your cheeks glow and your eyes shine.'' And Nargis would be right. The problem was, Nadia had no idea how to stop.

Chapter 9

Driving along the road to Black Rock Souk always made Nadia nervous. The bazaar, built on the ruins of an ancient trading center, was perched atop one of the highest cliffs in the region and could only be reached by a narrow road carved out of the side of the cliff.

On one side of the road rose a wall of rock that felt as if it could come crashing down on the car at any time. Even so, it was easier to fix her gaze on the cliff wall than to look at the other side, where the road sheared away in a dizzying drop to the sea, pounding the rocky shore far below.

At one point their driver had to slow almost to a crawl as a massive, yellow power shovel-tractor chewed chunks out of the cliff to widen the road ahead of them. Nadia saw more yellow vehicles parked along a new dirt siding they had gouged out of the cliff to keep the main thoroughfare clear while they worked.

"It's about time something was done about this road," Nargis commented, clutching a handful of scarf to her face although their car's air-conditioning system kept the choking dust from reaching them.

Nadia looked back. The car occupied by the other guests had almost disappeared in the dust churned up by the road-work machinery. She couldn't see Gage's car at all, although she told herself she hadn't been looking for him. In any case, he was well able to take care of himself.

"Do you have much shopping you want to do?" she asked her attendants to distract herself.

Nargis gave her the sort of look usually reserved for a backward child. "There is always shopping to be done, my princess. A new dress, a headscarf, some jewelry, gifts for friends."

For Nadia, shopping was something she did when she needed something, not a pursuit she found pleasurable, as well Nargis knew. She brightened. "I may buy some art supplies so I can paint the swans, as well as sketch them."

Nargis made a tongue-clicking sound of disgust. "Art supplies. What about the beautiful things you will need for your wedding?"

"Mother is taking care of everything to do with the wedding."

More tongue clicks. "She is not the one being married," Nargis said acerbically. "You might take a little interest in the proceedings, my princess."

Nadia traded looks with Tahani, knowing she understood. "Oh, but I do. I assure you I'm taking as little interest as I possibly can." She saw Tahani duck her head to hide her smile. On either side of Tahani, Thea and Ramana adopted bookend looks of confusion.

Muttering her disapproval, Nargis subsided against the butter-soft leather seat and said no more about wedding preparations, much to Nadia's relief.

Suddenly a new idea occurred to Nadia. "I know what I'll shop for—a gift for Father to commemorate his long tenure on the throne."

Her attendants approved of this, she saw as they burst into

an excited discussion of possibilities. Their suggestions ranged from gold and precious stones to daggers, Tamiri pearls and fine carpets, all of which would be available in abundance at the souk.

None of them were what Nadia had in mind. "I shall purchase new tools and order a special piece of marble to make a bust of the sheik," she announced.

The attendants stared at her, all but Tahani looking aghast. "But, Princess, surely you don't want to be carving statues now, when you are soon to be married?" Nargis asked.

Nadia read between the lines. What Nargis meant was that *she* didn't want to prepare the princess for her wedding day by picking chips of marble out of her hair and scrubbing the dust of the studio off her skin, as had happened the last time Nadia embarked on a major new work.

"Indeed I do," she said happily. "This bust will be the most special gift I have ever given my father."

"I think he would prefer grandchildren," muttered Nargis under her breath.

Nadia pretended not to hear. Her mind was already racing ahead to the bust she intended to create. At the Black Rock Souk she knew of a shop that specialized in supplying marble of all kinds, more usually for floors and columns. They were bound to have a piece that would suit her needs. In addition, she would need new chisels, hammers and bolsters, and sketching materials to make a preliminary plan. Oh, this would be wonderful!

She was so preoccupied that she hardly noticed when they crawled along the stretch of road she usually found most alarming, where the edge looked as if it might crumble at any moment, and there was barely room for one car to pass in either direction. They had reached the souk before she had finished outlining the new project in her mind.

Black Rock Souk was the largest of the Tamiri marketplaces, built according to traditional design and extended many times throughout the centuries. Bridges and staircases connected the older clifftop section with the newer sections, although even they were a century old by now. It was hard to tell old from new, because both featured intricate Tamiri architecture, Arabesque granite floors and spectacular skylights, as well as lovely murals on the walls.

In the old section, men gathered in coffee shops to play dominoes and cards, or waited on benches outside a traditional hairdresser, talking to while away the time.

One wing of the souk was reserved for gifts and electronic wares, while the other housed gold, gems and jewelry shops. Nadia knew there were more than six hundred shops arranged along the winding alleyways and atop the steep stone staircases. New merchants seemed to be opening stores all the time.

The upper floors were the most popular with tourists and offered antiques, fine carpets, Tamiri jewelry, curios and artifacts. On the lower floor could be found gold, precious stones, rosewood furniture and household items. A special section offered textiles and bridal wares, garments, cosmetics and leather goods. Here, there were also stores devoted to particular designers—Versace, Chanel, Tiffany and Gucci— which Nadia's sisters adored. Nadia was happy to replenish her store of jasmine perfume blended especially for her and stored inside an exquisitely handcrafted bottle.

She was surprised at how quickly she became caught up in exploring the lower floor. She even found herself enjoying inspecting some of the bridal wares, as bolts of exquisite textiles were unrolled before her, accompanied by thimble-size cups of coffee.

For once she was happy to follow Nargis's advice and refuse to buy at the first few shops they visited, although privately she thought the custom unnecessarily time-consuming. Left to herself, she would probably buy the first thing she saw that suited her needs and be on her way. As it was, she couldn't resist buying a dress she knew would be perfect for her sister Samira, without inspecting the dozen more that Nargis recommended.

''You would take all the pleasure out of the experience,

my princess,'' Nargis said reprovingly as they left the shop.
She gestured ahead of them. "At least your fiancé's guests
take my advice.''

Nadia felt her heart catch as she automatically looked for
Gage ahead of them, forgetting for a moment that he wasn't
the only one of Butrus's guests to join the shopping excur-
sion. And indeed, Nargis was referring to a married couple
Nadia had barely spoken to. They shook their heads and
lifted their hands as a merchant tried to thrust a Shirazi carpet
upon them. From where she stood, Nadia saw that it was an
imitation.

Stepping out of the shop with the merchant on their heels,
the couple gave the princess's party a helpless look. Nargis
stepped between the merchant and his victims, remonstrating
with him in voluble Tamiri until he rolled up the offending
carpet and returned to his shop.

Nargis turned away the couple's thanks, insisting she had
done nothing, but Nadia heard her attendant give them a few
more shopping tips before they plunged once more into the
heart of the bazaar.

"Maybe you should go with them," the princess suggested.

Nargis shook her head. "They were wise enough not to
be taken in by the carpet seller. They will be all right.'' She
looked at her mistress keenly. "Were you, perhaps, expecting
to see one of your fiancé's other guests, my princess? When
I pointed them out to you, you reacted as if you had been
stung by a bee.''

"You're imagining things.''

"No doubt. Shall I imagine your reaction this time, when
I tell you that Mr. Gage Weston has just entered the shop of
the gold merchant we are to visit next?''

Forewarned, Nadia was able to stop herself from reacting
so obviously this time, although she couldn't slow the racing
of her pulse or stop her hands from growing moist. "I have
no idea what you're twittering about," she said to Nargis in
her most regal tone.

The attendant gave her an assessing glance. "As Your Highness wishes." She lifted the embroidered hanging separating the gold merchant's shop from the busy alleyway and bowed slightly as Nadia passed her. Thea, Ramana and Tahani had paused to inspect a display of gold trinkets outside the shop.

"He is a most attractive man, your foreigner," Nargis said for the princess's ears alone.

Nadia shot her a sharp look. "He is not *my* foreigner. From the way you're going on about him, one might think you were the one stung by the bee."

Nargis let the curtain drop and spread her hands. "Alas, the bee of passion is unlikely to sting me, my princess. I am not such a beautiful flower as you, to attract men so easily."

"Maybe you're better off," Nadia said thoughtfully. Since Gage Weston had come into her life, she had known nothing but confusion. Allowing him to kiss her last night had only deepened her mental turmoil.

She knew she was letting him assume far too much importance in her life. That was what came from leading such a proscribed existence. Probably any man would have caused the same havoc within her, had they met under similar circumstances.

Or so she tried to tell herself.

One look at Gage, reclining easily on the cushions that edged the shop floor, his arm resting on a padded, boxlike affair, was enough to convince her of the folly of this idea. A coffee cup looked absurdly delicate in his masculine grasp, and Nadia couldn't help remembering how those same hands had felt holding her last night.

He uncoiled from the floor with all the grace of a hunting tiger. The slight smile curving his generous mouth suggested that he was remembering, too. She met his gaze directly, refusing to let him see how unsettled she was by his presence.

The gold merchant, Mr. Khalid, also sprang to his feet as soon as he recognized the princess. He bowed low. "This is a great honor, Your Highness. Let me make you comfortable.''

She was shown to cushions opposite Gage. As soon as she and Nargis were comfortable, the merchant clapped his hands and a servant materialized from the rear of the shop to offer her one of the small, bell-shaped cups that held a tablespoonful of very spicy coffee. She drank and answered polite inquiries about her father's health, her own health and the health of everyone in the royal household, then in turn inquired about Mr. Khalid's well-being and that of his children.

Throughout the ritual, she was aware of Gage relaxing on his cushions, watching and saying nothing. He didn't seem impatient with the performance; indeed he was enjoying it she saw, when she studied him covertly from beneath lowered lashes.

No doubt visiting the souk was a novelty for him. England had its share of marketplaces but none as rich and varied as the Black Rock Souk, not only for the breathtaking choice of wares, but also for the timelessness of the shopping experience.

While studying abroad, she had been bewildered to visit English stores and to see price tags for the first time. Such an idea was totally alien to her experience. How could prices be negotiated if they were already written down? For once Nadia found herself agreeing with Nargis, who believed such an outrageous concept allowed no room for the delicious art of haggling, which the merchants enjoyed as much as their customers. According to the attendant, the cut and thrust of arriving at precisely the right price to suit both parties was what made shopping the adventure it was.

Nadia wasn't as enthusiastic as her attendant and often found herself wishing every transaction didn't have to take quite so long, but she had to agree that the process had its pleasant moments.

The coffee ritual began again when Tahani, Thea and Ramana joined them. Nadia's cup was refilled twice from a brightly polished brass pot. At last she shook her empty cup and said, "Bass—enough." The server then collected all the cups and departed, one hand looking like a chandelier from the cluster of cups hooked onto his fingers.

Only then did the merchant bring out trays of gold wares for the women and Gage to inspect. As the agreed bargainer for the group, Nargis recoiled in horror every time a price was mentioned. Gage looked amused, but went along with the process, Nadia was pleased to see. Nargis would have been highly affronted had he contradicted her at any stage.

Nadia found her eye drawn again and again to a necklace made of heavy gold links in the shape of the Greek key pattern. At the center of the chain was a tiger's head the size of her thumbnail, the eyes made of gleaming emeralds. She had never seen anything to compare with it.

Had she been alone, she would have paid Mr. Khalid's price, but she didn't wish to incur Nargis's wrath a second time. When the attendant signaled, Nadia took a last regretful look at the necklace, then followed the group out of the shop. After a moment's hesitation Gage shrugged and followed them.

Mr. Khalid pursued them along the footpath until Nargis managed to convince him that no one in her entire life had ever offered her such inferior wares at such inflated prices. Seemingly cowed, the merchant returned to his shop.

"Wasn't she a bit hard on him, considering we'd accepted his hospitality?" Gage asked Nadia in a low voice.

"In Tamir hospitality is not considered a favor, but an obligation. By the time this day is done, you will have drunk many cups of coffee or tea and probably bought very little."

"Sounds like an expensive way to do business," he observed. "I was hoping you would buy that tiger necklace. It looked superb on you."

Nadia felt her face grow warm. She had seen him watching as the merchant placed the necklace around her throat and had also caught the nod of approval he gave, as if the combination pleased him. "If I had agreed to buy it so quickly, Nargis would have had my head on a platter. I already suc-

cumbed to impulse and bought a dress for Samira. Two impulses in one day are more than Nargis can cope with.''

"Tough lady, your Nargis.''

"She has served my family well for many years, and has
only my best interests at heart.''

As if to prove the point, Nargis moved closer to the princess, her frown disapproving of the whispered conversation
between her and Gage. "We will visit three more gold merchants, then we will return to Mr. Khalid and purchase the
tiger necklace.''

"Wouldn't it have been easier to buy it the first time
around?'' Gage asked innocently.

He might as well have asked Nargis why she made a habit
of breathing, Nadia thought, restraining her smile with an
effort. Her attendant drew herself up. "If you seriously intend
to improve trade relations between your country and ours,
Mr. Weston, you will do well to observe how things are done
here.''

He made an elaborate salaam. "My apologies, Mistress
Nargis. My words were ill chosen and I withdraw them. I
shall listen and learn.''

Mollified, Nargis let out the breath that had puffed up her
chest and addressed Nadia. "Come, we have many more
merchants to visit.''

She wasn't exaggerating, and by the time Nargis was satisfied they'd made enough comparisons, Gage's head was
spinning. He was ready to call for time-out when Nadia announced they would stop for refreshment at one of the many
cafés crowding the souk.

To Gage, one café looked much like the other, but Nadia
insisted they patronize a particular one, which evidently had
links to her family for generations back. The food was certainly good, Gage thought. They ate spicy roast lamb carved
from a giant vertical spit, with flat bread and fragrant sauces,
followed by honey-drenched baklava, the meal washed down
with springwater, which he found a welcome antidote to the

copious amounts of coffee he'd drunk that morning. The beverage may have been served in tiny cups, but they added up.

Afterward Nadia announced that she intended to order the marble and hammers for her new work.

"I'll forgo the tiger necklace and have those, instead," she said.

Nargis made a face. "Butrus will not appreciate seeing you on your wedding day wearing marble and hammers."

"Perhaps not, but my father will be thrilled with his gift."

The princess had spoken. Nargis fell silent but kept up a moody sulk all the way to the marble seller. Only Tahani showed any interest in this stage of the proceedings, Nargis and the twins remaining outside to rest on wooden benches. Gage accompanied Nadia and Tahani into the shop, wishing he could convince Tahani to stay outside, as well.

When the merchant brought out the coffee cups and brass pot, Gage had to work at looking pleased, not sure he could handle much more caffeine. He wondered if that was the source of Nadia's dazzlingly bright eyes, then decided the credit was hers alone. She was easily the most engaging and lively woman he'd ever met.

If he hadn't been preoccupied with what was going on back at Butrus's estate, he would have enjoyed the shopping expedition, if only for the pleasure of watching Nadia. She was enough to distract any man, especially as she was now, engaged in a quest that commanded her full attention.

After they had drunk coffee and exchanged the required small talk, the merchant automatically turned to Gage. "I am honored to be asked to supply marble to the royal palace, Your Highness. My grandfather, may he rest in peace, supplied marble to the princess's grandfather, may he rest in peace. May I be permitted to ask, how many columns are we discussing?"

Nadia sketched a foot-square cube in the air. "One piece, about so large."

The merchant hid his disappointment well, but still insisted on honoring Gage with a title. "Your Highness, I understand why you would wish to order a sample—"

"It isn't a sample. It's for a sculpture of my father, Sheik Ahmed," Nadia said in a voice with an edge that Gage thought the merchant would do well to heed. Although the merchant had recognized the princess on sight, he obviously didn't know her very well. Addressing his remarks to the male in the party was probably automatic, but wasn't going to get him anywhere with her.

"I think you'd better talk to the princess," Gage advised, keeping his voice low.

The merchant looked flustered but did as bidden, eventually promising to supply a piece of marble of the size and quality she required. The stone would be shipped to the palace without delay.

When Nadia began to discuss chisels and hammers with the expertise of a stonemason, Gage saw his chance and excused himself from the discussion. He didn't think she saw him leave, so caught up was she.

Slightly breathless, he returned to the party just as she and Tahani emerged from the marble seller. Nargis and the twins rose as one, and rejoined them.

"Did you get everything you needed?" he asked.

Nadia inclined her head. "Of course, *Your Highness.*"

For a moment alarm bolted through him. Had she discovered the truth about him? The sparkle in her eye told him she was only mimicking the marble seller. He concealed his relief behind a shrug. "What can I say? The man recognizes quality."

"The man recognizes another man," she snapped.

He caught her wrist. "Hey, it was hardly my fault."

She looked coldly at his hand, but he didn't release her. "I note you didn't mind."

The pulse he felt racing under his fingers was a potent reminder of how he had made her feel last night. How she had made *him* feel. He pulled his hand away as if burned. "I told him to talk to you, didn't I?"

Her face gave nothing away, but he saw her rub her wrist as if feeling something similar. "Precisely. You had to tell him to."

"I don't make the laws, Princess." If he did, she wouldn't be surrounded by attendants and they would be miles from here, lying on a beach somewhere, sharing an intimate meal and then... He snapped himself out of the reverie. Nothing of the sort was going to happen, and as long as he didn't know how much she knew of Dabir's affairs, it never would.

The thought left him feeling edgy and unsatisfied, in no mood for more shopping and, saints forbid, more coffee.

Nadia evidently agreed. She directed Nargis to locate the rest of their party and have the cars fetched for them. While the attendant was gone and the others window-shopped, Gage slipped a velvet box into the princess's hands.

She looked at it in confusion. "What is this?"

"I guessed you wouldn't have time to go back for it, so..." He left the explanation hanging as she opened the box. Inside was the tiger necklace.

She closed the box with a snap, her expression clouded. "You bought me a gift. Why?"

He wasn't sure. He still didn't know which side she was on, and he had almost no control when he was around her, breathing in her heady jasmine scent. Why he should feel motivated to give her anything was beyond him. But he did.

"You remind me of a tigress," he said, explaining to himself as much as to her. "Outwardly you're subservient to the males in the pride, but you're actually the huntress who takes care of everybody."

She gave him a look that said she didn't like being known more than she wanted to be. "You presume a great deal, Mr. Weston."

"That name again. In my country, once two people have kissed, they're usually on first-name terms."

Her hunted glance found Tahani and the twins, but they gave no sign of having heard. "I thought we agreed not to speak of that," Nadia hissed.

"You agreed not to speak of it, Princess. Yet today you've spoken of it with every look."

"Then I shall try not to look at you."

"The way you're not looking at me now?"

His huskily voiced challenge made her lift her long lashes and face him, as he had intended. His loins tightened as he felt himself drowning in her lambent gaze. Her lips curved into a reluctant smile. "You are an impossible man, Gage."

Better. Now all he had to do was prove that she was one of the good guys, deal with Butrus Dabir and whisk her away from all this, so he could taste more of the passion he knew simmered beneath that compliant exterior.

Which of the Herculean tasks would he find most difficult? he wondered. He wasn't sure he wanted to know the answer, but was afraid he already did.

Chapter 10

A few minutes later Nargis returned, shepherding the other members of the party. The petite, black-haired attendant was frowning. "A thousand apologies, but your car is proving difficult to start, Your Highness."

The man Nargis had rescued from buying the fake carpet stepped forward. "Please take our car, Your Highness. We can wait until the second car is fixed."

Before she could answer, Gage offered, "I'd be delighted to drive the princess back to the estate in my car—with her attendant, naturally."

Nadia schooled the turmoil out of her expression. "Thank you, but I'm sure my car will be ready soon. I don't mind waiting a little longer."

"Not afraid of riding with me, are you?" he asked her in an undertone.

She bristled, furious that he could think she was afraid of him when she had an entire army at her command if she so wished. Not that she needed one to handle such a presumptuous man. To prove it, she said through gritted teeth,

"Rather than inconvenience my fiancé's guests, I shall accept your offer. Tahani will attend me."

Nargis looked as if she would prefer to accompany her mistress, but Nadia quelled her with a fierce look. Bad enough to have to ride in the same car with Gage, without having Nargis reading omens into every word that passed between them.

She saw Gage's mouth twitch as she said as regally as she could, "Come, Tahani."

She swept ahead of him to the waiting Branxton, but somehow he reached it before her, opening the rear passenger door for her with all the aplomb of a professional chauffeur, although no servant would dare look at her so boldly as she brushed past.

At least he had the sense not to expect her to ride in front, Nadia thought. It was unthinkable for her to travel beside any man not her husband. Equally unthinkable for her to be alone in the car with him. So why did she feel a faint sense of disappointment that Tahani was sharing the journey?

She needn't have worried. Tired after the long shopping expedition, Tahani began to nod off almost as soon as they were under way.

"Looks like you wore out the hired help," Gage said, watching them in the rearview mirror.

She glanced at Tahani. "She told me she was troubled by bad dreams last night and didn't get much sleep." Nadia didn't add that the maid's dreams had worried her or that Gage himself had figured in them. He didn't seem like a man to believe in what he couldn't see, feel, taste or touch, so the premonitions were unlikely to impress him.

"I didn't get much sleep, either," he admitted. "Guess I don't need to tell you why."

She pursed her lips. "Dare I hope that your conscience was troubled?"

He shook his head. "Not a bit, Princess. Was yours?"

"It should have been."

"Which doesn't answer my question."

She summoned her voice with difficulty, unable to be less than truthful. "No, my conscience wasn't troubled. But my mind was uneasy." She had been kept awake last night, not because she felt guilty for having kissed Gage, but because she *hadn't* regretted it.

In truth she had wanted much more and had lain awake long into the night suffering from a bad case of frustration. Her penance for being disloyal to Butrus. Unfaithful was more accurate. Not only had she lost herself in Gage's embrace and enjoyed it, she had craved more of his attention. What kind of wife would she make when it took so little to turn her thoughts away from her duty?

"Don't look so troubled, Princess," Gage said softly, his gaze darting from the winding cliff road to her and back to the road again. "Lots of people succumb to a moment of curiosity. It doesn't mean you're beyond redemption."

"Perhaps not where you come from." And probably not in Tamir. It was Nadia herself who was letting the moment of weakness disturb her, mainly because she knew it was becoming far more than a moment. Every time she was near Gage, her thoughts turned in directions they shouldn't be going.

Could she really blame her response on curiosity? If it had been, surely the kiss would have satisfied her. Instead, it had set up a hunger that was becoming a fever in her blood.

She saw Gage's smile reflected in the mirror and thought she saw a tinge of sadness there. "You'll marry your attorney and have lots of kids," he said, "and look back on this as a test that you passed with flying colors."

He didn't sound happy, she noticed, her spirits lifting in spite of herself. "Do you enjoy wreaking havoc in people's lives?" she asked, well aware of how much havoc he wreaked in hers.

"Only the ones whose beauty takes my breath away."

Did she really do that? Heat radiated through her, although she tried to subdue it. "You mustn't say such things. And you can't give me gifts, either. You must take back the necklace."

"Sorry, the style wouldn't suit me at all."

She wished he wouldn't mock her. "Is there no one in England you could give it to?"

"Fishing, Princess?"

"No!" She knew her denial sounded forced. "You mentioned your sister..."

"If I start giving Alexandra jewelry, she'll think I've lost my mind."

Nadia tried to tell herself she didn't care that there was no other woman in his life, but her feeling of elation argued against it. "What kind of gifts do you give her?"

"Horse-riding gear, painting equipment. She's an artist like you."

"And a sportswoman, from the sound of it."

"She was part of the British equestrian team at the last Olympics."

The pride in his voice was unmistakable. "What about your parents? What do they do?"

He hesitated. Somehow she sensed it wasn't because he needed to give the hairpin turns his full attention. She could almost hear him trying to decide what to tell her. Why? Was he afraid the truth would repel her? She didn't care if his father was a street sweeper and nearly said so, until she stopped herself, not wanting to betray any more interest in him than she had already.

As the road straightened a little, he said over his shoulder, "My father advises our government on policy."

Hardly a street sweeper, so why the hesitation? She wished she could shake off the feeling that Gage was being secretive. "Like Butrus?" she said.

"Hopefully with a little less self-interest."

"You don't like Butrus, do you."

She saw his fingers tighten around the steering wheel. "Why do you ask?"

"You never mention him without sounding disapproving."

"Has it occurred to you there could be a good reason for that?"

Thinking of what the reason might be, she turned away, feeling her cheeks heat. They were approaching the steepest part of the road, she noticed. Her attention had been too focused on Gage for it to register before.

She remembered that Tahani's dream had concerned a road and cliffs, although she had been unable to specify where they were. Nadia became aware that Gage's attention had become totally fixed on the driving. The rigid set of his back and neck told her something was wrong.

"Aren't we going too fast?" she asked, fear gripping her as she saw the cliff face hurtling past much, much too close.

He didn't take his eyes from the road. "I don't want to alarm you, Princess, but you'd better brace yourself. We don't seem to have any brakes."

Tahani was awake and upright now, the car's swaying movement disturbing her doze. She looked at Nadia with wide frightened eyes, "Are we going to die, my princess?"

Gage heard her. "Not if I have anything to do with it. Hang on."

Gage knew his confident words belied the empty sensation that had hit him when he felt the brake pedal sink all the way to the floor without affecting the car's speed.

Instinct made him pump the pedal rapidly several times to try to build up brake-fluid pressure, but it was useless. Praying, he downshifted to the lowest gear and groped for the parking brake, easing it up. Just as well he kept a hold on it, because the car skidded into a four-wheel slide that took them perilously close to the crumbling shoulder. He had to spring away from the brake and put all his muscle into keeping the car from becoming airborne.

Loose stones skittered away from their wheels as he wrenched the car out of the careering dive at the last second.

Then he braced himself for the screech of tortured metal as he deliberately sideswiped the stone of the cliff side.

Sitting closest to that side, Tahani screamed and scrambled to the center of the seat, hunching away from the stone fragments peppering her window. "What is he doing?"

Struggling for calm, Nadia wrapped her arms around her attendant and friend. "I don't know, but I trust Gage."

"I'm using the friction of the cliff against the car to scrub off some of our speed," he ground out, steering against the stone again. Metal screamed and stone chips rained on the car. They slowed a fraction. Not nearly enough for Gage's liking, and he wasn't sure how much more of this the car could take before the body ripped open like a sardine can.

"The roadwork," Nadia remembered. "We shouldn't be far from it."

He nodded grimly, wondering if they would last that long. In the corner of his mind that wasn't fully occupied with keeping them alive, he had to admire her courage. The princess must be as terrified as her maid, but she was the one comforting Tahani and assuring her that Gage would get them out of this if anyone could.

He wished he shared her confidence.

Two more encounters with the cliff slowed them a little more. There was no time left to lose. Gage's arm muscles screamed with the effort of keeping the car on the road, instead of letting it launch itself into the space over the rocky shore.

With each catapulting turn his shoulders felt as if they would be wrenched from their sockets. It was becoming a race to see which would come apart first, car or driver.

Nadia's life and that of her attendant were in his hands, he reminded himself. It was his fault the princess was in the car with him. If he hadn't persuaded her to let him drive her home, she would be safely back at the souk. He wasn't about to let her die as long as he had breath left in him to prevent it.

He set his teeth against the pain in his arms and shoulders, and fought the car with everything in him, and a bit more besides. He couldn't have said how far they'd hurtled down the mountain. At each turn he expected to meet someone coming the other way and thanked providence when the road remained clear. How long could their good fortune hold?

The emptiness of the road started to make sense when he saw a blur of yellow filling his vision. Automatically he rode the brake pedal, then cursed himself for the futile gesture. They had reached the roadwork. If he ploughed into the giant machine blocking the road ahead, they were all finished.

Seconds before impact seemed unavoidable, he spotted the red-earth furrow of track off to the side, which the workers had gouged out to give them somewhere to park their machinery so they wouldn't obstruct traffic.

Saying a prayer to the gods that protected intelligence operatives, he steered for the side track, slewing past the machine close enough to hear the driver let loose with a string of colorful Arabic expletives.

"I'm with you there, pal," Gage muttered. The tires clawed for purchase on the earthen surface, the incline of the track further slowing them. Ahead was one of the yellow machines, the cabin empty this time.

Just as well, because they were still moving fast when the Branxton plowed into the yellow monster, coming to a shuddering stop that Gage felt in every muscle in his body. He slammed against the seat belt with bruising force, but wasted no time releasing it and swinging around. "Are you two okay?"

White-faced, Nadia fumbled for her own seat belt. "We're all right, thanks to you."

The attendant was slumped across Nadia. "Tahani?"

"She fainted when we were about to hit the yellow machine, but her seat belt saved her from harm."

As they spoke, Tahani began to stir, her eyes turning luminous as Nadia assured her they were all still alive. Gage heard her mutter a prayer of thanks and added his own. Nadia continued to murmur encouragement, and Gage was pleased to see a little color seep into the women's faces.

He needed all his strength to open the damaged door and climb out. Nadia was struggling with her door and smiled her appreciation as he grappled it open for her. Relief swept through him as he saw she was uninjured. He reached in and lifted her out, reveling in the feel of her living body in his arms. She gave a cry of surprise, but clung to him as if to reassure herself that he, too, was in one piece.

He had a momentary glimpse of a different scenario, one in which he cradled her lifeless form and her eyes were closed forever. The vision had come so close to being a reality that his heart almost stopped.

She was having similar thoughts, he saw, as her arms linked around his neck and she held on for dear life. Dear life. Suddenly it was more than a trite phrase.

Her huge eyes looked moist, but she didn't give in to tears and even managed a brave smile. "You saved my life. Thank you," she said in a husky voice.

He glanced at the car. "I still have to work out why it needed saving." Brakes sometimes failed without warning, but he couldn't shake off the suspicion that there was more to it this time. Dabir had insisted Gage go to the souk. While he was inside, Dabir could have arranged to have the brakes tampered with, ensuring that the culprit couldn't be connected with him.

Nadia shivered. "You think this wasn't an accident?"

"I don't know, but I intend to find out."

Sorely tempted never to let her go again, he made himself set her on her feet, leaning against the car, while he assisted Tahani. The attendant was quivering like an injured puppy. She had recovered from her faint, but was still paler than Gage liked. Shock most likely, Gage concluded. He knew just how she felt.

Men in coveralls raced toward them from the road-making machine, shouting and gesticulating. Gage had never felt so weary, but forced himself to face them, groping for the right words in Arabic to assure them this wasn't his idea of a joke.

"The car's brakes failed," he repeated, wondering if he was using the right expression. His Arabic wasn't bad, in fact, it was pretty good, but right now he was barely staying upright and his thinking processes were far from reliable.

Nadia levered herself away from the car and addressed the men. Immediately they came to a sort of ragged attention, murmuring her title in amazement. Gage could see them wondering how on earth their princess had come to be hurtling down a cliff at a million miles an hour with this incoherent foreigner.

He pulled himself together and reached into the still-steaming car for his cell phone. Like its owner, it had taken a beating during the rough ride, but looked to be functional. Unfortunately he wasn't, and he couldn't make his fingers hit the right keys to put through a call for help.

Nadia's fingers gently closed around his, closing the phone at the same time. "It's all right, Gage. The other cars will pass by soon and see what has happened. In the meantime, the workers have said they will summon help for us."

"For you, anyway." He wasn't sure they'd have been so enthusiastic about helping him after he'd slammed into one of their multimillion-dollar machines.

Folding chairs were brought and placed in the shade of a canvas awning the workers had rigged up between machinery and cliff for their own use. Gage was too keyed up to sit, but he helped Nadia and Tahani to the chairs and gratefully accepted the cool water that was offered. The drink washed away some of the dust and bile clogging his throat, although he needed both hands to hold the cup steady.

The car was a mess. Looking at the crumpled side, scraped down to bare metal but still essentially intact, he made a mental note to stick to Branxtons in the future. He had rented this one when he arrived in Tamir because he owned a couple of similar models back home in Penwyck. He was going to have some explaining to do when the agency saw what he'd done to this one. But they were alive. He'd settle for that, for now.

On a sudden inspiration, he located the foreman of the team and took him aside for a few private words. The man took pity on his inadequate Arabic. "My friend, you've had a great shock. We can speak English if it's easier for you."

"Thanks. Right now, any language feels beyond me. I want you to do me a favor. I'm willing to pay well."

The man shook his head. "You have saved the life of our princess. Any service I can do in return is my pleasure, although I can think of nothing that would repay the great debt we owe you."

Impressed by the love and devotion Nadia inspired in her people, Gage nodded, knowing he wasn't far from feeling the same way himself. It was reassuring to find he wasn't the only one falling under her spell. At the same time, he hoped he would never have to shake the faith of this man and others like him by unmasking her as a traitor.

He rubbed his hand over his jaw. "Do this one thing, and we'll call it even. As soon as we're gone, check the car over and let me know what you find."

The foreman looked at the damaged car in disbelief. "You think someone tampered with your car to try to harm the princess?"

"Not her. She hadn't planned to be in the car. Her own broke down."

"Then someone wished to do you harm. Why?"

"If it was deliberate sabotage, I can think of a few reasons. But first I need answers."

The foreman clapped him on the shoulder. "You shall have them, my friend. Where can I reach you?"

Gage gave the man his number at the British Embassy. "If you can't contact me, you can leave a message and someone will make sure I get it."

"Consider it done."

By the time Gage returned to the princess's side, the rest of their party had caught up and she was explaining what had happened. Nargis and the twins threw up their hands in horror, exclaiming over their lucky escape.

"It was Gage's doing. He saved our lives with his skillful driving," Nadia said, reaching for his hand to pull him into the circle.

He saw Nargis's disapproving look go to their joined hands. She could worry about morality even now? Well, to hell with that. Nadia's hand in his felt good. He tightened his grip, his frown daring the older attendant to interfere.

Summoned by the workmen as soon as they recognized Nadia, another limousine arrived soon afterward, dispatched from Butrus's estate. Rather than scandalize Nargis too much, Gage helped Nadia and her attendants into the spacious rear compartment and climbed into the front seat beside the driver. He had never felt so bone-weary in his life. He let his head drop back against the leather headrest and closed his eyes.

Watching him through the glass partition separating them, Nadia felt her heart squeeze into a giant fist. She felt as if the jolting ride had bruised every part of her body, but none ached as poignantly as her heart. She knew she was verging on shock, and her judgment was impaired, but she felt more drawn to Gage than she had ever been to any man.

She had thought herself in love before, but nothing compared to the strength of her feelings for this Englishman, with his forward manner and powerful kisses. She had never been overjoyed about the prospect of marrying Butrus, although she had been resigned to doing her duty. Now she felt sick inside, as if some part of her that had only newly awoken would shrivel and die the day she exchanged wedding vows with Butrus.

What was she thinking? She was a princess of Tamir. Her life was devoted to duty. There could be no room in it for the sort of foolish love she was afraid she was starting to feel for Gage Weston.

No, she wouldn't allow it. In any case, he didn't return her feelings. Kissing her wasn't the same as loving her. His society put far less store by kisses than hers did. Just because the feel of his lips was imprinted on her own and she ached to feel his arms around her again didn't mean he felt the same. In time he would return to his own country and forget her. She should try to do the same where he was concerned, although it was amazingly difficult to contemplate.

"I dreamed of this road," Tahani said in a tremulous voice, startling Nadia out of her reverie. "I saw us hurtling down the cliff, barely missing the edge. I should have stopped you from getting into that car, Your Highness."

Nadia covered the girl's hand with her own, noting that Tahani's fingers were icy. "I won't permit you to blame yourself for something you couldn't control. You had a dream that could have meant anything. It's only now the drama is over that you see it as an omen."

Nargis looked affronted. "Omens are not to be taken lightly. I wish you had listened to Tahani, my princess."

Nadia gave a weary sigh. If she had listened, would she have refused to travel with Gage? She doubted it. She wasn't much good at making predictions herself, but she would stake a lot on her future being intertwined with his. Wishful thinking? she wondered. More like something about him that kept him in her thoughts constantly. Maybe that would change once she was married.

She fervently hoped so, hating to think she would have to endure a lifetime married to one man while dreaming of another.

Chapter 11

Butrus Dabir was pacing up and down Zabara's main court-yard when the convoy pulled in. As soon as Nadia's driver opened the door for her, he rushed to her side. "My dear, are you sure you're all right?"

"Perfectly, thank you, Butrus," she assured him, but her pallor contradicted her assertion.

"A doctor is waiting inside to check you over. Those dolts working on the road told me you weren't injured, but I couldn't rely on their word."

The princess gave a faint smile. "Those dolts saved our lives, along with some brilliant driving on Mr. Weston's part."

Dabir's eyes became lethal slits as they slid over Gage. "Then you and the roadworkers have my gratitude for saving Her Highness's life."

Butrus didn't sound especially grateful, Nadia thought. He sounded—she searched for a suitable description—upset to see Gage. She shivered, reminded that Gage thought the brakes might have been sabotaged. Surely Butrus couldn't have had anything to do with it, could he?

Nadia tried to persuade Gage to let the doctor examine him, but he insisted he was fine. He didn't look fine, she thought worriedly. Steering the runaway car at breakneck speed down such a tortuous road must have drained him. She knew she would have bruises from neck to thigh from being jolted around, as well as where the seat belt had cut across her when they ran off the road. What injuries had Gage suffered?

The rigidity with which he carried himself suggested how close he was to collapse, although he would probably never admit it. She couldn't help thinking about the crumpled, stripped metal along the side of the car. The slightest miscalculation on Gage's part, and they would have crashed into the cliff face or soared helplessly over the edge to their deaths.

Where had he learned to drive like that? Not in any diplomatic corps she knew of. As she allowed herself to be steered inside where a female physician waited to examine her and Tahani, she wondered again about his background and his true purpose in Tamir.

Gage waited until she was safely handed into the doctor's care before he turned in the direction of his suite, wanting nothing so much as a hot shower and a stiff drink.

His host had other ideas. "I would like to speak with you in my study, Gage."

He didn't say "right now," but Gage heard it in his voice. Dabir sounded like the headmaster at the prep school Gage had attended as a boy, only this time, instead of shivering with apprehension at the summons, he felt utter loathing.

He masked the feeling with a perfunctory smile. "I wouldn't think of sullying your presence in this condition. Permit me to shower and change first."

"This will only take a moment."

In a country where a guest could do no wrong, Dabir wasn't playing by the rules. Gage decided to go along for now, wondering how much Dabir knew. Could the attorney possibly have learned his real identity? Today's near miss made him think it was possible. But how had he found out? And how much of the whole picture did the other man possess?

He followed Dabir across the courtyard, their footsteps loud on the mosaic tiling. A servant opened a heavy carved door into a sparsely furnished chamber that led to a larger chamber. Dabir's office, Gage guessed.

He hadn't been in here before, and his swift assessment missed nothing. The sophisticated computer equipment, satellite-communication devices and other paraphernalia of the modern office contrasted with the ornate wall hangings, mahogany furniture and Persian carpets overlying one another with the lavishness of merchandise in a souk.

The carpets were edged with cushions and armrests, but Dabir gestured toward an upright chair in front of the massive desk. "Sit."

No polite chitchat? Just "sit"? Too shell-shocked to do anything else, Gage sat. Dabir chose to pace.

"You sounded surprised to see me still in one piece," Gage said.

Dabir wasn't to be drawn out so easily. "Relieved, yes, but hardly surprised. Why should I be?"

Gage crossed his arms and tried to appear relaxed. "I thought you might not be expecting me back."

Dabir affected a shrug. "Your fate is in the hands of the Almighty. Today your life was spared. Tomorrow, who knows?"

A threat or simple local philosophy? Gage was too tired and bruised for verbal sparring. "If you have something to say to me, just say it, Dabir."

The other man's expression hardened. "Very well. Have you any idea what you just did?"

"Saved the princess's life?" Gage asked, striving to play the British diplomat to the hilt.

Dabir whirled on him. He was wearing a hand-tailored suit,

so there was no robe to swirl dramatically, but it was implied in his movements. "Had she not been in your car, her life would never have been put at risk in the first place."

"I wasn't the one who cut the brake lines," Gage snapped.

That stopped Dabir. "Are you suggesting someone sabotaged your car?"

"I'm not suggesting it. I know it." He didn't, but Dabir's reaction was making him more convinced all the time. Was Dabir so shaken because Nadia had been in the car and his attempt on Gage's life—if such it was—had almost killed the other man's ticket to power, as well?

Dabir looked convincingly shocked. "Why would anyone do such a thing?"

"I thought you might have some idea."

Dabir slowed, looming over Gage. "You are a guest in my house. I do not like—or accept—any insinuation that I am somehow involved in your misfortune."

"Then I withdraw the suggestion," Gage said smoothly, knowing he didn't sound in the least repentant.

"Why was Her Highness traveling with you?" Dabir demanded.

"Her car refused to start."

"So you gallantly offered to drive her home."

Gage nodded. "That's about it."

"There was nothing more to your offer than simple courtesy?"

Now who was implying impropriety? Gage stood up, exhausted, and tired of having Dabir loom over him. They were evenly matched in height, although Gage was broader of shoulder and probably fitter.

He gained a little satisfaction from seeing Dabir shrink away from him. "What's really bothering you, Dabir? That your fiancée isn't as devoted to you as you'd like? I understood yours was to be a marriage of convenience." Mostly Dabir's, but Gage managed not to add that part.

"Our marriage plans are none of your concern."

"Then why are you letting a little thing like my giving the princess a ride bother you so much?"

"You don't understand Tamiri ways. A woman driving with a man who isn't her husband is inviting scandal. If she is royal, the potential for scandal is much worse."

"Even if her maid goes along for the ride?"

"It is still unseemly."

Gage raked a hand through his hair and his fingers came away caked in dust. Dabir's preoccupation with appearances was getting to him. Didn't the man realize his fiancée had come within a hairbreadth of being killed today? That didn't seem to bother him half as much as having her flout convention by riding with Gage.

"Look, Dabir, I've had a day out of hell. My car's a crumpled mess stranded halfway up a mountain. It's only by the grace of that Almighty of yours that Nadia, Tahani and I aren't in the same state. We can continue this discussion later if you insist, but right now, I'm going to take a shower."

Only when he saw his host's eyes darken did Gage realize his mistake. By referring to the princess so familiarly, he had fueled Dabir's suspicions about them. He decided it didn't matter. If the man already suspected him of being interested in Nadia and wanted him dead, the extra ammunition wasn't going to make much difference.

Dabir inclined his head in a parody of graciousness. "I see no need to discuss the matter further. I think we understand each other."

Gage knew his gaze was as cold as his adversary's. "No doubt."

"After sustaining such a shock, I understand that you would wish to take your leave tomorrow. Go in peace."

Gage remembered a line his partner had often used: "Don't go away mad." Implied was the tag line "Just go away." Gage heard it now in Dabir's words. He allowed himself a moment of frustration. The conference was finally becoming interesting. He was convinced that the meetings up to this point had been window dressing. With the arrival of the underworld types, Gage felt certain Dabir was settling down to the real business of the conference.

Since he could see no way to prolong his stay and learn more, he gave the expected response, "Peace be with you, too." At least, until he had enough evidence to hang the man.

Dabir pressed a button on his desk and a servant appeared silently, prepared to escort Gage back to his suite. So he wasn't to be allowed the freedom of the estate any longer. That meant he would probably be watched until he left. No problem. If Dani learned anything, she knew better than to tell him so in plain words. That left the foreman and whatever he uncovered from Gage's car. With luck, that message wouldn't reach Gage until he was safely back at the British Embassy.

He decided to relax and enjoy being alive.

Nadia was resting on a chaise longue in the shade of a colonnaded veranda when she saw Butrus approaching. He waved away her attempt to get to her feet. "Please stay where you are. You must be exhausted."

She set aside the magazine she'd been looking at without really seeing it. "I am tired, but the doctor says there is no lasting damage."

"Praise be. How is your maid?"

"Tahani is fine, too. She's gone to her room to rest."

Butrus frowned. "Leaving you alone?"

"It was my wish. I needed time to think, to deal with what happened today."

Butrus pulled up a chair close to Nadia. "I understand. It was a most unfortunate accident."

"According to Gage, it may not have been an accident."

"He has proof?"

She shook her head. "Not really, but he seems fairly confident."

Butrus's smile vanished. "Mr. Weston is a little too confident about many things. It is fortunate that he is leaving us tomorrow."

Nadia struggled to keep her disappointment to herself. She should be glad, she knew. She was finding Gage far more attractive than was proper, and she suspected Butrus knew it. All the same she couldn't help asking, "Was it his idea to leave?"

"Does it matter? I imagine he is needed at the British Embassy."

"He didn't say anything to me about having to go so soon."

Butrus took her hand. "Much more of this, little one, and I shall fear that my presence alone is insufficient to make you happy."

Instead of the expected reassurance, she said, "You must agree, you have been preoccupied with your business affairs lately."

Her fiancé sighed. "Regrettable, but necessary. I shall make it up to you as soon as my guests leave."

"Those men who arrived yesterday?"

He nodded. "They are only here for one more night. We had much business to discuss today."

"What kind of business?"

"Nothing you need worry about. You have had enough excitement for one day."

She shifted restively. "Hearing about your discussions will help take my mind off…what happened."

He spread his hands wide. "We talked of many things, mostly international affairs."

"This morning I heard you tell Gage that your discussions would concern purely local matters."

Angry color washed up Butrus's neck into his face. "What we spoke about is none of Gage Weston's concern."

Or hers, she heard, although he didn't say it. Butrus knew that she had a brain and opinions of her own and couldn't be relegated to a decorative role in his life. "Those men look more like criminals than businessmen," she insisted. "I can't imagine what you have in common with their type."

Butrus reined in his temper with a visible effort. "In my

work, it is sometimes necessary to deal with people other than one's own kind.''

"Then you don't like them, either?''

"Liking them is not the issue. The important thing is that I can deal with them when I must.'' He stood up. "They will only occupy me for another few hours, then I can devote my time to you. Your father agreed to allow you to come to the estate because he thought you needed the rest. He will never forgive me if I return you in worse condition than when we arrived.''

Fueled by the knowledge that Butrus and her father had made plans for her without consulting her, she felt her impatience grow. She had thought the invitation was Butrus's idea alone. "Surely where I go and what I do is up to me.''

"Of course. Before today's misadventure, I thought you were enjoying your small vacation.''

"I have enjoyed myself. The souk was wonderful.''

He smiled indulgently. "Did you buy a great many new clothes and jewels?''

She shook her head, deciding not to mention the tiger necklace, which she intended to return to Gage as soon as she could. "Nargis and the others bought clothes. I ordered the most wonderful piece of marble.''

He frowned in confusion. "You bought marble? Whatever for?''

Didn't he know even now that her passion for painting was equaled only by her enthusiasm for sculpting? "I intend to make a bust of my father as a gift to celebrate his long tenure on the throne.''

He regarded her as if she'd lost her mind. "Wouldn't you rather commission such a piece? I know an artist who—''

"I know an artist,'' she said, modulating her voice with an effort. "As do you—the one you're about to marry.''

"I understood that after our marriage—''

"I'd give up all this foolishness?'' she supplied for him. "If I did, you wouldn't want me, because I'd be unbearable to live with.''

He took her hand. "You are far too beautiful to be unbearable, my dear. We'll work this out, I have no doubt."

She had plenty of doubts but didn't voice them. "Let's hope so." Extricating her hand from Butrus's hold, she got to her feet. "I think I shall go to my suite and rest, after all."

"Excellent idea," he commended her. "This has been a difficult day for you."

She looked away. "More than you know." Almost getting killed had a way of sharpening one's thoughts, she had discovered. She wondered if Butrus had any idea of the direction hers were heading in. She would petition her father to release her from the engagement when she returned to the palace.

She had thought she was prepared to marry Butrus, but his persistent refusal to understand her filled her with misgivings. More worrying still was his involvement with men she was sure were criminals. Nargis had heard that the Americans were linked with a crime syndicate in that country and had reported that another servant had overheard them plotting. Although Nadia didn't encourage Nargis to relay gossip, this time she had listened with alarm. Why was Butrus entertaining such men? His evasiveness had only added to her unease. She was sure her father didn't know or approve.

"I'll see you at dinner," Butrus said.

She hesitated, reluctant to sit at the same table as his guests. "Will you forgive me if I don't join you tonight? As you say, it has been a difficult day. I'll have something brought to my room."

Butrus seemed almost relieved by her decision. "It's probably wise. Rest well, little one. I'll see you tomorrow."

As she made her way to her suite, she found herself wondering how Gage would choose to spend the evening.

The object of her thoughts had retired to his suite, citing his need to prepare for his departure the next day. In truth he felt as if he had gone several championship rounds in the boxing ring. The last thing he felt up to was sitting cross-legged on a divan for hours, drinking coffee and making polite conversation with Dabir and his guests—when he would have preferred to get his hands around the man's throat.

Why was he so antagonistic toward Dabir? In the intelligence field, Gage had dealt with all kinds of people, good and bad. Where Dabir was concerned, all he had were suspicions. Not enough to feel so violently inclined toward him.

Gage suspected the real reason for his antagonism, and its name was Nadia Kamal. He was starting to hate, really hate, the thought of her marrying a man like Dabir, sharing his bed, bearing his children, when the man didn't deserve to breathe the same air she did.

Looking down at his hands, Gage saw they were tightly clenched and made an effort to unclench them. Dabir wasn't worth the expenditure of so much energy. There was a better solution. Find proof that he was the traitor in the Kamal ranks and solve both his problems at once. Sheik Ahmed would hardly want his daughter to marry a traitor.

After he finished packing, Gage had a servant bring a tray of cheese, fruit and pastries, as well as a jug of chilled water to his room so he could graze at his leisure. Afterward he spent a long time standing under the steaming spray of a shower, letting the hot water unknot his aching muscles.

"Nice set of bruises, Weston," he told his reflection. Tomorrow he was going to be an interesting shade of black and blue from neck to hip. He had just finished zipping up a pair of chinos but was still bare-chested, when his cell phone rang.

He slung a towel around his shoulders and picked up the phone, flipping it open in the same movement. "Dani here," came the unceremonious greeting.

"Darlin', you've no idea how good it is to hear your voice," he told her. "How's your dear father?"

It was their agreed code for "Do you have any information for me?"

"He's not at all well," she said, sounding cheerful for someone with such news.

No news yet, Gage interpreted. "Is he still in the hospital?" he asked.

"I'm afraid so. He's in intensive care."

Intensive care meant Dani was still investigating and would report back as soon as she had more news.

Disappointment swamped Gage. He had hoped Dani would be able to link at least one of Dabir's recent arrivals to the Brothers of Darkness. "At least your father's in good hands," he said, trying not to communicate his disappointment.

Dani heard it, anyway. "I'm sorry not to have better news."

"Not your fault. How are your brothers holding up?"

Dani had no brothers. She would know that Gage was asking after the organization. "Quiet for the time being, thank goodness. I thought one of them was in those holiday snapshots you sent me yesterday."

Gage felt his tension increase. "And was he?"

"No, he only reminded me of my brother. I'll show it around and see if the rest of the family sees the resemblance."

"Good girl." Dani was telling him she wouldn't rest until she had identified all the men in the photos Gage had e-mailed to her.

"How are things at your end?"

"I'm living the diplomatic high life, rubbing shoulders with royalty." Almost getting killed, he was tempted to add but didn't. No sense alarming Dani when there was nothing she could do. "I'm returning to the embassy tomorrow," he finished.

"I thought you were staying for another few days."

"Let's say I wore out my welcome."

Her musical laugh lifted his spirits. "Next time keep your roving eye to yourself."

Dani was closer to the truth than she knew, he thought as

he ended the call. Shoving his open suitcase to one side, he
threw himself onto the four-poster and linked his hands behind his head. Was Gage being asked to leave because Dabir
suspected his real mission, or because he didn't want Gage
anywhere near his bride-to-be?

If Dabir knew who he was, Gage was sure he wouldn't
have been allowed to leave the man's office alive. That left
Nadia. Had the lawyer somehow found out about the kiss
they'd exchanged last night and sabotaged the car to get Gage
out of the way? It would explain Dabir's shock at hearing
that his plan had almost killed Nadia, as well.

Gage wondered if he should have told Dani the truth. If
anything happened to him, she would know his demise was
the result of foul play.

And do what? Come racing to Tamir to avenge him? Forget it, he instructed himself. Allowing Dani to do research
for him was one thing. Involving her in the dangerous side
of his work was another.

He hadn't wanted her to be involved in any of it, but she
had insisted after overhearing him and Conrad planning a
mission together. With her contacts in the rock-music scene
all over the world, some with dubious connections of their
own, she had proved more adept at ferreting out information
than Gage liked. Since he hadn't been able to stop her from
getting involved, he had tried to keep her out of anything
remotely risky, starting with limiting the people who knew
she had anything to do with him.

Nadia knew, he thought, sitting up with a jolt. What sort
of fool was he, telling her about Dani's role in his life, when
the princess herself was still a suspect? Putting himself in
danger because he was attracted to Nadia was one thing, but
if he had endangered Dani because he couldn't control his
hormones, he would never forgive himself.

Chapter 12

He jolted awake to find the room lit only by the spill of moonlight from the window. Some nightmare, he thought, rolling to his feet in a swift movement that brought a stab of pain. His ribs felt as if they'd been used as a trampoline.

Snapping on a light, he poured himself a glass of the now-tepid water at his bedside and sat on the edge of the bed to drink it. In the nightmare he'd been riding a magnificent filly that had bolted toward the edge of a cliff, jerking awake as the horse gathered herself and leaped into the void.

No need to wonder where that dream came from, he thought. The runaway horse had been his mind's way of dealing with the runaway car. Then he remembered reading that in some schools of dream theory, runaway horses were also powerful sexual symbols.

"That's what you are, frustrated," he told himself, getting up and peering in the dresser mirror to finger a bruise blossoming on his cheek. Time he wrapped up this mission and headed home to Penwyck, where he could find a nice woman of his own kind, a woman who wasn't promised to a lowlife like Butrus Dabir.

The thought was oddly unsatisfying, not because Gage didn't have his pick of women back home. One of the advantages of being a duke, even if you didn't use the title, was its attractiveness to the fairer sex. In Gage's experience, half the women he knew would kill to be able to call themselves a duchess.

One or two of them he liked enough to imagine bestowing the title on them.

He wasn't exactly in his dotage, but he wanted to have children while he was still young enough to keep up with them. So why hadn't he done anything about it?

Because liking a woman wasn't enough, he thought, repressing a sigh. He was an idealist, who wanted the whole brass band and fireworks of being in love. He wanted to put stars in his woman's eyes and feel them in his own. To make vows about "till death do us part" and mean them with all his heart. He was probably setting himself up for a lonely future, but he couldn't change how he felt, and didn't really want to.

Restless and uncomfortable, he began to wish he'd taken the princess's advice and consulted her doctor, after all. She could have prescribed a painkiller and maybe something to help him sleep. It was too late now. He didn't have as much as an aspirin in his luggage, and he was so wide awake he felt like jumping out of his skin.

It was the aftereffect of the brush with death, he knew. Going back to sleep didn't appeal after coming as close as he had to never waking up at all. So why try? He reached into the suitcase and put on the first shirt he grabbed, tucking it into his jeans with decisive movements. He thrust his wallet into his back pocket, pulled a pair of ripple-soled moccasins on his bare feet and he was ready, although he couldn't have said for what.

He prowled to the door of the suite and listened, hearing the restive stirring of the guard posted in the hallway. He would have to use the other exit. Luckily the terrace off his living room was only a dozen feet off the ground, with lawn underneath. He waited but saw no sign of another guard, so he climbed over the balustrade and jumped.

He swore aloud as the landing made his bruises sing a song of pain. Instantly he melted into the shadow of the building and waited, but no challenge came. He was free to walk off some of his restless energy.

The direction was decided for him when he saw another figure gliding along the moonlit path leading to the swan lake. Recognizing the figure, he felt a grin play across his features. So he wasn't the only one being kept awake by their near miss.

He tracked her silently, in no hurry. Once, she stopped to listen, looking around as if sensing his presence. By the time she turned in his direction, he had become one with the bushes beside the path. He saw her shrug and continue on. He counted a couple of heartbeats before following.

It came to him that she could have her own reason for being out here. He would feel like a complete fool if she was meeting someone else, or was on some errand for her fiancé.

She had almost reached the filigreed metal pavilion when she spun around. "Who's there? I know someone's following me. Show yourself before I scream for help."

Gage stepped into a pool of moonlight and held up his hands. "No need to scream, Princess. Not that anyone would hear you from here. But it's only me, your faithful stunt driver."

She clutched a hand to her chest. "Gage, you scared me out of my wits."

She sounded remarkably in possession of them, he thought. He had heard that the princess had been schooled in self-defense and wouldn't have been surprised if she had decided to get in some practice on him. She looked more than capable.

"I didn't mean to frighten you," he said, lowering his hands.

"And I'm not usually so nervous. I'm still feeling jumpy, after what happened."

He moved closer. In the moonlight, the contours of her

face were outlined like the lines of a classic sculpture. She was dressed in a long, lemon-colored robe that rustled with her movements. Moonlight reflected off the gold embroidery at her throat, wrists and hem. She swayed a little in the light breeze, as a swan called to its mate in the reeds at the water's edge.

Without conscious intention, he put an arm around the princess's shoulder and urged her into the shelter of the pavilion. She felt fragile but strong, as if she possessed an inner core of steel. Candle lanterns and matches stood ready on a side table. He crossed to them and lit a couple, hanging them from brackets on the pavilion walls. Soon the dancing flames filled the structure with soft golden light.

Nadia had seated herself on one of the velvet-covered divans that edged the pavilion. She leaned back. "I couldn't sleep."

He resisted the temptation to sit beside her and took a seat opposite. "Me, neither. Rough day, huh?"

She opened her eyes and nodded. "Not the sort I'd care to repeat. I told Butrus you thought the car had been sabotaged."

"Let me guess—he didn't believe it. What other explanation did he suggest?"

"None. He was more concerned that I was in the car with you."

"Were you? Concerned, I mean?"

She pulled some cushions toward her and arranged them as an armrest. "I shouldn't have agreed to ride with you."

"Because of the danger?"

She dropped sooty lashes over her night-dark eyes. "Certainly because of the danger." Suddenly she lifted her head and looked directly at him. "You are the most dangerous man I have ever met, Gage."

He found the statement curiously encouraging. If she had known who he really was, she would never have risked such a betraying admission. "Most men would take that as a compliment," he said.

"It wasn't meant as one."

"I don't mean to frighten you," he said.

"You don't, not in the usual way. But you upset many of my beliefs and customs. Tamir society is orderly, predictable."

"And I'm not," he guessed.

"Not in the least. You remind me of Gordon."

Gage wished he knew whether that was good or bad. "Who is Gordon?"

"Was," she corrected gently. "Like you, he was English."

In the sudden softening of her tone, he heard what she wasn't saying. "And you were in love with him."

Without the intimacy of the flickering lanterns keeping the balmy night at bay, and the fact that they had nearly died together this day, Gage doubted she would have continued. Now she nodded. "He was a man of great talent and sensitivity. We met while I was out painting and arranged further meetings without anyone knowing what was really going on. As far as anyone knew, he was teaching art to me and my sisters. They helped me to keep our secret."

Gage found his insides clenching involuntarily as he imagined what this Gordon might have taught Nadia. He reminded himself she was speaking in the past tense. "What happened to him?"

"One day my father caught us together in my studio and ordered Gordon to leave Tamir. I heard no more of him until I saw a television news report that a foreign visitor had drowned while swimming off a treacherous stretch of our coast. Even before they identified Gordon, I knew it was him."

"You think he killed himself?"

She shook her head. "I think he was so distraught over being forced to leave that he took less care than he should, and drowned as a result."

"But you blame yourself."

She turned brimming eyes to him. "Why shouldn't I? Had we never met, he might still be alive today."

Again Gage was thinking of himself. "I wonder if he

would agree with you. You know what they say about it being better to have loved and lost, than never to have loved at all?''

She drew her knees up and wrapped her arms around them, the robe pooling over her slippered feet. ''I've tried to tell myself that, but my heart doesn't agree. Although seven years have passed and the pain has receded, the guilt lingers. I don't expect you to understand.''

''Why shouldn't I?'' Gage asked, wounded that she should credit him with so little feeling. ''I know how it feels to lose someone you care about and to feel responsible.''

She regarded him with renewed interest. ''Someone you loved?''

''Not in the same way you loved Gordon. I lost my friend and partner, Conrad Drake. We were closer than brothers.''

He watched her carefully, but she gave no sign that the name meant anything to her, other than as someone Gage had cared about. Her response strengthened his conviction that she was unaware of Dabir's true nature. Gage knew he needed to believe in her innocence, but right now, he couldn't make himself believe anything else.

Her eyes were huge with empathy. ''I have two brothers. Losing either of them would be like losing a part of myself. Why do you feel responsible for Conrad's death?''

''He got into some trouble in America. I wasn't there to help him.''

The harshness he couldn't screen out of his tone brought Nadia to her feet. She crossed to his side, the aura of her distinctive perfume fogging his senses. ''How long ago did you lose your brother-of-the-heart?''

''A few months ago.''

She touched his arm. The lightest of caresses, meant to communicate her understanding of his loss. Instead, he felt a sense of arousal that only made him feel worse.

''Not enough time for the grieving to stop,'' she said.

He placed his hand over hers. ''Does it ever stop?''

''Perhaps not, but it becomes bearable with time.''

''For you, too?''

She nodded. "At one time I thought I would never feel whole again. Now I do. We must accept the will of the Almighty and go on."

"Conrad would have agreed with you. He was a great fatalist."

"And you?"

"I'm with Dylan Thomas when it comes to raging against the dying of the light."

"So you don't see yourself going gently?"

He gave a sharp laugh. He might have known she would recognize the quote. "Hell, no. When the time comes, I'll have to be dragged kicking and screaming every step of the way."

Her fingers curled around his, her no-nonsense artist's fingernails teasing his palm. "Now I understand why you fought so hard for our lives today. I haven't had the chance to thank you properly."

Before he knew it, she had bent down and found his mouth. The kiss should have been a thank-you, sisterly and chaste, but he couldn't help himself. He had to have more.

He got to his feet and wrapped his arms around her, putting into the kiss all his love of life and thankfulness that he had been able to preserve hers for her. And for him.

Nadia felt her head spin as Gage deepened the kiss. What on earth had possessed her to kiss him, when there were far more suitable ways she could have shown her appreciation? She had known she was playing with fire the moment she crossed the pavilion to his side. Had she hoped he would take control of the situation and give her what she craved in her most secret heart?

This.

The night, the stars, the call of the swans, all combined to create the most magical backdrop she could imagine for a kiss. Held in Gage's strong arms, she felt at once peaceful and caught up in the most exquisite turmoil. How could she feel both at once? Somehow he made it possible.

His lips roved over her face, her eyelids, her forehead, tasting every inch of her as if he could never get enough. As his questing mouth returned to hers, fire tore through her, the flames consuming what was left of her reticence. They had nearly died today. But for Gage's skill and fast thinking, she wouldn't have the choice of whether to kiss him or not. She wasn't sure she had the choice now.

Her senses swam and she let her head drop back. He trailed a line of kisses over her exposed throat, his tongue gently lapping at the fast-beating pulse and sending it into orbit.

"Oh, Gage," she breathed, panting with the exhilaration he made her feel.

"Am I going too fast for you?" he asked. "Should I stop?"

She almost panicked, fearing that all the unbridled emotion was on her side—until she saw the answering fire in his eyes. "Please don't stop. I couldn't bear it, not now."

He threaded his fingers through her hair. "I don't think I could, either." He cradled the back of her head in his palm, his gaze clouding. "This wasn't why I followed you here."

"Does it matter?"

"It matters to me. I have strong principles against moving in on another man's woman."

Her heart raced in instant objection. Was he going to abandon her, after all, in the name of principle? "You're wrong," she said huskily. "I may be engaged to Butrus, but I don't belong to him."

"Engaged will do," he said unsteadily, and moved as if to release her.

She clung to him. "You don't understand. The marriage is my father's wish. I agreed to it to please him. Today I realized I can't go through with it. I intend to tell my father."

Gage lifted her hand and grazed her knuckles with his teeth, sending shivers of sensation rebounding through her. "Sheik Ahmed won't like that."

"Neither will Butrus, but they'll have to accept my decision."

"Won't they ship you off to a harem, or something?"

"I don't care. It would be better than marrying a man I don't tr…love."

She saw Gage's interest sharpen. "You were going to say you don't trust Butrus, weren't you?"

She looked away, but he caught her chin and gently turned her to face him. The compassion and caring she saw in his gaze was almost her undoing. "Yes," she whispered.

He slid his thumb along the line of her jaw. "Why not?"

It was hard to think straight when he did that. She made the effort. "According to Nargis, those men who arrived to meet with Butrus are American criminals. He won't say why they're here or what connection he has with them. This...this isn't the first time he's had dealings with such people. I'm afraid he may be involved in something bad. He may be betraying Tamir."

"He was keen enough to get us out of the way before the meeting began," Gage added thoughtfully. "In fact, we were nearly put out of the way permanently."

"Oh, Gage." Her throat closed as she remembered how close they had come. She slid her hands around his back. He felt so strong, so alive. The steady beat of his heart reaching her through her robe was like a celebration of life. Tremors rippled through her and she never wanted to let go.

"Have you told anyone your suspicions?" he asked.

"How can I? My father would think I was trying to discredit Butrus as a suitable husband."

"And are you?"

"That would go against all I have been taught about my duty," she said, drawing herself up. "I would rather face my father's wrath directly than try to undermine his confidence in Butrus without just cause."

Gage's hold tightened. "I'm sorry for suggesting it. I needed to know."

"Why?"

He debated how much he could safely tell her. "Some of us in the...diplomatic corps suspect Dabir, as you do. We would like to find proof of any illicit activities on his part before he harms your country's interests." It was the truth, as far as it went.

He saw her lovely eyes narrow. "I thought there must be more to you than meets the eye. Are you some kind of spy?"

"Sure," he said in a low-pitched Scottish brogue. "The name's Weston, Gage Weston."

She took a swipe at him. "Be serious. Someone tried to kill you today. Could it be because of your interest in Butrus?"

"Possibly."

"Gage, you must stop this before you are hurt or killed. Tell the police about your suspicions and let them handle this."

"Doesn't Dabir serve as your minister of police?"

She understood immediately.

He felt a shiver take her and held her closer. "Don't be frightened, Princess. Whatever can be done is being done. As long as you're not involved, you're safe." Dabir wasn't going to risk harming the person who could bring him ultimate power. His horror at today's near miss was proof enough.

Gage's use of her title had been mocking before. Now he said it like a caress, and her blood heated to fever pitch in response. "I don't think I want to be safe," she said on a heavy exhalation of breath.

"What do you want?"

She shuddered again. In her society what women wanted was rarely a consideration. Being expected to articulate her needs so boldly filled her with confusion, but she saw that Gage really wanted to know.

"I want you," she said in a voice barely above a whisper, knowing she had never spoken more truly in her life.

"Are you sure?"

The churning inside her made her wonder, but she said firmly, "I've never been more sure of anything."

When he didn't seem shocked, she became bolder. "What do *you* want, Gage?"

He took so long answering that she wondered if she had miscalculated. At last he said unsteadily, "You know I want you."

She was heartened to see that he was as uncertain about

this as she was, although she suspected their reasons were very different. For all her thirty-five years, she was still hopelessly inexperienced. Her only taste of seduction had been with Gordon, and theirs had been such a whirlwind affair that she wondered now if the forbidden nature of the liaison had made it seem more intense than it really was. These days she had difficulty remembering what he had looked like.

She would never feel that way about Gage. Every sharply delineated line of his ruggedly handsome features was imprinted on her mind. Ten years from now she'd be able to paint him from memory and no one would doubt the subject's identity.

She knew well the source of Gage's uncertainty. Her royal status made many people feel uncomfortable around her. Normally she did all she could to make them feel at ease. Now she wished desperately that she could cast aside her crown for this one night and come to him as an ordinary woman.

"I know this isn't easy…" she began hesitantly.

Questions sprang to his eyes. "What do you mean?"

"Can't you try to forget that I'm a princess? Treat me as you would any woman. It's what I want, honestly."

She was puzzled by the laughter infusing his expression. She drew herself up angrily. "I don't see what's so funny."

He caught her hands in one of his and lifted them to his mouth, kissing her fingers. "I'm not laughing at you," he assured her.

"Then what?"

"You think I'm worried because you're royalty?"

"It has a way of coming between me and other people."

"Not this time." His dark warm gaze lent weight to the assurance. "If you must know, I was worried about…consequences."

She felt her cheeks heat and was grateful for the shadows cast by the flickering lanterns, shielding her embarrassment. "I see." She couldn't keep the defeat out of her voice. How could he satisfy the aching need vibrating between them without the risk of pregnancy?

He couldn't, and she wasn't so much of a rebel that she would take such a risk. When she had a child, it would be loved and wanted and welcome in the world, not conceived in moonlight with a man she might never see again.

She half turned away, a thick knot of despair filling her. "I'd better return to the house."

He caught her by the shoulders and spun her back. "I have some protection with me in my wallet, but I don't want you getting the wrong idea."

"I'm sure it's all right," she said stiffly. What was the matter with her? A moment ago she'd been plunged into despair because she thought he couldn't make love to her. Now she knew he could, she was as nervous as a serving girl about to cope with her first royal banquet.

Watching her, Gage wondered if he was going crazy. He wanted to make love to Nadia more than he had ever wanted anything. Yet something held him back. Despite her belief, his reluctance had nothing to do with her royal status. She didn't know it, but his blood was every bit as blue as hers.

It was Nadia herself who terrified him. She was younger in experience than her years. He gathered she'd only known one man in her life, and he wasn't too sure how far that had gone. She was bound to have dreams of what love should be like. Gage hated the thought of disappointing her.

He touched her cheek. How flawless her skin was. How dark and compelling her eyes. Surely if he shared with her all that was inside him, it would be enough. It had to be. He didn't know how to give more than all he had.

Chapter 13

Not giving himself any more time to think, to doubt, he swept her up into his arms. She lay as lightly as thistledown, laughing as she linked her hands around his neck. "There's no need to carry me, Gage."

He smiled down at her lovely face. "You wouldn't deny a man who nearly died today this simple pleasure, would you?"

"When you put it that way..."

For pure enjoyment, he swirled her around the pavilion, delighting in the way the moonlight kissed her raven hair with silver and turned her skin to silk. One jeweled slipper went tumbling to the floor. She kicked the other off and wiggled her bare toes, which were painted an opalescent pink. "This feels amazing."

"It does, doesn't it?" He kissed her gently and placed her on the divan, gathering cushions to support her head. His heart thudded with anticipation.

Lying against the cushions, she looked every inch a fairy-tale princess, her diffident expression part of her charm. He reminded himself to take things slowly, give her time to adjust to this new experience, to him.

She smelled of jasmine, roses and something else, a faintly musky scent that tantalized his senses, challenged his self-control.

Nadia had never before been so conscious of a man's appraisal. In her society it simply wasn't done for a man to gaze so openly at a woman. Husbands and wives might do so in the privacy of their boudoir, but in the open air and the moonlight, far from the forbidding eyes of a chaperon, it was unthinkable.

She knew she should feel ashamed for letting Gage look his fill, for encouraging his attention by stretching her arms over her head so that the swell of her breasts was outlined by her yellow robe.

Instead, she felt womanly and alive, desirable and wanton, cherished and beautiful all at the same time. She told herself she had no need to be nervous. She had invited this and she wanted him with all her heart. She knew he would be careful.

Knowing that didn't stop the nerves from leaping inside her, constricting her breathing and making her heart pound. Anyone would think this was her first time. In a sense, it was. She and Gordon had had so little time to explore, to touch, to discover each other. Of necessity, their lovemaking had been quick and furtive, not at all satisfying because of the fear of being found out. Why didn't she feel that fear now?

Because the man was Gage. How could she be afraid of anything when he was strong enough and sure enough for both of them?

Keeping one leg on the floor for balance, he knelt beside her on the divan and leaned over her. The heady male scent of him washed over her as his mouth found hers.

This kiss was different. Deeper, more giving but more demanding. He teased her lips apart, sending spirals of need eddying through her as he explored with tongue and teeth, tasting, nipping, enticing, until she felt drugged by desire.

The night air whispered against her legs as he slid her robe up her body. She felt herself go rigid. Years of conditioning urged her to deny him such intimacy, to cover herself and escape.

"It's all right, my princess, I won't hurt you," he said softly, feeling the tension coiling through her. "I won't do anything you don't want me to do."

She summoned the strength to allow his touch and was glad when she heard him murmur, "Beautiful, so beautiful." She began to relax, to open to him.

Suddenly his muttered oath made her eyes widen. He was seeing her bruises from today's helter-skelter ride, bending his head to kiss each one in turn. "My poor princess."

She didn't feel like a poor princess. She felt like a queen as he kissed each faint blemish. She was almost glad they were there, so delightful were his ministrations. When he returned to her mouth, she gave a sigh of pure satisfaction.

He seemed to have all the time in the world, losing himself in her kiss as if that alone could satisfy him. She fervently hoped not, because she could feel building within herself such a volcano of need that she could burst into flame at the slightest spark.

His clever hands were everywhere, stroking, teasing, as if he was blind and exploring her by touch alone. Each gentle caress brought new shivers of pleasure until she was a mass of them, floating, dreaming, drifting, wanting.

Over and over he murmured her name. Not her title this time, but her name, as if it was the most beautiful name imaginable. She found herself repeating his name until the fragrant night air sang with the wonderful sound of it.

More words poured from him, reassurances, although she needed none now. For the first time in her life she understood why such words were called sweet nothings. They meant nothing of consequence, but they were so very sweet.

When her English became insufficient for the words she wanted to say to him, she used beautiful, poetic Arabic, calling him the sheik of her heart and other ancient endearments.

She wasn't sure he understood all the words, but his kisses and caresses told her he understood what she meant.

Touch became their common language, and she began to wonder how she had communicated without it for so long.

When Gage undid the fastenings of her robe and let it fall away, she felt no fear or shame, only intense pleasure at being so blatantly appreciated. His mouth became more eager to explore, and she arched beneath him, barely able to stop herself from crying out for sheer joy. He undressed her lovingly and she helped him, eager to remove all barriers between them.

Feeling sublimely desirable, she pulled his shirt out of the waistband of his pants, her fingers busy on the buttons, wanting to look and touch her fill of him, too. When she saw the mottled stripe the seat belt had seared across his chest, she drew a gasp of dismay. She skimmed her fingers over the mark. "Does it hurt very much?"

"The bruise? No. This waiting? Pure agony."

He reared back long enough to strip off the shirt and toss it to one side. His remaining clothes followed, and she had her wish. Only one barrier remained.

He was not eager to cross it, taking endless time to bestow more of the delicious kisses that pushed her to the brink of endurance, on her mouth, her breasts, even those most secret places that made the color flood her cheeks even as she readied herself to receive him.

She was aware that he retrieved something from his pants pocket and heard his labored breathing as he put on the protection he had assured her he would use. In the next moment passion tore through her like fire. Her breathing sounded loud in the night air, but she didn't try to hold back. She was where she most wanted to be, and nothing else mattered. It came to her that Gage was awfully skilled at this, knowing exactly where to touch, to kiss, to arouse. She decided not to care. His skill was his gift to her, and her very inexperience was the offering she gave him in return, allowing him the pleasure of showing her how wonderful it could be between a man and a woman.

Higher, higher, he took her until she felt as if she had left the earth and was floating in the night air, the magic carpet of her culture's mythology becoming real as she was carried aloft.

How could anything feel more wonderful than this?

Amazingly it was possible, she discovered as Gage eased himself over her. He came to her gently, so gently that she wanted to beg him to be strong, to assure him she was strong, too. He made her strong, even as he weakened her with passion. The heat, the momentary pain that made her gasp with shock was nothing compared to what waited beyond the pain.

She could hardly believe one could experience such pleasure and live.

She wasn't at all sure she had lived until Gage's mouth on hers told her so. His heart pounded in time with hers, and his hand felt damp as he stroked her hair, holding her through the tremors rocking her.

Holding her, stroking her hair away from her forehead, Gage could hardly believe what had just happened. Because of who she was, he had known she wouldn't have much experience and had driven himself nearly insane trying to pace himself to her needs. But he had never expected to be her first. The privilege both humbled and exalted him beyond belief. Just as she was, she was a man's dream, but this… He felt his eyes swim with the wonder of it.

The lantern light danced over her body, making him want to touch her again, take her to heights beyond her wildest dreams. Too soon, he cautioned himself. Give her time to recover.

But this time she was the one exploring with hands and mouth, pulling his head down to her and molding herself against him until his restraint became ragged and his breathing shallow.

"Not yet, you need time," he murmured, pulling away from her mouth.

She shook her head, her hair making a soft halo around her face. "There is no time, not for us. This night may be all we have."

A pang gripped him. She was right. They may never have more than this precious moment in the moonlight. He wanted more, and was astonished at the intensity of his desire. Afraid it might make him savage when she deserved better, he forced himself to be careful, although he wanted to plunge into her sweet depths and carry her to heights undreamed of in her imagination.

In the end the carrying was mutual. Ancient instincts guided her to touch him and move with him until he was no longer sure who was teaching whom, the experience melding into a feast of pleasurable sensation until they were both utterly spent.

The candles had sputtered low by the time he brought her back to earth, or she brought him. Or both. He only knew breathing had never been such an effort, and his heart felt as if it would beat right out of his chest. But she looked happy. Satisfied, like a cat curled into itself after a surfeit of cream.

He had given her that.

She had given him so much more. He had never known it could feel like this, be like this. How could he leave her, now that he knew what they could be to one another?

He dropped butterfly kisses on her brow. Her eyes fluttered open and her lips curved into a smile. "Wonderful," she said dreamily.

He kissed her open mouth, tasting her. "You're wonderful, my princess."

She smiled teasingly. "More wonderful than any woman you've ever known?"

He affected an innocent look. "There has been no other woman like you." True enough. None like her.

She touched a finger to his lips. "I believe you."

He closed his lips around it, drawing the finger into his mouth, taking delight in her gasp of response. When she pulled away, he said, "You surprised me tonight."

"In what way?"

"I thought Tamiri princesses led sheltered lives."

"We do."

"Then who do I thank for your education?"

She smiled, taking his meaning, and touched the back of her hand to his cheek. "You."

"Not—" what was the name of her first love? "—not Gordon?"

"You should know better by now."

He did. Whatever had passed between her and the other man, they had never really made love. Gage decided not to take too much satisfaction in his own part in her awakening. Pride was a sin even in his culture. Better to humbly appreciate the gift she had given him.

Trouble was, he didn't feel humble. He felt like a giant killer, and he knew she was the reason. "You're bad for me," he murmured.

Her dark brows came together in an expression of concern. "Was I such a disappointment?"

"The very opposite. I've never known a woman like you. You make me feel more of a man than is good for me."

She sat up, shaping herself to the curve of his arm. "I'm not sure I understand the problem."

"The problem is, I have to leave tomorrow. Today," he amended, noticing for the first time the faint fingers of dawn creeping across the sky. "How can I leave you now?"

"If it is in our stars to be together, we will be together. For now, we will both do what we must."

"And that makes you happy?"

She shook her head, resting it against his shoulder so that her silken hair brushed his chest. Her face was hidden from him, but he heard the thickening in her voice. "What would make me happy would be to go with you, but we both know I cannot."

"When will I see you again?"

"At the palace, when you become again Gage Weston, diplomatic attaché."

"By then you'll be Her Royal Highness, Princess Nadia."
The untouchable princess. How could he stand it?

"We can't change who we are, Gage."

He could and did. He wondered what she would think if
he revealed his true identity…. But too many other lives were
involved. He couldn't put them at risk to satisfy his own
desires. "You could run away with me." Even as he said it,
he knew it wasn't an option.

She knew it, too. "I would be turning my back on my
family and my country, never welcome here again."

"That's why I would never ask it of you. But I can dream,
can't I?"

"As can I," she said. "You gave me a wonderful dream
tonight, Gage. Let's not tarnish it with regret for what we
can't have."

He tightened his hold on her and rained kisses on her up-
turned face. "Whatever I may feel about tonight," he assured
her, "it will never be regret."

That came later, as he was stowing the last of his belong-
ings in his suitcase. He picked up the crumpled shirt that had
spent the better part of last night on the floor of the pavilion.
Unable to stop himself, he lifted it to his face, smelling her
jasmine perfume in the folds. His heartbeat quickened and he
let the shirt drop, closing the suitcase and wishing he could
do the same with the memories.

He hoped Nadia had been able to return to her suite safely.
Having more experience of getting in and out of places un-
detected, he'd had no trouble climbing the balcony and letting himself into the room. As far as the guard outside his
door was aware, Gage had never left.

Nadia had told him that she had slipped away by pretending to go to the kitchen for a cool drink. Her sleepy servants
hadn't protested when she assured them she could manage.
The rest had been easy. But if any of them, that nosy Nargis,
for instance, had monitored how long she was away, she
might have some explaining to do.

Nadia was a strong independent woman, Gage reminded himself. Strong enough to be suspicious of Butrus Dabir. As his parting gift to her, Gage had asked her not to share her suspicions with anyone else. She hadn't understood at first, and he'd had to remind her that Dabir was the most likely suspect behind the sabotage of the car.

"Why would he do that?" she had asked.

"Someone may have reported our first kiss."

"He would kill you for that?" Nadia's tone had revealed that she knew as well as Gage did that Dabir was capable of such an action. If he suspected that Gage had made love to Nadia, who knew what would happen.

The thought that he had put her in danger to satisfy his own needs made Gage furious with himself. No matter how extreme the temptation, he should have kept her at arm's length for her sake and his, until he had sorted out this whole mess. Once Dabir was safely behind bars, then maybe Gage could justify getting involved with Nadia.

It was too late now. He was already involved with her. He not only had to find enough evidence to convict Dabir, he had to protect Nadia, as well. He fought the impulse to barge into her suite and take her away to safety right now. That was one sure way to get both of them killed.

As long as Dabir thought she knew nothing, she was safe. Gage had to hang on to that and start working with his head, instead of his heart. Not easy when he kept thinking of her in his arms, remembering the heaven they'd shared.

A sudden flash of the bruises marring her perfect body had his hands clenching into fists. Dabir would pay for every one of them, Gage promised himself. Not today, but as soon as Gage could arrange it.

Chapter 14

Three days later Gage was still no closer to bringing Dabir to account. He'd learned little more from Dani about his host's American visitors and established no definite links to the Brothers of Darkness.

He looked at a message lying on the desk he ostensibly occupied at the British Embassy. He had underlined the three words: "Brake lines cut." The note was signed Hamad, the name of the foreman of the road-construction gang.

No news there, Gage thought, feeling his mouth twist into a grim smile. Hamad hadn't found any clues as to who the perpetrator was, but then Gage would have been surprised if he had. Dabir was proving annoyingly efficient at covering his tracks.

Arranging to retrieve the car and smoothing things over with the rental agency had taken time Gage would have preferred to use to further his mission. When he reported back to King Marcus, the king had sounded frustrated at the lack of progress. That made two of them, Gage thought. As much as Marcus wanted the traitor in the Kamal household caught,

Gage wanted Conrad's killer more. Neither of them looked as if they'd get satisfaction anytime soon.

He looked up as his godfather, Sir Brian Theodore, walked into the office. At sixty the British ambassador was an imposing figure, still strikingly good-looking, with a lion's mane of black hair, silvering at the temples.

From Gage's desk the ambassador picked up a bullet between thumb and forefinger, and examined it before returning it to Gage's desk. "Still contributing to international relations, I see," he said in his clipped British accent.

Gage fitted the magazine back into the gun he'd just finished cleaning and grinned. "In my own way, Sir Brian. It's good of you to let me use the embassy as my cover."

"Your father would never forgive me if I hadn't." The ambassador's ties to Gage's family went back to before Gage was born. His wife, Lillian, was from Penwyck, and was a cousin of Gage's father. The ambassador frowned. "I don't know what Sheik Ahmed will make of King Marcus hiring you to investigate his family."

"He won't know until it's over. Then I imagine he'll thank King Marcus for uncovering the viper in his nest."

Sir Brian nodded. "You're probably right, provided you can find enough evidence to convict this viper."

Gage had already shared his suspicions with his godfather, who had turned out to be no fan of Dabir's. Sir Brian's greatest concern was that the attorney would gain sufficient power to take over control of Tamir, ruining what Sir Brian called "a perfectly good country" in the process.

Sir Brian saw Gage's gaze flicker to the royal palace framed in the view from the embassy window. "You're not getting personally involved in this case, are you?"

Gage pulled his gaze back with an effort, aware of a strong reluctance to do so. Nadia was home now, behind one of those carefully screened windows. He hadn't been able to see her again before leaving Zabara, and he felt as if some crucial part of himself was missing. "What makes you ask?"

"Lillian noticed it at dinner yesterday, actually. You know

how women pick up on these things. She thinks you're becoming attracted to Nadia Kamal.''

Not by a flicker did Gage let his expression betray him. ''Lillian is a romantic.''

''Then she's wrong about you and the princess?''

Gage saw no point in dissembling. Along with his father, his godfather was one of the few people in the world with whom he could be honest about who he was and what he did. ''She isn't wrong,'' he said heavily.

Sir Brian sat down opposite Gage and steepled his hands on the desk. ''Have you considered that Nadia could be in league with Dabir?''

''I've considered it. She isn't.''

Sir Brian's eyebrows lifted. ''You have evidence?''

''I don't need evidence. I know Nadia.''

''I won't ask how well. Just be careful. Dabir won't give her up easily.'' The ambassador picked up the note from Hamad and frowned. ''You already know how far he's prepared to go to secure his future within the royal family.''

Gage still had the bruises to prove it, as his godfather was well aware. He and Lillian had been horrified when they heard about Gage's near miss. ''I know,'' he said shortly. ''I won't take any unnecessary chances.''

The ambassador stood up. ''It's the necessary ones Lillian and I worry about.''

''Thanks, but there's no need. I know my job.''

''Does King Marcus know how fortunate he is to have you on his side?''

Gage holstered the gun, easing his specially tailored jacket over the top. ''I'm only on his side to catch whoever killed Conrad. Then it's up to Marcus and the sheik to sort out their own politics.''

Sir Brian's mouth softened. ''A lot of people would believe you, but not me. You'll do whatever you can to help secure a lasting peace in this part of the world. Even as a boy, you took it upon yourself to broker agreements between your friends, occasionally cracking heads if that's what the situation required.''

''Are you telling me I haven't changed much?''

''These days you broker more agreements and crack a few less heads. It's called growing up.''

Gage grinned. ''Or an increasing sense of self-preservation.''

Sir Brian sobered. ''Quite possibly. Just don't let your personal feelings get in the way of this mission.''

''About Conrad?''

''About everything.''

His godfather meant Nadia, Gage knew. It was good advice. All Gage had to do was remember to take it.

In her apartment at the royal palace, Nadia curled her feet under her on the divan, watching Samira try on the dress she'd bought for her at the Black Rock Souk. She had felt strange not buying anything for their younger sister, Leila, but then, she had married a Texas oilman, Cade Gallagher, and gone to live in America. It was impractical to exchange small gifts on impulse, the way they had done when Leila lived at the palace. From her sister's letters and phone calls, Nadia knew that Cade would give Leila the moon if he could. What would it be like to be the focus of one man's desires?

She wasn't fooling herself that Gage Weston felt like that toward her. To him, she was forbidden fruit. Now that he had made love to her, he probably wouldn't want to see her again, even if it was possible. It wasn't, of course. Nadia's father would never permit a man like Gage to court his daughter. The sheik would be horrified if he knew what they had already done.

For herself, Nadia had no regrets. Twinges of conscience, yes, but no regrets. The hours she had spent with Gage remained in her mind like a glimpse of paradise. If she never knew such sublime pleasure again in her lifetime, at least she had known it once, and that was more than many women experienced.

Or so she tried to make herself believe. Only, the ache inside her told her that she would give a great deal to know such ecstasy again. To see Gage again. She found her gaze straying to the window, to where she could see the British Embassy in the distance. Was he there now? Was he thinking of her?

Chiding herself for behaving like a lovestruck adolescent when she knew there was no future in it, she forced her thoughts back to reality. "I knew that dress would be perfect for you the moment I saw it," she told Samira, pleased with the way the color emphasized the sparkle in her younger sister's eyes.

Samira twirled in front of the mirror. "I suppose it's too much to hope you bought something gorgeous for yourself."

Nadia hid her smile. "Of course I did."

Samira bounced to her side. "Where is it? What color is it?"

"It's a glorious shade of coral pink."

"Long or short? Formal or casual? Let me see."

Nadia laughed. "I can't because it hasn't been delivered yet. It's a piece of marble I plan to sculpt into a bust of our dear father."

Samira's face fell. "I might have known. Honestly, Nadia, you'll be the only bride in the kingdom to be married with marble dust in your hair."

"Nargis said much the same thing. She thoroughly disapproved of my buying marble, instead of gowns and jewels."

"You did buy some jewelry, though," Samira said. She gestured to where a jewel case sat on Nadia's dresser. "That's new since you came home. Aren't you going to show me what caught your eye?"

Trust Samira to spot the case. "It was a mistake. I mean to send it back."

Samira's keen glance caught the flush of color Nadia was unable to hide. "It was a gift, wasn't it. From Butrus? Surely not from another man.'' She swirled around the room, chanting, ''Nadia has a secret admirer.''

''Stop it. I don't have any such thing.''

''A lover, then. You *do* have a lover. I can see it in your eyes.''

''You're fishing, and I'm not going to tell you anything if you keep needling me.''

Samira picked up the jewel case from atop the dresser. Nadia had left it there, intending to return it to Gage. She should have done it by now. Why hadn't she?

Before Nadia could say anything to dissuade her, her sister opened the box. ''It's magnificent,'' Samira said on a sharply indrawn breath. She lifted the tiger necklace from its velvet nest and held it up to the light. ''Whoever your admirer is, he must care for you very much to give you such a stunning necklace.''

''He saw me try it on in a shop in the souk. He thought he was doing me a favor by buying it for me, not knowing how shocked Father would be.'' Not to mention Butrus, Nadia thought uncomfortably. She was sure her fiancé had tried to kill Gage because he knew Gage had kissed her. What might happen if he knew about the necklace or the hours Nadia had spent in Gage's arms beside the swan lake didn't bear thinking about.

''Then there is a man involved,'' Samira concluded. She replaced the necklace in its case, replaced it on the dresser and sat down beside Nadia. ''You have to tell me the rest now.''

''You're as bad as Nargis when it comes to gossip.''

''This isn't gossip. It's my sister's happiness.''

Nadia passed a hand over her eyes. ''If you really care about my happiness, you won't ask me anymore.''

Samira took her hand. ''This sounds really serious. What are you going to do?''

Nadia was afraid her expression revealed the truth to Samira, who knew her better than most. ''It is serious, and I haven't decided what I'm going to do. Until I do, I'd rather you didn't say anything about this to anyone.''

''Of course I won't,'' her sister said. Her eyes narrowed. ''This doesn't have anything to do with why you were nearly killed on the cliff road, does it?''

Nadia clasped her hands together. ''It might.''

Samira looked shocked. ''You don't think Butrus…''

''I don't think anything. Please, we mustn't discuss this anymore.'' She looked around as if the walls themselves might have ears.

Samira saw the look. ''You don't think someone's listening to our private conversations, do you?''

''I don't know anymore. All I know is I can't marry Butrus. I simply don't love him.''

''You've never loved him, but you were committed to marrying him. What has happened to change your mind?''

Nadia got up and paced to the windows opening onto a screened balcony from where she could observe the comings and goings in the palace gardens. She knew there was only one figure she hoped to glimpse among the fountains and flower beds, because she had been watching for him since returning from Zabara.

But Gage was nowhere in sight.

She wondered what Samira would say if she knew that Nadia was half in love with the English diplomat. He made her feel things she had never experienced before, made her yearn for a life beyond the palace walls, beyond even Tamir's borders. Like the eagle in her paintings, she had always wanted to stretch her wings and fly. Gage was the first person to make her feel that was possible.

She knew that making love wasn't the same as being in love and hoped she wasn't confusing the two. What he had made her feel was so wonderful it would be easy enough. Since returning to the palace, she had felt different, as if the doors of a new world had been opened for her and there was no going back.

Her conscience should have troubled her, but instead, she

yearned for more of Gage's touch. He was in her thoughts as she lay in her solitary bed at night and when her attendants woke her to a new day. In between, he haunted her dreams.

She couldn't sketch, couldn't paint, could barely manage to eat properly. Already her mother had expressed the hope that her daughter wasn't coming down with something. How long before her father noticed and demanded to know the reason?

Soon she would have to tell him that she couldn't marry Butrus. The sheik's wrath would come down on her head as never before. He might even carry out his threat to exile her to a harem miles from anywhere. After what she had experienced in Gage's arms, she knew she could live with that more readily than with a man she didn't love.

"Why is life so difficult?" she asked Samira. "Leila dreamed of going to America and seeing Hollywood and Rodeo Drive and Texas. It happened for her. You dream of someone so secret you won't even share his name with me. What's wrong with wanting what we don't have?"

At the mention of the mystery man occupying her thoughts, Samira shook her head, her dark hair cascading around her face in a satin curtain, hiding her expression. "There's nothing wrong with dreaming. It's wanting the dreams to turn into reality that causes problems."

"And for that reason, we shouldn't dream?"

Her sister put a hand on her arm. "Nadia, what's the matter? You've always had big dreams, bigger than either Leila or me. But you were always a realist when it came to your life. What happened at Zabara to change you?"

Gage happened. Since she couldn't very well tell Samira so, Nadia gave an enigmatic smile. "Coming close to death has a way of revealing what is important in life." It was the simple truth, perhaps not the whole truth, but enough to satisfy her sister.

Samira nodded thoughtfully. "I think I understand. And I hope you achieve whatever this important thing is. When will you tell father you can't marry Butrus?"

Nadia gave a slight shudder. "I should tell him soon. Mother already suspects that all is not well between Butrus and me, so I may tell her first. She has a way of charming father into seeing things her way, without actually contradicting him."

"The perfect wife. Do you think we'll ever be that perfect?"

Nadia knew she hadn't a hope. She was far too outspoken and independent to let a man think he ran things, while getting her own way through guile. She didn't really think her mother did that. Alima was quite capable of speaking her mind when she thought it was warranted. But she knew her place, something Nadia doubted she ever would. "You might, but not me," she told Samira with a rueful smile.

Nargis chose that moment to bustle in, reminding them that it was time to prepare for dinner. Nadia knew the private moment with her sister was at an end. She didn't dare express her thoughts so openly in front of Nargis. They would be all over the palace in a day. She didn't blame the attendant for taking pleasure in gossip. Nargis had few other joys in life. But Nadia had no wish to be the focus of that gossip. Not when her desires were so new and tender—and so unlikely to be fulfilled.

The ringing of the phone on his desk pulled Gage away from the embassy window. Night was falling and lights were springing on all over the city, turning the royal palace into a fairy castle. Which window was Nadia behind? he wondered. What was she doing now? Probably being fussed over by that dragon lady of a maid. Nargis. And the beautiful twin servants who hardly ever said a word.

He reached for the phone, having to fumble with it before getting a hold of it, so distracted were his thoughts. He made an effort to concentrate. "Weston."

"You sound as if you're a million miles away," came the laughing response.

He felt something inside himself loosen. "Dani, me darlin' girl, how are you?"

"Don't change the subject. What were you thinking about when you picked up the phone?"

"You're much too young to understand."

"Nineteen is hardly young these days, oh, ancient one," she teased. "But I get the message. Butt out of your love life."

"Exactly," he said, cursing inwardly as he realized he'd been neatly trapped into confirming her suspicion. He was glad the embassy phones were secure, the lines being swept regularly for bugs and protected by state-of-the-art encryption systems. It meant he could talk openly to Dani for once. "How's your own love life?"

He imagined her shrug. "You know me, wedded to my music."

And gun-shy when it came to relationships, he knew. Hardly surprising, considering her experience of family life to this point. He wasn't setting much of an example himself, come to that. "No one on the horizon for you yet?" he probed gently. "Not even that drummer with the eye patch?"

To anyone who didn't know Dani as well as Gage did, the hesitation would have been imperceptible. "Nothing I want to talk about yet."

The yet gave him hope. "When you're ready to talk, I'm here," he reminded her.

"Same goes for me," she said. "By your reckoning, I may be just out of the cradle, but I know a thing or two about life."

More than he wanted her to know. "I'm a long way from the cradle and I'm still learning, but thanks for the offer, darlin'. Now tell me, to what do I owe the pleasure of this call?"

He heard papers being shuffled. "I've found out some interesting stuff about that orphanage you told me about, the one where the doctor and the princess hang out together."

"They don't hang out together, at least not in the way you make it sound."

"Gotcha." Dani sounded triumphant. "I knew from the way you spoke about her that the princess was more than a lead in this case to you."

First his godfather, now Dani. Was everybody in the world pairing him with Nadia? He must be losing his touch. "You're imagining things."

"Whatever you say, boss. But she must be affecting your thinking processes. You still haven't asked what I've discovered."

He *was* losing his touch. "What have you discovered?"

"You won't like it."

"Dani…"

She heeded the warning in his voice. "I took the list you e-mailed me of people working at the orphanage and ran it through your computer. One of the women, Sitra Wahabi, rang alarm bells. Her maiden name is Salim."

Gage's mind leaped ahead. "Any relation to Jalil Salim, aka Kevin Weber, confirmed Brothers of Darkness agent?"

"None other than his sweet little sister," Dani supplied.

Gage frowned at the phone. "I didn't know Salim had a sister."

"He kept his family in the background. After he was caught, she must have decided to go into the family business."

Kevin Weber's real name and connection to the Brothers had been established when he was captured in America by Max Ryker Sebastiani, a nephew of King Marcus's, and his bounty-hunter partner, Cara Rivers. Gage remembered the details from reading the files on the case before he came to Tamir.

Disappointment stabbed through him. "So the orphanage does have a connection to the Brothers." He hadn't known how much he wanted the opposite to be true until he felt the bile rise in his throat. Did Nadia know about the connection?

"Unless Sitra is a sweet innocent and you're completely misjudging her."

In Gage's experience, it was unlikely, given the octopus-like spread of the Brothers' influence. The more hotheaded younger members even used the octopus as their secret symbol, which Gage felt was extraordinarily appropriate. "We can't be sure of anything until I can find more evidence," he said.

"Your princess friend may not know about the connection," Dani said, reading his mind. "It doesn't mean she's involved."

Gage's grip on the phone intensified. "It doesn't mean she's innocent, either."

"Until proved guilty at least."

"Yes." Gage let his breath out in a gust. He had to grant Nadia that much. She might not know that the orphanage was a possible safe haven for the Brothers of Darkness.

And she might be in it up to her beautiful neck, along with her fiancé.

"What will you do now?" Dani asked as his silence continued.

He had always been careful to keep his protégé out of the active side of his work. Tracing information for him was one thing. She was damned good with a computer, better than Gage himself. And thanks to the traveling she did with her band, her network of contacts stretched all over the world. But he wasn't about to let her risk her life out in the field. "You know better than to ask. The less you know about my plans, the safer you'll be."

"Hey, take care, man. You're all I've got."

He forced a smile into his voice. "What about Patch, the drummer?"

"Okay, maybe you can be replaced in time. But not easily."

Did Nadia feel the same way? Had Gage already been replaced by an earlier allegiance, one that had motivated her to let him make love to her? Lord, he hated that thought. It meant that all the time she lay in his arms, she had been serving a cause he hated with everything in him.

All the sweetness and sublime passion would have been a lie.

She had shared her doubts about Dabir with him. Did she genuinely suspect her fiancé, or was that a clever ruse to throw Gage off the scent?

"You still there?" Dani asked anxiously.

For all her worldly wisdom, Dani was still only nineteen and had precious few people she could rely on. "I'm always here for you, me darlin' girl," he said blithely. He had no intention of sharing his personal heartache with her, although he suspected she might be way ahead of him this time.

"Anything else you want me to do?" Dani asked.

"You've already done wonders. Now get back to that band of yours and knock 'em dead in Heidelberg."

"Frankfurt," she corrected good-humoredly. "Our next gig is in Frankfurt, but I'll be available daytimes if you need me."

"I'll try not to let my concerns interfere with show business. The show must go on."

The phrase haunted him as they said their goodbyes and hung up. No matter how he felt about Nadia Kamal, and he was starting to suspect he felt a lot more than he admitted to himself, he had a job to do.

He refused to accept that Sitra Wahabi's presence at the orphanage was coincidence. He had to find out what she was up to, and what role the orphanage itself played in the Brothers' schemes. If Nadia was implicated, not even his feelings for her would be allowed to stand in the way of seeing justice done. Later would be time enough to deal with the consequences to himself.

First he was going to pay another call on the orphanage.

Chapter 15

Getting in unseen and planting a listening device in the orphanage's infirmary was the easy part, Gage discovered. He'd done the deed the next morning while everyone was still sleeping. He hadn't counted on how hard it would be to listen to Nadia working with the children and not be able to see or touch her.

Maybe Dani was right and he was getting too old for this work, he thought as he sat in his car a short distance from the building, concealed behind a thick screen of bushes. Not surprisingly, the rental company was less than keen to entrust another car to him after what had happened to the last one. His godfather had come to his aid, assuring Gage that the ambassadorial limousine took care of his driving needs, so he was welcome to take their compact sedan.

Gage wished his own needs were as easily met. Listening to Nadia persuading little Sammy to let the doctor check him over, Gage found himself dreaming of her in his arms and had to direct his thoughts elsewhere fast in order to keep his mind clear.

He had to admire her skill with the child. By making a game of the checkup, she soon had Sammy chuckling and cooperating.

The examination apparently over, Gage heard a door slam, signaling the child's return to the play area. "You're good at this, Nadia," Gage heard the doctor say. "I've never had a more able—or lovelier—assistant."

Clenching his fists, Gage focused on Nadia's response. It was playful and sweet, not exactly encouraging, he heard with some satisfaction. Evidently she didn't return the doctor's obvious interest. Just as well, or Gage might have had to storm into the orphanage and tell Warren where to get off.

Now where had that thought come from?

He wasn't in love with Nadia, Gage told himself. He couldn't afford to be until he knew more about her role in Dabir's affairs. The assurance didn't stop him from remembering how wonderful she had felt in his arms. The scent of jasmine would forever remind him of how he had taken her to the heights of ecstasy.

No matter how he tried to keep some mental distance from her, he couldn't bring himself to regret the hours they had spent together beside the swan lake. Knowing he had been her first real lover was enough to make his heart pick up speed. The thought that she would always compare other men to him was little consolation. He didn't want to imagine her with anyone else. Didn't want her to be with anyone but him.

But he wasn't in love with her.

He sat through an hour of listening to more children coming and going, being reassured by Nadia as she cajoled them into letting Warren look after them. The doctor's easy familiarity with her had Gage gritting his teeth, especially when he heard Nadia respond in kind. Not that Gage was jealous. He was merely protective of the princess. Warren obviously needed a lesson in how to treat royalty.

In a pig's eye, he admitted to himself. He was jealous. The very sound of her voice, like a musical instrument played by a virtuoso, was enough to turn his insides to mush. On a sudden impulse he grabbed his cell phone and dialed, hearing the orphanage phone ring a couple of seconds later.

To avoid a feedback loop, he turned the monitor speaker off before Nadia answered. Satisfaction coursed through him as he heard her pleased response to his suggestion that he visit the orphanage later that day. She sounded as if she couldn't wait to see him.

That could have been because he had said he might know of a suitable adoptive family for Sammy, but Gage liked to think he was at least part of the reason. And he did know someone interested in adopting Sammy. Himself.

The more he thought about it, the more attracted he was to the idea of giving the little boy a home. Back in Penwyck Gage could provide a child with everything he would need, including a loving father. He was already thinking about staying at home more, concentrating on his investments while someone else took over saving the world. Which should give him ample time to raise a child as his son and heir.

A wife would have been nice, too, but seemed impossible. The one woman he would like to carry home to Penwyck was strictly off-limits. Gage could imagine Sheik Ahmed's response if Gage were to ask for his daughter's hand in marriage. Gage told himself he was only interested in what great parents they would make for Sammy, but couldn't hide from the truth—he wanted Nadia for himself.

He was still smiling as he closed the phone and turned the speaker on again.

What he would do if she turned out to be on the side of the devil, he didn't know. He could only pray it wouldn't come to that.

He shifted restively in the car seat, which was too small for his six-foot frame. He had adjusted the seat as far back as it would go, but he still felt cramped. Getting up and walking around wasn't an option. Too much chance of someone from the orphanage spotting him. He began a series of yoga breathing exercises designed to convince his body that he was comfortable and relaxed.

They were about as successful as telling himself that he wasn't in love with Nadia. Time he faced facts. He had fallen for her hard the day she stopped to help him when she thought he'd crashed his car on the Marhaba road. His feelings had only intensified since then. Making love to her had been an expression of his feelings, not the cause of them. Thinking of her and marriage in the same breath felt as natural as breathing.

Could he be in love with her and still do the job he'd come to Tamir to do? He had an awful sense that he was going to find out soon.

Nadia and Warren's voices began to fade, and Gage turned up the volume on the miniature speaker he'd positioned above the steering wheel. "Time for lunch," Warren was saying. Gage heard Nadia agree with the doctor. Her sigh had Gage clenching his fists again. She sounded tired. Was it the pressure of leading a double life between the orphanage and her royal responsibilities? He was conceited enough to hope he might be the one keeping her awake at night, but doubted it. There was no reason she should have given him a second thought since returning to the palace.

The infirmary door opened, closed, then silence. They had gone to lunch. Maybe it was time for Gage to do the same. He was reaching for the ignition switch when he heard the infirmary door open again, creaking a little as if it was being pushed slowly and carefully. He pulled his hand back and listened.

There was the sound of footfalls across the floor. Very light. Female, then. Nadia? Gage's sixth sense told him it wasn't. His intuition was confirmed when he heard the phone being dialled and a woman's voice said, "It's Sitra. You wanted to know when she came here again. She's been here all morning, but this is the first chance I've had to call you."

Gage couldn't hear the other end of the conversation, but he was sure "she" meant the princess. Sitra had to be Sitra Wahabi, sister of the terrorist, Jalil Salim. Gage sat forward, straining to hear more.

''No, he isn't with her this time,'' Sitra said. ''As they passed me in the corridor, I heard her tell the doctor that he's coming here this afternoon. It seems he's interested in one of the children.''

The woman laughed unpleasantly, chilling Gage's blood. Sitra had to be talking about him. Who was she informing of his impending visit? Butrus Dabir? Someone in the Brothers of Darkness? How had they caught on to him?

His mind raced. If Nadia hadn't betrayed him directly, she had probably done so indirectly. Gage's suspicion that Dabir had been having her followed cemented into certainty. It would explain how Dabir had known about their first kiss in time to sabotage Gage's car. Did Dabir know they had made love? Probably not, or Gage doubted if he would still be alive to ask the question. Dabir wasn't a man who would take kindly to being cheated on.

Gage was surprised to feel an unfamiliar flash of sympathy for the man. They didn't have much in common, but Gage knew if any man laid hands on his woman, that man's life wouldn't be worth living.

Sitra was speaking again. He made himself pay attention. ''Just don't do anything inside the orphanage. We don't need police swarming around, finding out what else goes on here.''

She hung up and then Gage heard her depart, leaving him gripping the wheel in fierce concentration. So he was to be ambushed when he left the orphanage this afternoon. His gut tightened in automatic response as he thought of all the ways they could disarm, then dispose of him. Not that he intended to sell his life cheaply, or at all, if it could be avoided. His veins sang with the adrenaline coursing through him at the prospect.

It was small consolation to be right about the place being used as a front for illicit activities. Given Sitra's connection with the Brothers, they had to be involved. What more-innocent venue could they hide behind than an orphanage? How did Dabir fit in with their activities? Gage decided he had to live long enough to find out.

A cold sweat broke out on his brow as another thought drove through him. Nadia was in there. Somehow he had to get her away before all hell broke loose.

She was going to see Gage again. Nadia hoped her elation wasn't too obvious, but she felt as excited as a child on the night before a birthday. Ever since he had made love to her at Zabara, her thoughts had been filled with him. How he touched her, how he held her and kissed her, the masculine scent of him that lingered on the yellow robe she had worn that fateful night.

When Nargis found the robe folded under her pillow, Nadia had pretended she had put it there by mistake, earning a curious look from the servant. In truth she had hoped to dream of Gage and the marvellous way he had made her feel.

She had been so preoccupied that she hadn't even started the bust of her father, although the coral marble had been in her studio for several days. Normally she would have been unable to stop herself from making preliminary sketches and staring at the marble until she could see the sculpture in her mind's eye. Then she would have started to chip away at the marble until the shape in her mind was mirrored in the stone.

Instead, she had mooned around her studio, making desultory sketches that were all of one face, one pair of hands, one set of penetrating eyes. Gage Weston's. Thinking his name filled her with anticipation.

"Better eat your lunch before it gets cold," Warren urged, drawing her back to reality.

She looked at her plate. Today Sitra had cooked spinach stew with chicken pieces and rice, one of the children's favorites and usually Nadia's, too. Today she had little appetite. "I'm not very hungry," she confessed. "Sammy will help finish my portion, won't you, Sammy?"

Sammy didn't need a second invitation to help himself to her lunch. Warren jokingly called him a bottomless pit, but Nadia was aware the child had known many days of hunger after his mother died of a heart attack while hanging out washing. His record showed that the boy had been alone in the house for a week, eating whatever he could find and open from the cupboards, before he was brought to the orphanage. There was no sign of his father.

She hoped that Gage really did know someone who could adopt the child. She tried not to play favorites. All the children were worthy of love and attention, but she couldn't help being seduced by Sammy's cheeky charm.

She had a sudden vision of herself, Gage and Sammy as a family, and felt her cheeks grow warm. Nothing of the sort was likely to happen, so she might as well stop fantasizing about it.

"I hope you're not coming down with something," Warren said, giving her what she called his doctor's look.

She mustered a smile. "With the medical care available here, how could I?"

"Nevertheless, you look a little flushed."

"I'm fine, honestly." She would be even better after Gage got here.

Supervising the children's hand washing and helping the other women to settle them for an afternoon nap took enough of her attention that she was able to avoid checking the front gate every few minutes to see if he was approaching.

So successful was she that he was able to come up behind her in the play area, where she was collecting the children's toys, without her being aware he'd arrived.

"Gage, you startled me!" she said, spinning around, her arms full of toys. She was afraid her expression must have given away how glad she was to see him.

If so, he didn't react. "It's good to see you again, Your Highness."

She shot a concerned look around them, but no one was within earshot. Why was he being so formal suddenly? "You mustn't call me that now. To everyone here, I'm plain Addie," she said.

Nadia couldn't be plain if she tried, Gage thought. He assumed that the *galabiya* she wore belonged to her maid, who was probably standing in for her mistress right now. The white dress, embroidered with dark-blue cornflowers, fell over flowing pants caught at the ankles with more embroidery. In it Nadia looked heartrendingly beautiful. The delicate color of the traditional gown made her dark eyes shine like stars, and set off her high cheekbones and full lips so that he ached to kiss her right here and now, and to blazes with what anybody thought.

It took almost more willpower than he possessed not to take her in his arms, but he dared not. Not if his plan to get her away safely was to have any chance of success. If she had the slightest notion of the danger facing him, he was sure she would refuse to budge. That left him only one option. Somehow he had to convince her that she had been no more than a memorable one-night stand to him.

"Very well, Addie, then," he said, keeping his tone cool. "You must get quite a kick out of slumming here, pretending to be an ordinary person."

Her shocked gaze shot to his face and her arms tightened around the toys. "I beg your pardon?"

His gesture took in the humble surroundings. "You have to admit, this place is a long way from the royal palace. It must be a novelty for you to spend a few hours here, knowing you have all that luxury waiting for you back home."

She drew herself up, looking every inch a royal princess, although the hurt and puzzlement in her expression was heart-wrenching. "It is a contrast certainly. That's why I come, to remind myself that there are many people in the world less fortunate than I, and to do what little I can to redress the balance," she said.

He nodded. "The rich can afford to be charitable."

She frowned. "This isn't charity, Gage. It's a choice. I work here because I love the children." She piled the toys into a wooden chest and closed the lid carefully. "I thought you, of all people, would understand."

He retrieved a stuffed camel from beneath a potted palm and handed it to her. "Why me, of all people?"

"Because you and I...because we..." Color suffused her face and she stumbled over the obvious explanation—that she had allowed him to get closer to her than any other person.

"All we did was have sex. It doesn't have to signify anything," he said, keeping his tone neutral, although he longed to tell her that she had made far more impact on him than he could possibly have made on her.

"What are you trying to tell me, Gage?" she asked as calmly as if he hadn't just wounded her to her core.

He took her arm and stepped into the shade, towing her with him so they were both shadowed by the wall of the building. Hugging the toy camel, she looked so young and vulnerable that he almost betrayed himself by giving in to the urge to kiss her. He released her arm. If he kept hold of her, he *would* kiss her, and he wasn't at all sure he'd be able to stop.

"After that night, I realized that you might read more into it than I wanted you to. Women do that, I know."

Her face remained impassive, her voice cold. "Do they?"

"It's different for men. With us, sex doesn't have to be about love. More often, it's merely an expression of physical desire, without any strings attached."

"Go on," she said levelly.

"I don't expect you to understand."

"Oh, but I do," she said, all chill regal fury and splendor now. "You decided it would be—what did you call it?—a novelty to sleep with a princess. Something to boast about to your men friends when you return to England. You hadn't expected to be my first, and now your conscience is troubling you, so you've come to apologize."

He raked a hand through his hair, torn between being relieved that she had swallowed his lie and wishing desperately that it hadn't been necessary. "Something like that," he agreed, feeling as low as he'd ever felt in his life. Only the awareness of what awaited him outside the gates of the orphanage prevented him from telling her the truth.

"Then you've wasted your time. No apology is necessary.

I am a grown woman and I knew what I was doing. Has it occurred to you that I might also have found the experience a novelty?''

He hadn't expected that. ''I hadn't considered such a thing,'' he admitted frankly, aware of a stab of discomfort. Hurt pride? Their situation didn't entitle him to it, he thought as he pushed the feeling away.

''Perhaps it's time you did. I am to be married within a few weeks. One night with you was a last fling for me, as you say, with no strings attached. You can return to your own country with a clear conscience, knowing that both of us got what we wanted from the experience.''

He was fairly sure she was lying to save face and decided he owed it to her to go along. ''No hard feelings on either side?''

''None at all.''

He couldn't help himself. ''All the same, I am sorry, Prin...Addie.''

Abruptly she thrust the toy camel into his hands. ''I hadn't realized the time. It's late and I must be getting home. If you want to discuss an adoption, you'll have to do it with Warren. Goodbye, Gage.''

The toy was still warm from her hands and he found himself caressing it as he watched her walk swiftly to her car, which was parked to one side of the courtyard. The faintest hint of her perfume lingered in the synthetic fur and he inhaled deeply. Be careful what you wish for, he thought. He had wanted to send her away as fast as possible, and he had done so. He had also made her hate him.

He tried to tell himself he was relieved when she drove out of the gates at a less-than-moderate speed. All he felt was an aching emptiness at seeing the joy in her face turn to misery in the space of a few minutes, knowing he was the cause.

''Nice work, Weston,'' he said to himself. What came next? Taking candy from babies? He carried the camel to the chest and placed it among the other toys, feeling as if he closed the lid not only on the contents, but on something good in his life that he might never find again.

He had moved his godfather's car so it was parked well away from the orphanage gates, where it couldn't be missed if someone came looking for him, but where he could be sure the children weren't in any danger. Now he braced himself to walk back to the car, knowing that there was very little chance he would reach it before Sitra's friends intervened.

He almost welcomed the prospect of some action to burn off the distaste he felt at the way he'd been forced to treat Nadia. *They* were responsible—Dabir, the Brothers of Darkness, all the forces of evil that contaminated everything that was good in life. They were responsible for the death of his friend, Conrad, and for making Gage put the despair on Nadia's face. He looked forward to evening the score.

Chapter 16

She did not care. She did not care. She did not care. Nadia repeated the mantra to herself as she drove away from the orphanage. She considered herself a modern woman. That meant she could enjoy Gage Weston's lovemaking without requiring a happy-ever-after, couldn't she? He obviously could.

Her fingers tightened around the steering wheel. No love, no strings, he had said. Well, what had she expected? A marriage proposal? A declaration of undying devotion? In her experience, living happily ever after only happened in fairy tales.

She still intended to ask her father to release her from her engagement to Butrus. Gage had left her one legacy. He had shown her that she couldn't commit to a loveless marriage. The sheik would be furious, and she regretted the hurt she knew she must cause him. Butrus would be even angrier, but if he was involved in shady dealings, as she suspected, it served him right. For herself, she would rather endure the storm of their wrath for a time, even if it meant spending her future alone, with only her art for company.

Her thoughts were so busy that she almost drove past the field where she had left Tahani and Mahir, her driver. She looked around at the empty landscape. Surely this was the right place. In her confusion, she could have been mistaken.

Adjusting Tahani's scarf over her head, she put on her dark glasses and got out of the car, walking across the field in bewilderment. Her foot kicked a small object, and she stooped to pick up a tube of bright red paint, which she studied for a moment before slipping it inside her *galabiya*. This was the right place, but why would Tahani have left before they could change places again?

Her heart almost stopped. Something must have happened to her father or mother and the palace had sent someone to find her, taking Tahani back to the palace in her place. Her parents were visiting the island of Jawhar, inspecting a new oil field. There could have been an accident. Nadia stumbled back to the car. She had to return home quickly.

But there was no sign of a problem at the palace. Removing the scarf and glasses, she was recognized at once, although the guard looked bemused to see her behind the wheel and unescorted. She didn't feel inclined to explain. "Where is Mahir?"

"Mr. Dabir sent a car to fetch you. I saw it return a short time ago with Mahir and…and you, I thought, Your Highness."

"Obviously it wasn't me," she snapped, her nerves stretched to breaking point at hearing that Butrus was behind this. "Can you not tell the difference between me and Tahani?"

The man turned beet red. "Of course, Your Highness." But he had been fooled, she saw, although she took little satisfaction in the knowledge. Nadia had used her trick once too often, and today she was to pay the price.

"Is everything all right with my mother and father?" she asked.

"Certainly, Your Highness. Before I came on duty, I saw a news broadcast that showed that your father's inspection of the oil fields on Jawhar is going well."

Her apprehension grew. If nothing was amiss, why had Butrus had Tahani brought back to the palace? Their deception must have been discovered. Nadia's heart was beating double time as she gave her car into the care of a servant and made her way to her apartment.

"How good of you to pay us a visit," Butrus drawled as she let herself in past a saluting guard.

He was seated at the desk in her living room, his fingers drumming on the leather surface. On the sofa sat a white-faced Tahani, visibly trembling.

Nadia ignored Butrus and went to the attendant. "Are you all right?"

Tahani nodded, biting her lip to hold back tears. "Mr. Dabir sent a car for you, and they insisted I return at once. I wanted to wait for you."

Nadia took her friend's hand. It felt icy in hers. "It's all right. You did the right thing." The only thing, if Butrus's implacable expression was any guide.

Tahani brightened a little. "Thank you, Princess."

"You can go now. Please fetch cool drinks for me and Mr. Dabir."

With alacrity, Tahani jumped up from the sofa, giving Butrus a wide berth, Nadia noticed, as she headed for the door. The princess waited until the door closed behind Tahani, then turned her attention to her fiancé. "What is the meaning of this intrusion?"

He folded his arms and glared at her. "I thought you could tell me. Quite the adventuress, aren't you, little one?"

"I have no idea what you're talking about."

His dark brows arched. "No? Then why was your servant disguised as you, painting at your easel, while her mistress was nowhere to be found?"

"I had an errand to run."

"What could possibly be so urgent that you had to go in person, rather than send your maid?"

She stood up. "Why don't we stop playing cat and mouse, Butrus. Say what you came here to say."

He stood up, too, and moved to stand over her, his closeness daunting. She refused to back away. "Very well. I've known for some time that you have a habit of changing places with the maid and going off on your own for hours at a time."

Horror made her skin crawl. "You had me watched? How dare you do such a thing to a member of the royal family?"

"Oh, I dare." He reached into the jacket of his impeccably tailored suit and pulled out a handful of photographs, dropping them onto the couch beside her. "You forfeited any protection due your royal status when you assumed the guise of a humble maid. No one could blame me for treating you as such. Look at you!"

He was referring to her simple attire and disheveled state after her stint at the orphanage. She drew herself up, refusing to look at the photographs. "One does not have to appear royal to *be* royal."

"But one does have to maintain certain standards. You can hardly be said to have maintained them today."

"Are you worried about my actions or my image?" she asked wearily.

He placed his hands on her upper arms. "Since we are to be married, both are of concern to me."

She glared at him. "Remove your hands from me. We are not going to be married."

She had not intended to be so blunt, but Butrus had left her no choice. His attitude confirmed what she had long suspected—that as his wife, she would be no more than a chattel to him, her royal status a convenience that would be ignored when they were alone. She would tell her father of her decision as soon as he returned.

Butrus's grip tightened to bruising force as he urged her

to her feet. "That's where you're wrong, my princess. We are going to be married, and soon."

She caught her breath. "You can't make me marry you."

"No, but your father can. Once he hears what you've been up to…"

She felt the color rush to her face. "You wouldn't tell him." Her father would be devastated by her behavior, especially when the tale was slanted to show her in the worst possible light, as Butrus was sure to do.

Butrus's eyes lit with purpose. "Not unless you force me to."

"He will never take your side against his own daughter."

"Once he sees these photographs, you'll be lucky to claim that status."

She made herself look at them, horrified when she saw that the photographer had captured her in Gage's arms the first time they had kissed under the colonnade at Zabara. The odd lighting suggested some kind of security camera or infrared device, but there was no mistaking the scene. There were more pictures of her changing places with Tahani, driving alone in her car and, worst of all, entering the orphanage at Marhaba.

"How did you get these?" she asked, her throat so tight that speaking was an effort.

He grinned, running his hands along her arms from wrist to elbow. "Changing your tune a little, are you? As you should. I've had you followed for some time, but saw no reason to interfere in your activities until now."

Until it was beneficial to him, she interpreted. She pulled free of him and moved away, feeling cold in spite of the day's warmth. "I'm surprised you would want to marry a woman who has so dishonored herself," she said, her voice dripping sarcasm.

He chose to ignore her tone, taking her words at face value. "I'm glad you agree that your behavior is dishonorable, my princess. I confess, I did think of baring my soul to your father. No woman has been stoned for immoral behavior in

Tamir for centuries, but Sheik Ahmed might be persuaded to revive the custom if the transgression is sufficient. You must agree, your transgressions are more than sufficient.''

She shook her head, refusing to entertain the vision of herself being so punished, although her blood chilled at the very thought. ''You sound like someone from the Dark Ages, Butrus. My father would never condone such a thing.''

Butrus began to gather up the photographs. ''Shall we put his response to the test when he returns from Jawhar tomorrow?''

''No, wait.'' She couldn't let her father see the photos.

Butrus paused, the photos fanned in his fingers like a hand of cards. The one of Gage kissing her was uppermost, she noticed. Remembering how special he had made her feel, she couldn't bring herself to regret the moment. She only regretted that Butrus had found her out. What sort of woman did that make her? Was Butrus right about her lack of morals?

No, she thought defiantly. No matter how sordid Butrus made this look, she cared about Gage, even if he did not return her affection.

She loved him.

The realization left her thunderstruck. She had thought herself infatuated with him, driven to find out what his lovemaking was like, but never in love with him. Now she made herself face the truth. From the moment she had set eyes on him, he had begun to capture her soul.

That he had thrown her feelings in her face didn't stop her from having them, any more than she could stop the sun from rising in the morning.

Did Butrus know that she and Gage had made love? If he did, nothing on earth would have stopped him from seeing her punished as cruelly as he could devise, she knew. Apparently he did not know, not yet.

''What do you want from me?'' she asked.

The gleam of satisfaction fired his gaze. ''What I've al-

ways wanted from you—membership in the most exclusive
club on earth, the royal family.''

"Power and prestige mean so much to you that you would
marry me, knowing how I feel toward you?"

"You don't understand, do you? You've always had
power, always had people rushing to do your slightest bidding. Yet you throw it all away to pretend to be less than
you are. You would not be so eager to do so if you knew
what it's like to be truly less than others."

She clasped her hands together. "You're right, I don't understand."

A timid knock interrupted them. At Nadia's distracted
command, Tahani entered with a tray containing two glasses
of chilled fruit juice and a plate of sweetmeats. The glasses
rattled as she edged past Butrus and placed the tray within
Nadia's reach. "Thank you. You may lay out my clothes for
this evening," Nadia told her.

Tahani gave her a grateful smile and disappeared into the
bedroom, closing the door carefully behind her.

"That's what it's like to be less than others," Butrus said,
gesturing toward the closed door. "It means being at the beck
and call of your betters, jumping when they say jump and
being terrified of making the slightest wrong move."

Nadia refrained from pointing out that it was Butrus who
had caused the other woman's fear. "You sound as if you
speak from experience," she said, knowing it was impossible.

He crossed to the tray and picked up one of the glasses,
drinking deeply before returning his attention to her. "Bitter
experience," he confirmed. "The man you know as my father is really my uncle. He took me in when I was orphaned
as a small boy."

Her hand went to her mouth. "I had no idea."

"I don't want your pity," he said savagely. "I had enough
of that as a child. Pity and condescension, always aware that
I wasn't a son of the house, but a charity case, taken in on
sufferance."

"Your father…your uncle's behavior never suggested he thought less of you than his natural children," she said, striving to think of a time when she had noticed any discrimination between adoptive father and son. Butrus's family had socialized with hers often enough that she would have noticed some difference. She could remember none. In fact, she had occasionally thought his adoptive father favored Butrus over his other children. Couldn't Butrus see that?

Apparently not, because he shook his head. "Perhaps not to you. To me, the difference is always there."

"In you, not in your family," she insisted. "Can't you see, you're fighting phantoms. You don't want to marry me. You want to marry what I am. That makes your actions worse than those you attribute to your father."

He swept the glasses off the tray onto the floor, making her jump. "You will not judge me. As my wife, you will do my bidding and put a glad face on it. Understood?"

"I will never lie with you willingly," she said in a low tone, more shaken than she wanted him to know.

He gave a guttural laugh. "No matter. Unwilling can be even more exciting."

She couldn't stop a shudder from rippling through her. After the joy she had found in Gage's arms, how could she resign herself to the travesty of a marriage Butrus meant them to have? She would rather die first, and she let her resolute gaze tell Butrus so. "Even though my heart belongs to another?"

Butrus looked as if he would like to kill her there and then. She saw his hands actually flex and reach out for her before he brought them back to his sides. When he spoke, his voice was as rigidly controlled as his pose. "When I saw the photo of Weston kissing you, I told myself you had been coerced by him. You have not tasted a man's love yet—that boy, the art teacher, was barely a man—so it is natural for you to be curious about such things. And a man from the West has little compunction about despoiling such innocence as yours. I have decided to forgive you."

Knowing she was flirting with danger, she could not keep silent. "I don't want your forgiveness, Butrus. I was not coerced, nor a victim of curiosity. I am in love with Gage Weston."

Butrus's expression turned to stone. The coldness in his eyes froze her blood as he said, "Then you are in love with a dead man. Weston is already being hunted by my agent."

She stared at Butrus, aghast. "You were the one who tried to kill Gage before by sabotaging his car brakes, weren't you?"

His mouth thinned. "Unfortunately I was unsuccessful. This time there will be no mistake. He sealed his fate by touching my woman."

"How many times must I tell you I'm not your woman, and never will be? If you harm Gage in any way, I won't rest until you are made to pay."

Butrus was not as discomfited as she thought he should be. "Without proof that I had anything to do with it, who will believe you? I'll deny we ever had this conversation."

Suddenly everything fell into place. Appalled, she remembered Gage's determination to convince her that their lovemaking had meant nothing to him. Had he found out that Butrus meant to have him killed and decided to remove her from harm in the only way he could—by driving her away?

How could she have fallen for his scheme? Her body had known, if her mind had not, that their lovemaking had meant more to him than a casual experiment. He had been willing to sacrifice their love to save her. She had to get to him.

As soon as she gained her feet, Butrus motioned her to sit again. "Whatever you are planning will be too late to save Weston. By the time you can reach him, his body will be lying in a ditch and my agent will be on his way to claim his payment."

She felt her eyes brim and she blinked furiously. She refused to accept that Gage was dead. "I can't believe you would stoop to paying someone to do murder."

"Believe it. I have done worse, and doubtless will again in the future. It is not your concern."

This time she would not remain seated. "It will certainly be my father's concern after I tell him what you are."

"Are you sure he does not know?"

Horror overcame her. She and her father had had their disagreements, but he would never endorse Butrus's crimes. Her father could be hard, but he was just and he always upheld the law. "No, he isn't like that."

"Of course he isn't. So I undertake the causes he cannot support publicly, using ways and means not open to him to achieve his aims."

"You're mad. My father would never condone what you're doing."

Butrus gave an ugly sneer. "How prettily you defend him, my princess, for all the good it will do either of you. Sheik Ahmed benefits from my actions, therefore he is a party to them by default, at the very least."

Her head swam with the effort to make sense of Butrus's ramblings. He had taken her father's lack of objection for approval, convincing himself that the sheik supported his actions, when the sheik knew nothing of what his adviser was doing. When he learned the truth, Butrus's reign of terror would be over, she knew.

"How are you going to prevent me from telling my father what you've told me at the first opportunity?" she demanded.

"The guard at your door is one of my men. He is under orders to see that you remain in seclusion here for the next few days. By the time you are recovered from your…indisposition, Weston will be long dead, and our wedding will be only days away. Any hysteria you exhibit will be blamed on prewedding nerves."

The thought of being unable to save Gage turned her heart to lead. Was her fate always to have her love snatched from her by the cold hand of death? How could she go on living, knowing that Gage was lost to her forever, the last words they shared a repudiation of the love she was sure he felt for her? Why else had he tried so hard to drive her away, if not to keep her from harm?

"My parents will never take your word over mine," she said bitterly.

Butrus patted his jacket pocket. "I still have the photographs as a last resort. Once Sheik Ahmed sees them, he will think you are accusing me to deflect censure from yourself. He will be happy to expedite our marriage in order to have such a troublesome daughter off his hands."

"You really mean to go through with this, don't you? Even though it means I will hate you for the rest of your life."

"That is a long time," he said equably. "Ample for me to change your opinion of me."

"Never. You will have to drag me to the ceremony, for I shall not go any other way."

"Not even knowing that your dear Tahani will be standing in the wings with a knife pressed to her throat?"

Butrus knew she would never let anything happen to Tahani to save herself, and his smug expression told her he knew he had won. "Cheer up," he added, as if he had not spoken of murder and mayhem the way other people discussed the weather. "When you are my bride, I shall build you the finest studio, where you can dabble in your art to your heart's content."

"With bars on the windows," she threw at him.

Her anger rolled off him. "That depends entirely on how you behave." He consulted his watch. "Much as I would like to stay and discuss our plans for the future, I must go. I have an appointment to keep with your beloved's killer."

"Butrus, wait. Why must Gage die? I could tell Father that he accosted me and forced me to kiss me. He would be banished from Tamir instantly, never to cross our borders again." Bleakness gripped her at the thought of never seeing him again, but at least he would be alive.

Butrus favored her with a wintry smile. "I wish I'd thought of that. It would have been far less trouble. But I'm afraid you're too late. His body should be discovered within the hour, the victim of an unfortunate robbery. Since your family knows you were acquainted with Mr. Weston, they won't be surprised if you withdraw to your apartments and don't want to see anyone. Very sad, really. I wish there was something I could do to help you get over your grief." He brightened suddenly. "Fortunately the prospect of our wedding will restore your mood."

She grabbed one of the glasses lying on the carpet and flung it at him. He ducked and the glass shattered against a wall, the remaining juice spilling like blood over the costly drapery. "I'll see you in hell before marrying you," she vowed.

His laughter mocked her. "Princess, this *is* hell." The second glass exploded against the door, but he had already closed it behind him.

Chapter 17

The old fort that housed the orphanage had been built on a rocky promontory overlooking the town of Marhaba. Once, the fort would have commanded unlimited vistas over the surrounding area, but in modern times, greenery had grown up around the old stone walls, although the view was still spectacular from some parts.

Gage was in no mood to enjoy the scenery as he scanned the bushes for signs of an attacker. Every rustle of a bird made his nerves strain almost to the breaking point as he readied himself for anything. He knew that dealing with whoever was sent against him wouldn't be a picnic.

Too bad he hadn't brought his gun along on what he'd believed would be a simple surveillance exercise when he left the embassy this morning. A weapon would have gone a long way toward evening the odds. But thinking that an orphanage wasn't the place to bring a loaded weapon, he had left it behind. He hoped his concern for the children's safety wasn't going to cost him too dearly.

He consoled himself with knowing that Nadia was safe.

The specter of her hurt expression as he convinced her she meant nothing to him haunted him, but at least she was back at the palace by now.

She couldn't know how much she really meant to him, couldn't be allowed to know, as long as it put her in danger. Every time he imagined her here dealing with this, he felt himself break out in a cold sweat. He wasn't afraid for himself, but he was terrified for her.

He continued walking back to where he had left the car, trying not to betray his tension in his movements. Thinking of Nadia was a welcome distraction. When had she started to mean so much to him? When he kissed her beneath the colonnade at Zabara, he decided. She had been so uncertain, yet she had kissed him back with surprising enthusiasm.

In spite of his unease, a warmth spread through him. He'd never come across such a wondrous mix of worldly wisdom and inexperience before. She charmed, delighted and challenged him in a way no other woman ever had. By the time they made love, she had already found a place in his heart.

His sense of well-being evaporated. By now she was probably cursing his name and wishing she'd never set eyes on him. Even if he lived through the next few minutes, and he intended to do his level best, she would probably never speak to him again.

A rustling sound in the bushes just ahead and to his left drove all other thoughts out of his mind. He kept his pose relaxed, kept his feet tracking, while fixing every shred of his attention on the source of the sound.

Not birds this time, something far larger, moving stealthily toward him. Whoever it was had waited until Gage was out of sight of the orphanage entrance, not out of consideration for the children, but to ensure the minimum number of witnesses.

He braced himself.

The man who confronted him belonged to one of Tamir's hill families, judging by his wide shoulders and swarthy complexion. A head taller than Gage, he wore his people's tra-

ditional outfit of coarsely woven shirt and loose pants tucked
into leather boots, with a wide sash around the waist, hear-
kening back to a Tamir of a century before.

Gage had a split second to absorb this information before
the man was on top of him, large hands reaching for his
throat.

Gage leaped aside, slashing the side of his hand down on
the man's shoulder with all his strength. The blow glanced
off the muscle as if he'd merely patted the big man on the
back.

No picnic, he reminded himself, dodging out of the path
of the man's bull charge. His adversary had the advantages
of weight, size and blood lust. All Gage could do was try to
exhaust him, hopefully before he finished Gage.

Head down, the man charged at him again. Gage twisted
in the air and landed on his feet, getting in a rabbit punch to
the back of his attacker's neck. The man staggered, shook
himself as if momentarily groggy, then came back at Gage,
his eyes fiery with the desire to exact payment for the blow.

Some distant part of Gage's mind calculated the odds of
getting out of this alive and found them depressingly stacked
against him. No matter. He had beaten the odds before. He
would do so again.

This brute was the reason Nadia never wanted to see him
again, he thought, goading himself to fury. A haze of red
darkened his vision. This man and whoever had sent him
were responsible for Gage's being forced to hurt her, and for
the pain in his own heart as a result.

He stopped dodging and moved in, looking for an opening.
The mountain man swung at him. Gage ducked and came
back with his hands locked together, slugging at his adversary in double-handed blows that should have been lethal but
seemed merely to increase the other man's fury.

Another pass and Gage caught only a handful of shirt for
his trouble. He found himself staring at the man's shoulder
where the ripped fabric had exposed a symbol that made
Gage's blood roar.

"You're one of the Brothers," he ground out as he and the man circled each other. He knew that the younger, more hotheaded members of the Brothers of Darkness had adopted the tattoo of a black octopus as their personal symbol, but had never seen it on a living person before now.

Most of the men wearing that tattoo had been in the morgue.

"What of it?" the man demanded, seemingly disconcerted that Gage had recognized the symbol. As the shoulder muscles of its owner twitched, warning Gage to brace himself for another rush, the creature seemed to writhe with an evil look of purpose.

Keep him talking while you formulate a strategy, Gage told himself. "This is a mistake. I'm one of you," he said, fighting his distaste for the admission, even if it was a pretense to buy himself some time.

The big man blinked his confusion but for the moment held off on another charge, giving Gage a few precious seconds to slow his laboring breath.

"Prove it. Show me the sign."

Gage thought fast. Did he mean the tattoo or some other code signal used between members of the Brothers? Since he didn't have a clue, he rode another hunch. "I'm working undercover for Butrus Dabir."

The look of confusion changed to blind rage. "Now I know you lie. Dabir himself hired me to kill you."

With a bull roar, the mountain man charged, locking his great arms around Gage's ribs, squeezing tighter and tighter until Gage felt as if he was in the grip of a boa constrictor. He felt his ribs start to give way under the relentless pressure. Black fringed his vision, and his lungs screamed for air. The octopus writhed close to his face, its tattooed death's head mocking his fight to breathe.

He—would—not—give—in—to—such—evil.

Desperately he brought his knee up, finding his target unerringly. He felt a grim satisfaction as his attacker's arms fell away and the man doubled over.

The sudden release of pressure on his ribs brought a new burst of agony, but Gage staggered for a moment until he got his feet centered under him. Determinedly he advanced on his attacker, the pounding in his temples and the ache in his ribs driving him on. The big man was trying to pick himself up when Gage drove his head back with a right to the jaw.

"This is for Nadia," he snarled as he sent the man doubling over again with a blow to the midsection.

As he moved in to finish the job, he caught the gleam of metal and dodged the blade barely in time. He should have known the man would come armed. Gage had not so much as a dinner knife on him, while the stiletto being waved in his face looked wickedly purposeful.

He weaved out of its deadly reach. The man wasn't as vanquished as he'd encouraged Gage to think. He came up remarkably easily and balanced on the balls of his feet, jabbing the air in front of Gage's face.

Trying to buy himself some time, Gage retreated behind a pile of boulders, but the mountain man followed him, stalking him, confident that his knife gave him the upper hand.

Gage allowed him to think so, not at all sure that his attacker wouldn't turn out to be right. Think, he ordered himself. That's what his training for this work had taught him to do. Too bad his training hadn't anticipated such unequal odds.

He kept retreating until he reached the bushes where he'd waited this morning while he listened in on the activities at the orphanage. Was it only hours ago? It felt like an eternity.

Backing the clearing, he remembered, was a rock wall hidden by greenery. He stepped out into the middle of the clearing, noting the tracks of his own tires from earlier in the day. By a miracle he was in the right place.

As if directing traffic, he held up his hands, flexing his fingers toward himself, inviting the other man to come at him. If he had judged the situation accurately, the rock wall should be only a couple of yards behind him.

The giant obliged him by rushing in for the kill. Head down, blade extended, he never saw the rock wall until he drove headlong into it, Gage stepping out of his path at the last second. Then the crunching sound of bone against rock jarred Gage's senses. The mountain man went down.

Moving in cautiously, Gage felt for a pulse. The man still lived. Good. He was only a hired gun, and Gage had never meant to kill him.

For a moment during the fight, he had wanted to, he thought grimly. Thinking of the distress this man's cohorts had caused to Nadia had made Gage furious enough to kill. Even now, as he thought about the hurt he had inflicted on her this morning, Gage had to struggle against the urge to keep going until the man was not only defeated but dead.

She was worthy of much nobler impulses, he told himself. He stripped away a length of the pliant strangle-quick vine clinging to the cliff, using his attacker's own knife to cut the thing to size. He used the vine to bind the attacker hand and foot, before slicing another chunk off the man's shirt to use as a gag when he came to.

Propping the man's trussed body against the rock wall, Gage dropped to the ground beside him and waited.

Only then did he allow himself to take stock of the injuries he'd collected from the pounding. His ribs weren't broken but were severely bruised by the man's boa constrictor grip, and every breath hurt. Something wet dripped into his eye. He touched the spot tentatively and his finger came away red. Mountain Man must have nicked him with the knife without his noticing.

Gage pressed a handkerchief to the spot until the bleeding stopped. Considering the size of his attacker, Gage counted himself lucky to be the one sitting up.

As soon as his breathing slowed enough to make movement less arduous, he levered himself to his feet and headed for the car. A bottle of tepid water lay on the front seat and he took a swallow, then poured some on to the handkerchief and swabbed the knife wound. Squinting into the driving mirror, he was glad to see the injury felt worse than it looked.

By the time he returned to the clearing, the mountain man was awake and pulling at his bonds. "The more you strain, the tighter they'll get," Gage warned him. The vine he'd used for rope wasn't called strangle-quick for nothing. Under strain the fibers kept contracting until there was no give left.

If looks could kill, Gage would be dead where he stood. "Why didn't you kill me when you had the chance?" the man demanded

"That may be how the Brothers of Darkness do things, but not how I work. As long as you tell me what I want to know, you'll be allowed to live."

The man spat on the ground. "I'll tell you nothing."

Gage flicked the knife against the octopus tattoo on the man's shoulder. "This thing offends me. It ought to be surgically removed." Pressing just deeply enough to make his point without breaking the skin, he traced the tattoo's outline delicately with the blade.

In spite of his bravado, the man shrank away from the deadly blade. "Butrus Dabir will kill me, anyway."

"Not if I let him think you're already dead. You'd have time to escape back to the mountains before he finds out the truth."

The man tossed his head. "You think I'd be safe there? The Brothers are everywhere."

Like the tentacles of their chosen symbol, Gage thought. "Then I'll turn you over to the police and you can ask for protection in return for giving evidence against the Brothers. It's your problem, not mine. All I want to know is where and when you're supposed to report to Dabir and collect your payment for this job."

The man hesitated, weighing whether it was better to die now at Gage's hands or later at Dabir's. Deciding that later at least offered him a fighting chance, he let out a whistling breath. "I am to meet him in the alleyway behind the Old Souk in Marhaba in one hour."

Gage's sigh mirrored his captive's. "All I needed to know."

The man offered his bound hands. "Untie me now."

"Not until I've settled with Dabir. Until then, you're my insurance policy. Don't worry, I won't forget where I parked you."

The man began to protest, but Gage wadded up the piece of shirt he'd souvenired and used it to silence any further objections. Gage knew the man's best hope for life was to throw himself on the mercy of the police. He planned to tell them where to find him and also suggest they pick up Sitra Wahabi for questioning, but not before he confronted Dabir.

He finally had the link he'd been searching for between Dabir and the Brothers of Darkness. King Marcus was going to be very pleased with the news when Gage eventually shared it with him.

First there was Dabir's complicity in the murder of Conrad Drake. Before he died, Conrad had left a clue to his killer in the letters DOT he'd scratched in the dirt. Gage had followed the killer's trail to Tamir and found the Octopus—the Brothers' symbol. That left only D for Dabir. For once, Gage wished he was the vigilante type, who could mete out his own brand of justice without waiting for the law to act. He wasn't, but Dabir didn't know that.

Before handing Dabir over to the authorities, Gage intended to give the other man a taste of the suffering he had put Conrad through at the last. First he had to track down a traditional hill-family costume. Since he was meeting Dabir at the Souk, that was as likely a place as any to find what he needed.

Tahani watched her mistress pace. "A thousand apologies, Princess. When the car came for me—for you—I tried to make the driver wait, but he insisted Mahir and I were to return to the palace immediately. With your father and mother away, I thought something must be wrong with them. I had no idea what was to unfold."

Nadia rested a hand on her attendant's arm. She was sure when Butrus posted the guard on her apartment, he had forgotten that Tahani was in the bedroom, preparing the princess's clothes for the evening. The irony wasn't lost on her. He had objected to being treated as an inferior by his family, yet he was the one who had treated the servant as if she didn't exist.

The princess smiled at her attendant. "It's all right, Tahani. You did the right thing. The fault is mine for thinking I could change my situation."

"You have changed it, my princess. The children at the orphanage adore you. Your paintings command high prices."

"Because they are sold for charity, not because of their artistic merit," Nadia said on a deep sigh. She wished Tahani would stop fretting and allow her to think. She knew the other woman was distressed. Butrus's anger had shaken the princess, too, more than she was letting Tahani see. But she was more terrified for Gage. If she was too late to save him— and a tight fist of pain closed around her heart at the idea— she could at least make sure Butrus paid for his crime.

"I'm going out," she said resolutely.

Tahani was on her knees, collecting the last of the glass fragments and placing them on the tray. She stood up. "But the guard…"

"Did he pay you any heed when you came and went before?"

"Of course not, my princess." Her tone said she would have been surprised if he had.

"Give me a moment."

Nadia took out a palm-size tape recorder she often used to capture her thoughts about future works of art. Going into the bedroom, she recorded two messages, rewound the tape and returned, handing it to Tahani. Then she made Tahani stand still while her long hair was tucked out of sight under one of Nadia's beautiful scarves. Nadia was staking a lot on the guard's not noticing her clothes, but they didn't have time to change.

As she pushed a last strand of Tahani's hair under the scarf, the princess felt her attendant trembling. "All will be well," she assured her, wondering in her own heart if anything would ever be well again.

Tahani fumbled in her *galabiya*. "Please take this, my princess."

Tahani held out a jeweled knife in a carved leather scabbard. It was the sort of knife one would use to peel fruit or whittle a piece of wood, but the sight of it heartened Nadia. "Thank you, I shan't forget your loyalty," she said. tucking it into her own garment. Then she pulled a scarf over her head, shadowing her features.

She bid Tahani stand near the window with her back to the door, then opened it a little, balancing the tray in her free hand. As instructed, Tahani played the tape Nadia had made. "Guard, kindly come in here."

The man looked around the crack, ignoring Nadia's downcast head. "I'm sorry, Your Highness. My orders are to remain outside until Mr. Dabir returns."

Nadia saw her maid's hand go to the tape again and heard her second message. "Kindly permit my maid to fetch refreshment for me. The first she brought was unacceptable."

The man must have heard the shattering glass, because Nadia saw him nod from under the fringe of her lashes. She adjusted the scarf over her hair and kept her head down as she carried the tray past him. He was so intent on watching Tahani's back that he barely gave Nadia a glance.

She kept her head down until she was out of his sight, then set the tray on the nearest table and ran the length of the corridor and across the courtyard to her car. A servant was cleaning it and looked astonished when she snatched the keys from his hand. But he was too well trained to intervene. As she got in and drove toward the main gates, in the mirror she saw the man resignedly gather the cleaning things.

Butrus was already out of sight. She pulled up beside the sentry box at the main gate. The guard was the same one she had passed on her return earlier. This time he looked less surprised to see her behind the wheel. "My fiancé forgot something," she said. "Did you see which road he took?"

"Mr. Dabir did not inform me of his destination, Your Highness, but he went right, along the main Marhaba road."

One way or another, that road seemed to lead to her destiny, she thought as she thanked the guard and drove on. Tears almost blinded her as she passed the place where she had first met Gage. She couldn't believe she would never see him again, never know the magic of his touch or the press of his lips on hers.

Would the outcome have been different if she hadn't allowed him to send her away this morning? She should never have believed his assertion that she meant nothing to him. In her heart she had known it wasn't true.

It had never been true for her.

Gage meant more to her than any man she had ever known, and she was sure she meant more to him. No man could have spoken to her, touched her, loved her so completely unless he cared. Now she might never know for sure.

If Gage had come to harm, Butrus would pay, she vowed as the turnoff for the orphanage slid past. A commotion up ahead made her frown. She soon saw what was happening. A farmer was herding cattle across the road and Butrus's car was stuck behind them, delaying him long enough for her to catch up. She stopped, not wanting him to recognize her car, although it was agony when everything in her wanted to race after Butrus and claw his traitorous eyes out. When the road cleared and he moved off again, she saw he was heading for the old town.

How long had he been following his own agenda while pretending to be serving the crown? Most of his life, if his story was to be believed. She had never known that he was adopted, or that he so bitterly resented his lack of status.

It would have made no difference to her if she *had* known, but she could see that Butrus would never believe her. He was too caught up in his quest to redress what he perceived as the unfairness of his lot. No amount of reassurance would make any difference to how he saw himself.

She thought again of Gage, so confident and self-assured. He had never let her royal status come between them. A sob welled in her throat, but she throttled it back. She would have time for tears later, when she knew what had happened to her beloved. For now, she concentrated on following Butrus's car.

Chapter 18

Marhaba's Old Souk had been built around the town's original customs house, and it still boasted the original massive wrought-iron gates. Alleyways led away from the building in all directions, their narrow cobbled stretches packed with furniture, wrought-iron wares, dusty coffeepots, wooden boxes and many more Arabian curios. Some of the alleyways were so narrow and shadowy they were lit by wrought-iron lamps even in full daylight.

The Old Souk had been the heart of the town many years ago and was one of the oldest in Tamir. The Gold Souk, a souk-within-a-souk, was still a center of local commerce, providing dowries for those families who still subscribed to the notion.

As he wove his way through the alleys, Gage's nostrils were assaulted by the scents of aromatic herbs, spices and incense, their purveyors assuring him they could be had for pennies. He shook off the hands clutching at him, importuning him to come in for coffee without obligation, and left the puzzled merchants wondering what sort of boor had no time for coffee and conversation.

He further offended the merchant from whom he bought the traditional mountain accouterments by paying the first asking price and refusing the man's offer of coffee. The merchant looked so offended that Gage wondered if he would be allowed to make his purchases at all.

Fortunately the man's instincts for profit won over his desire to see custom satisfied, although he muttered to himself in Arabic. Gage knew enough of the language to recognize that some of the words weren't normally used in polite company, and he summoned an equally earthy reply, silencing the merchant.

Sullenly, the man provided Gage with billowing cotton pants and a woven white shirt that would have done Errol Flynn proud. A scarlet sash and black boots completed the outfit, and Gage stowed his attacker's silver-handled stiletto into the sash, feeling better for knowing it was there. A white skullcap and scarflike head covering secured by a black band provided limited disguise potential, Gage found when he pulled the end of the scarf experimentally across his nose and mouth.

After his fight with the mountain man, Gage's own clothes were the worse for wear, so he felt no regrets about bundling them up and leaving them with the merchant.

His shopping expedition had left him barely enough time to find his way out of the maze of alleyways to the meeting point. Since his disguise was at best rudimentary, he decided to stick to the shadows and let Dabir do most of the talking to begin with.

The attorney was late. Gage fingered the handle of the dagger, wondering what was keeping him. Then he heard a movement behind him and whirled to find Dabir entering the alley. The attorney's shoulders were hunched and his eyes darted everywhere until he spotted Gage waiting in the shadows.

Gage performed a deep salaam and dropped his voice into the low register. "Your will has been done, Mr. Dabir."

Dabir looked around uneasily. "Don't use my name here, Rukn."

So that was his adversary's name. Gage grunted an affirmative that seemed to satisfy Dabir.

"Did he give you any trouble?" Dabir asked.

Gage shuffled his feet. "No trouble, Mr....sir." He couldn't resist adding, "He fought like a tiger, sir."

"But you were able to subdue him?"

Gage jerked his head back in the direction of the orphanage. "His body lies well away from the road, behind a curtain of strangle-quick."

Dabir gave a satisfied nod. "No one would be foolish enough to look for him there. Good work." Gage tensed automatically as Dabir reached inside his jacket, but it was only to withdraw an envelope. Rukn's fee, he assumed.

He accepted the envelope without a twinge of conscience, knowing how much the orphanage could use the money. Holding it by its corner to preserve any fingerprints, he tucked it inside his shirt. He wondered if Rukn would have opened the envelope and checked the contents. Dabir didn't seem to notice the omission.

"You have more work for me, sir?" Gage asked in the same husky voice.

Dabir flicked a glance back the way he'd come, but the alley remained deserted, although with so much of it in shadow, it was difficult to tell. "How loyal are you to Sheik Ahmed?" he asked.

Gage gave a careful shrug. "I am loyal to my brothers."

The answer seemed to satisfy Dabir who nodded. "Good. These brothers of yours grow tired of waiting for power. The sheik is talking of instituting reforms that will endanger our plans. He's starting to listen too much to his headstrong daughter."

"The princess Nadia?" Gage asked, surprise making him

almost forget to disguise his voice. "I understand she is soon to become your bride. Will you not be able to control her?"

Dabir gestured savagely. "No one can control that one. After we are married, she will meet with an unfortunate accident and will no longer be able to contaminate the sheik's thinking. As his son-in-law, I shall console him in his grief and then guide his mind until he speaks for the Brothers without ever knowing he does so."

Gage's hatred of Dabir spiraled into blood rage as he wondered what kind of vicious instincts were needed to contemplate marrying Nadia, while planning to have her killed. His hands itched to close around the man's throat and squeeze the life out of him for daring to threaten the woman he loved.

Gage mastered his urge by assuring himself that Dabir wouldn't be permitted to harm one hair of Nadia's head as long as breath remained in his body to prevent it. With every word he spoke, Dabir was incriminating himself further. All Gage had to do was keep him talking until the police arrived, which should be anytime soon. Before setting off for Marhaba, Gage had called to alert them to pick up Rukn, and had suggested that a bigger fish could be caught if they raided the alleyway behind the Old Souk right about now.

"I'm not sure…" Gage began, thinking that even a mercenary would balk at assassinating a woman.

"Then become sure. Or I will find someone who is."

"I will become sure, sir." Abruptly Gage threw off the disguise and straightened to his full height, clearing the huskiness out of his voice as he said, "In fact, I'm sure now."

Dabir's face drained of color. "What the…? You!"

"I'm afraid your hired killer, Rukn, is the one lying in the strangle-quick, where the police should have found him by now."

"I have no idea what you're talking about. I know no one called Rukn."

"And the envelope in my possession doesn't contain cash covered in your fingerprints," Gage threw at him. "Between the money and the testimony of one who wears the symbol

of the Brothers of Darkness, you're finished, Dabir.'' He
pulled the dagger out of his sash and held it so the thread of
light penetrating the alleyway glinted off it.

Dabir's throat convulsed as he saw the blade. Evidently it
was one thing to order someone to be killed, and quite another to be faced with the possibility of one's own demise.
''What are you going to do?'' he asked, sounding strangled.
He had flattened himself against the ancient stone wall as if
he needed its support to remain upright. His expression was
hunted.

''What I'd like to do and what I will do are, unfortunately,
different matters,'' Gage said. ''Gutting you like a fish has a
certain appeal, but I promised the police I would hand you
over to them in one piece.''

''So what happens now?''

Gage made a show of examining the deadly blade. ''We
wait. In the meantime, you can tell me about Conrad Drake.''

''That name means nothing to me.''

''How many men did you order to their deaths in America?''

He saw the dawning of recognition in Dabir's eyes,
masked by a thin-lipped smile of contempt. ''His death was
his own fault. He tried to join the Brothers and failed on his
first mission.''

Gage let his knife settle on the other man's throat, wondering how much pressure would be needed to sever the jug-
ular. Only a little more than he was exerting now. Only a
little.

Reluctantly he eased the blade back. Whatever Dabir had
done, the law would judge him, not Gage Weston. ''He
didn't fail. He took five members of the cell he'd infiltrated
with him,'' he said.

Dabir's eyebrows arched as he tried to make his breathing
shallow enough to avoid contact with the knife. ''Infiltrated?
What was this man to you?''

''My partner, my best friend, you could say my brother.
Like me, he was working deep undercover for King Marcus

of Montebello. The king asked us to find who, in Sheik Ahmed's circle, could have betrayed Prince Lucas and my partner. Before he died, Conrad left a message that led me to Tamir and to you. You're tied in with the American criminals who operated through that same cell of the Brothers of Darkness. It doesn't take a genius to know who was reporting to whom.''

Dabir shook his head, stopping the motion as he felt the press of cold steel against his skin. ''You have nothing that would stand up in a court of law. All I have to do is deny everything.''

''No doubt. But I'm just as happy to see you convicted of a charge of conspiracy to commit murder. And that will stand up in court when your hireling, Rukn, testifies that you sent him to kill me. Either way, you're finished.''

He saw the same certainty reach Dabir's eyes, but felt no shred of pity. The man deserved everything that was coming to him. In Gage's mind his crimes included the murder of Conrad Drake. It didn't matter what was read out in court.

Suddenly Dabir laughed. ''I suppose you think you've won.''

''I don't think it, I know I've won.''

''Then you sacrifice the most important prize of all. If I don't return to the palace within two hours, your beloved princess will die. I left one of my men guarding her, with orders to kill her if he doesn't receive my coded assurance that all is well.''

This time it was all Gage could do not to drive the blade home. His hand trembled with the need, but he dared not, as long as there was a chance that Dabir was telling the truth. ''What makes you think I care what happens to her?'' he asked carefully.

''I know you are in love with her. I had her followed all the time we were at Zabara. You were photographed kissing her in the colonnade.''

''A kiss doesn't have to signify love.''

''A man knows when another man desires his woman.''

"In this case, you're right. I do love her. But she was never your woman and never will be once she hears that you intended to marry her, then have her killed as soon as your position in the royal family was secure."

A gasp of shock brought Gage's head up, and a hint of jasmine reached his nostrils. Joy ripped through him as he realized that Nadia wasn't at the palace, under threat of death. In the same moment, his joy was engulfed by stark terror that she was here, where he couldn't guarantee to protect her.

He peered into the shadows in time to see a slight figure duck out from under a wall hanging. A moment later he saw Butrus give a start of recognition. "Nadia."

Making her way alone through the souk, Nadia had felt horribly exposed, although she had drawn her scarf over her face to avoid recognition. She was unaccustomed to being in such a crowded public place without Nargis, Tahani and the twins. Every time she was jostled, she was filled with apprehension, aware of the curious glances she drew from men as she scanned the alleyways for any sign of Butrus.

She had seen him leave his car and enter the labyrinthine complex. In the short time it had taken her to find somewhere to leave her car, he had disappeared. How was she ever going to find him and bring him to account for what he had done to Gage?

She was alerted by the sound of a man's voice, one so dear and familiar that tears sprang to her eyes. Gage. He sounded as if he had a heavy cold, and his British accent had been replaced by a rough Tamiri dialect, but she was sure it was him. He was alive and very nearby. She lifted her head, trying to determine where the sound had come from.

He was only a few feet away, separated from her by what she had taken to be a solid wall, but was actually a thick old carpet hung from a line.

She froze, listening hard, her joy turning to ashes in her mouth as she heard Gage say in the low unfamiliar voice,

"The princess Nadia? I understand she is soon to become your bride. Will you not be able to control her?"

Her heart solidified in her chest and she brought her hand to her mouth to keep from screaming. Had Gage's courtship been nothing more than an elaborate scheme to see her dead and Butrus ruling by her father's side? The possibility made her sick to her stomach, the words buzzing in her mind, beyond any possibility of denial. Her mounting horror drowned out Butrus's reply. Her thoughts whirled so fast that the rest of the conversation went by in a blur of sound.

After a few minutes she straightened. She was not going to let them get away with this. She wasn't sure what she could do, but she was determined to make Butrus and his charming accomplice pay for their treasonous plans.

She pulled out Tahani's knife, discarding the scabbard. As a weapon, it wasn't much against two grown men, but it was all she had. Taking deep breaths to slow the rapid beating of her heart, she ducked under the carpet into the alleyway. The deep shadows protected her, and her dancer's skill enabled her to move on silent feet until she was within sight of Gage and Butrus.

Relief shimmered through her, cool and sweet, as she saw that Gage held a knife to Butrus's throat. The two couldn't be in league, after all. But what had Gage meant about controlling her, and why was he dressed in the costume of the hill people? She forced herself to remain still and listen.

The more she heard, the more appalled she became at the thought of how close she had come to entrusting her future to Butrus Dabir. He was responsible for the death of Gage's best friend and partner. How many other crimes had he committed in his quest for power and glory?

Bad enough when she thought he suffered from a sense of inferiority because of what he believed he had lacked as a boy. She had never dreamed that his aspirations had led him to join the Brothers of Darkness, one of the most feared and hated organizations in her country's history.

Her heart ached for poor King Marcus of Montebello. He

was her brother's father-in-law, and she knew how badly the
king had suffered while his son was missing. All the time
Butrus had been paying lip service to concern for the king,
he had been helping the people who had tried to kill Prince
Lucas.

In the shadows, she pressed her hands together to stop
them from trembling. She had sensed all along that Gage was
more than he seemed. Now she knew he was some kind of
secret agent, charged with finding the traitor in her family.
She felt confused, on one hand pleased that he had unmasked
Butrus, but on the other wondering how much of his love for
her had been part of his cover story.

*"She was never your woman and never will be once she
hears that you intended to marry her, then have her killed
as soon as your position in the royal family was secure."*

This time she couldn't restrain her gasp of shock and saw
the two men turn toward her.

She moved out of the shadows. In the instant that Gage's
attention was distracted, she saw Butrus slam the blade away
from his throat and heard the dagger clatter to the cobblestones. Before she had time to react, Butrus had grabbed her
and spun her around to put her between him and Gage. Butrus's arm pressed painfully against her windpipe. "If you
really love her, you'll stay where you are," he ordered Gage.

She saw Gage freeze. She could have wept for knowing
she had helped Butrus to turn the tables. "Never mind me,"
she urged. "Do what you must." Then Butrus's hold tightened, silencing her.

She increased her grip on the knife and jabbed it upward,
hearing her fiancé's grunt of surprise as the small blade pen-
etrated his sleeve. "You little…"

She used the moment to twist free and held her knife between them. "Hurry, Gage," she implored.

In the narrow confines of the alley, he maneuvered around
her, but desperation made Butrus quicker. He slammed Nadia
against the wall and tried to shoulder past Gage to make his

escape. Gage shot a foot out and tripped the attorney, who fell heavily. He made a strange rattling sound and lay still.

"Stay there," Gage ordered Nadia, and went to Dabir, rolling him just enough to see what had happened. The stiletto had landed between two cobblestones with the blade pointing skyward, spearing Dabir through the heart when he fell. Gage let his inert body fall back. The police would have no difficulty working out how Dabir had died. Gage was torn between relief that it was over and regret that he wouldn't have the satisfaction of seeing the man brought to trial.

A whimpering sound brought his head around in time to see Nadia sliding bonelessly down the stone wall. Cursing, Gage went to her, collecting her in his arms. Had she realized what had happened to Dabir and fainted?

Her eyes fluttered open. "I think something's the matter with me," she murmured, her hand against her breast.

Gently Gage pried her fingers loose and felt his heart turn to stone in his chest. When she had been thrown against the wall, the knife she had wielded against Dabir had slipped. The jeweled handle now protruded from her breast, and a tide of scarlet was spreading outward from it.

"No, Nadia, dear heaven, no," he moaned, feeling as if the blade had pierced his own heart. "Don't do this to me. I love you. I can't live without you."

He saw her sweet beautiful mouth turn up in a gentle smile. "I love you, too," she said faintly, and slipped into unconsciousness.

Careful of the protruding knife, Gage compressed a handful of her gown against the wound, pressing hard, but unable to stem the spreading red tide. Moments later he heard the wail of sirens coming closer. Too late, he thought in anguish. He cradled the princess in his arms, rocking her gently backward and forward in a grief too soul-deep to be borne. He was still holding her when the sirens stopped.

Chapter 19

Nadia swam up toward the light. Although she was deep underwater, she felt no urgency to breathe. The crystalline water felt warm and welcoming, as if she was being cradled in loving arms.

She felt blissfully happy and knew why. Gage had told her he loved her and couldn't live without her. It was a dream of course, too beautiful and magical to be real, but oh, what a wonderful dream. She thought she had told him she loved him, too, then she had slipped underwater and drifted there for a long, long time.

Now some instinct told her it was time she returned to land. She started to swim toward the light, her strokes fluid and unhurried. Never had she known such lightness and joy. Her *galabiya* floated around her, pinpoints of phosphorescence clinging to the fabric like fairy lights.

"I think she's coming around," came a strange voice. She felt her eyelids being lifted back and a pinpoint of light shone in them. The hands were gentle.

She opened her eyes and the light was lifted away. She

was lying in a high narrow bed in an unfamiliar room. The walls and ceiling were white, but against them were banked huge vases filled with red roses. Their glorious perfume surrounded her, bringing a smile to her lips.

A woman dressed in white was bending over her. Then the woman was moved aside, and Gage leaned over her, taking her hand. "Nadia, thank goodness."

He exchanged a few words with the woman in white, and Nadia heard a door close as she was left alone with Gage.

His voice sounded strained, she noticed, and his eyes were red-rimmed. "Where am I?" she asked, her voice husky.

Gage heard and cradled her head in one hand while he lifted a glass to her lips with the other. She swallowed a few drops of water, and the rasp in her throat lessened. "Thank you."

He eased her head back to the pillow, letting his fingers trail through her hair as though touching her was a minor miracle. "You're in the hospital," he told her. "You were injured and you collapsed in the alley at the Marhaba Souk."

Memory came rushing back, displacing her sense of tranquility. She looked at Gage with wide unhappy eyes. "Butrus?"

"He's dead," he told her. "I'm sorry."

Now she remembered seeing her fiancé fall and land on the dagger he had knocked from Gage's hand. "It's hard to feel sorry," she said. "I had no idea he bore me and my family such ill will. My father was always good to him, yet he repaid us by collaborating with the Brothers of Darkness. How could he do such a thing?"

Gage caressed her forehead. "Many reasons can motivate a man to side with the forces of evil. Power, greed, the need to feel bigger than he is, are all reason enough if you want them to be."

She nodded. "Butrus told me his uncle adopted him. He never felt equal to the other children of the household."

Gage's face took on a faraway expression. "I knew someone in the same position. He never knew his father, and his

mother died when he was a child. He was farmed out to aunts
and uncles, then we became friends at school and my family
adopted him. We grew up together as close as brothers.''

"Your friend, Conrad Drake?'' she guessed, remembering
what she had overheard in the alleyway.

Gage seated himself on the side of her bed. "You heard
what I told Dabir?''

"Not everything, but a lot. I gather you hold Butrus responsible for the death of your friend.''

"Without a trial, I'll never have all the facts, but the evidence is there. Prince Lucas of Montebello identified one of
the Americans Dabir met with at Zabara as belonging to the
Brothers who held him prisoner in America. They kept their
affiliations well hidden. If Lucas hadn't identified the man in
the photos I sent to King Marcus, we still wouldn't have the
link.''

"You've been busy,'' she said dreamily, "for a minor English diplomat.''

He smiled self-deprecatingly. "You're entitled to know
that I'm neither English, nor a diplomat. The British ambassador and his wife are my godparents, and they kindly allowed me to use the embassy as a base, but my home is in
Penwyck and my business…well, I think you know what that
is by now.''

She nodded, finding she didn't mind as much as she
thought she would. Unlike Butrus, Gage hadn't deceived her
for his own benefit, but to ensure that justice was done. She
felt her eyelids grow heavy. "I forgive you,'' she murmured.

She was aware of the woman in white returning and checking her over, a doctor, she knew now, but her eyelids felt so
heavy she could no longer keep them open.

Gage watched her slip into sleep, pleased to see how
peaceful she looked. Her color was back to normal, and the
pulse he felt under his fingers was strong and steady. He
curled his fingers into hers, before bending and dropping a
light kiss on her slightly parted lips.

After the rigors of these last horrible few days, he felt as tired and battered as he ever had, but he didn't care as long as she was all right.

When he thought she had been fatally wounded, he had thought his own heart was going to stop. Cradling her, watching the crimson tide seep through her gown and knowing there was nothing more he could do, he had fought back tears of anguish, which had threatened to become a flood if he gave in to them.

He had not wanted to give her up to the care of the police and ambulance attendants who had arrived at the scene. When the paramedics told him she was only slightly injured, he hadn't believed them.

"No one bleeds that much from a slight injury," he had insisted, knowing that his control was a hairbreadth from snapping.

Not until one of the paramedics had taken Gage to the ambulance and shown him the tube of paint that Nadia's knife had ruptured did Gage start to believe she might live. He had no idea what she was doing with a tube of red paint tucked in her *galabiya,* but he thanked God that it was there. When Dabir threw her against the wall, the paint had absorbed most of the impact of the knife, so she was only slightly wounded. Gage had been right all along. She had fainted from the shock of Dabir's revelations and seeing him fall on his knife.

"The princess is exhausted," the doctor had assured Gage. "We will hospitalize her to treat the shock and the minor wound, but she will recover quickly."

After the police had confirmed his identity, he was allowed to ride in the ambulance with Nadia, and they agreed to take his statement at the hospital later. They would need to talk to the princess, too, but Gage could see they were prepared to await her pleasure. There were some advantages to being royal, he thought. He didn't mind as long as it meant he could be with her.

When next Nadia opened her eyes, daylight streamed into the room. Gage was asleep in a chair at her bedside, she saw, her heart filling with joy at the sight. During the night she had drifted in and out of awareness as doctors watched over her. She had known that Gage was there, a reassuring figure, willing her to recover.

His prayers had worked. She felt strong and well, and relieved beyond measure that Butrus hadn't succeeded in subverting the throne of Tamir to the will of the Brothers of Darkness. Thinking of how close he had come made her shudder. If she had forced herself to do what she thought was her duty and marry him, she would have been helping him to further his devilish aims.

Never again, she thought resolutely. From now on, she would be true to herself first. She had no illusions that Gage would sweep her off her feet. He had said he loved her, but that was in the heat of battle with Butrus. In daylight he would probably feel otherwise. They were from different backgrounds. Her father would never allow her to marry Gage.

She felt a smile start. Old habits died hard. She had just finished deciding to be true to herself, and already she was worrying about what her father would and wouldn't permit her to do. After all, he *had* allowed her sister Leila to marry an American just weeks ago. She might just tell her father that she was going to visit Penwyck. The former British colony was reputed to be a beautiful place. If she and Gage were to meet there, who knew where it could lead?

"You look pleased with yourself," Gage observed.

Her thoughts had been so busy, she hadn't seen him stir. "I was thinking of my future," she said. "Thanks to you, I have one to look forward to." She didn't add how largely Gage himself figured in her dreams.

He stretched and stood up, then padded to her bedside to take her hand. She felt some of his strength flowing into her. "Don't thank me. You were the one who attacked Dabir with the knife." He picked up a distorted piece of metal from the bedside table. "Thank God the blade went into this tube of paint, instead of into you."

She nodded, remembering. "I found it in the field where I'd left Tahani painting. Butrus had sent a car and taken Tahani and my driver back to the palace. Until I stumbled across the tube of paint, I thought I was in the wrong place."

"Picking up the tube probably saved your life."

Her hand went to her breast. The knife had pierced her *galabiya,* fatally she'd thought. She was pleased to find only a small dressing over the place and murmured a prayer of thanks.

Gage heard her. "Amen to that. But I wish you'd found another color besides red. When I held you in my arms, I thought you were bleeding to death."

"Would blue paint have made you believe that royalty is truly blueblooded?" she asked, hoping to defuse the tension she saw in his face and posture.

He leaned over and gathered her into his arms, being careful to avoid hurting her. She almost sighed with annoyance, wanting him to be anything but gentle. She wanted to be crushed against him, to feel his mouth hungry on hers and to hear him say he loved her now, when he knew she wasn't dying.

He didn't say it and she became aware that his embrace was stiff and awkward. She pulled back a little, looking at him anxiously. "What's the matter, Gage?"

"Your parents are due to visit at any moment."

She frowned. "I thought the sheik was still away." He and her mother were inspecting the new oil field on the island of Jawhar.

"They returned as soon as they knew you were hurt. They were here earlier, but you were still asleep, so they went out for some air. They'll be back any moment."

She gripped his arm. "Stay with me, please."

"Your father isn't very happy with my clandestine activities."

"I'm happy with you," she affirmed. "I want you to stay."

"You're certain?"

Another thought made her frown. "Is Tahani all right?"

"She's a little shaken by what happened to you, but she's fine. The police arrested the guard who was working for Butrus."

She chewed her lower lip. "Butrus had photographs of us."

"I know. I found them on him and destroyed all but one."

"To use as blackmail against me?"

"To remind myself of what a lucky man I am to have known you."

Past tense, she noticed with a stab of anguish. He sounded as if he was preparing to leave. What else had she expected? Declaring his love when he thought she was engaged to another man or dying was one thing. Saying it now would probably be more of a commitment than he wanted to make. Although she had prepared herself, the thought plunged her into the depths of despair.

Reading the unhappiness in her expression, Gage touched a hand to her cheek. "Don't worry, Princess. All will be well."

She had said the same thing to Tahani, and look what had happened. Then she had no more time to brood, because her mother and father entered the room. Sheik Ahmed looked astonished to find Gage there, but made no comment. Her mother was too busy gathering her into a loving hug.

"My dearest child, I was worried out of my mind. Are you all right?"

Nadia returned the hug. "Yes, Mother, I'm fine. It's good to see you both."

Sheik Ahmed moved closer to the bed and took her hand. "It's good to see you awake, my daughter. From what the police told me, we almost never saw you again."

Nadia's look included Gage. "Mr. Weston saved my life, and saved Tamir from Butrus's schemes."

The sheik's cool nod acknowledged Gage's role. "Since arriving in our country, Mr. Weston has been rather active, he tells me."

A doctor who had followed the ruler and his wife into the room bustled around the spacious suite, rearranging the comfortable chairs for them. Alima declined hers, preferring to perch on Nadia's bed and cling to her hand as if to convince herself that her eldest daughter was really safe and well.

Sheik Ahmed thanked the doctor curtly, his tone suggesting dismissal. The doctor took the hint and left.

"Gage has told me why he came to Tamir," Nadia said to her father. "He had nothing but our best interests at heart."

The sheik's lips thinned. "Mr. Weston and I will discuss this again later, Daughter. It is not your concern."

"But it is my concern," she insisted, a now-or-never feeling driving her to throw caution and years of royal education to the wind. "I want you to know that when I marry, it will be for love."

The sheik looked as if she wasn't telling him anything he hadn't suspected—and dismissed. "Love has little to do with making a good marriage. Your mother and I married for family reasons, and they were sufficient."

Nadia saw Alima's face dimple and knew that love had crept into her parents' relationship over the years. She was sure her father felt the same, although he would never admit it. She took a deep breath. "Your way was appropriate for your generation. I am of a new generation, and I wish to live my life differently."

"I told you so," Gage said, folding his arms and resting his back against the wall, his gaze soft on her.

She looked at her father in confusion. "What does he mean?"

"While you were asleep, Mr. Weston asked me for your hand in marriage," the sheik said. "He asked me not to tell you until you indicated that you wanted the same thing." He looked over his shoulder at Gage. "I think we may take this as an indication."

"Sounds like it," Gage said equably. He sounded insufferably pleased with himself.

Feeling as if she had been outmaneuvered, Nadia felt her face heat with annoyance. "So the two of you have already settled my future?"

Gage nodded. "Pretty well."

"Without bothering to consult me?"

"Uh-huh."

"That is how men decide matters," the sheik added loftily.

Nadia retrieved her hand from her mother and gesticulated in anger. "Men! Always men! What they want, think, decide. Can't a woman decide for herself what she wants and whom she will marry?"

Gage seemed unmoved by her tantrum. "I thought she already had."

"Is Gage wrong?" her father asked.

She subsided against the pillows. "No," she said sulkily. "But it would have been nice to have my opinion considered."

"Your opinion was considered," Gage said, moving closer. "Why do you think I asked Sheik Ahmed to withhold his news until I knew how you felt?"

As marriage proposals went, it had to be the strangest one in the history of Tamir, she thought. Then it came to her that she didn't really mind if it meant she and Gage could be together for always.

"I admit I wasn't pleased when I heard why Gage had come to our country," the sheik continued. "I had started to believe that relations between us and King Marcus of Montebello had reached a new level of understanding. Finding that the king had secretly arranged to have our family investigated hardly seemed a step in the right direction."

"I wish there had been another way, too," Gage agreed. "Your father now accepts that there was no other way to uncover the traitor who was working against your family's interests."

Alima touched a hand to Nadia's cheek. "You're not too distraught about Butrus, are you, child?"

Nadia shook her head. "I shudder to think of the havoc he could have caused Tamir if he'd achieved his aims."

"That isn't going to happen now," Gage said. "You're safe, and so is the peace process between your country and Montebello."

The sheik rose to his feet, adjusting his headdress and *'iqual,* and gathered his wife up with a look. "We'll leave you to rest now, Daughter. Your sister and attendants will visit later. They have been beside themselves with worry and will be relieved to hear that we found you looking so much better."

Alima placed Gage's hand into Nadia's. "Keep her safe for us."

His glowing expression was answer enough, but he said, "Believe me, I will." If it cost him his life, Nadia read into his expression.

Thinking of how close they had come, she tightened her fingers around his and sent her father a radiant look of gratitude. "Thank you for giving us your blessing, Father." Then a frown creased her brow. "Although I don't understand how you can be so pleased that I wish to marry a commoner of another country and faith."

The sheik's look went to Gage. "He is not as much a commoner as you think, my child. Tell her, Gage."

Gage shuffled his feet and looked uncomfortable. "It's true I'm from Penwyck, but from the royal part of it, although I don't use the titles much."

"I'm pleased to present His Grace, Gage Weston, Duke of Penwyck," the sheik said with a satisfied smirk. "As for his faith…"

"We share the same beliefs," Gage said quietly.

She blinked in surprise. "But you have godparents."

"An honorary role. The Theodores are long-standing friends of my father's and consider themselves my godparents. I have known them so long that I regard them in that role, too."

Alima clapped her hands in delight. "I must return to the

palace. There is much to be done to plan another royal wedding feast.''

Nadia didn't even try to mask her distress. The thought of her wedding reception being turned into a royal circus was not to be borne. ''Mother…,'' she said warningly.

Alima gave her a wicked smile. ''Permit a mother her pleasures, child. I promise to make the feast last no longer than a week.''

Nadia collapsed against the pillows, knowing when she was being teased. ''You are impossible, but I love you both.''

Her mother stroked her brow. ''As we love you, too, Daughter.''

Although they might frustrate and anger her beyond belief, Nadia had always known her parents loved her. She felt blessed to hear it spoken at long last. Murmuring a prayer of leave-taking over her, the sheik left with his wife in tow.

''They're quite a couple, aren't they?'' Gage asked. He got up and snapped the lock closed on the door. They were finally, blessedly alone.

''You should have told me you were a duke,'' she said reprovingly. ''How many other secrets have you kept from me?''

''Only one,'' he said with a seductive smile. ''How much I truly love you. I doubt if even your parents have any idea.''

He pulled her into his arms and found her mouth with a certainty that took her breath away. Just as well the medical staff had unhooked her from the monitoring equipment over her bed while she slept, because the heart monitor would have gone crazy, she knew. She could feel her pulse racing and knew the cause was far from medical.

''I love you, too,'' she whispered, linking her arms around his neck. How strong he felt. The prince of her heart, now and for all time. ''For a moment there, before my parents arrived, I was afraid you were preparing to leave me.''

''I was,'' he confirmed, his kiss silencing her indrawn breath of alarm. ''I knew how I felt about you and I had your father's blessing. But I wanted to be sure you felt the same way. As you must know by now, I'm not your average royal, and I have my own ideas about equality between men and women.''

He was giving her a gift greater than anything she had ever dreamed of receiving—the right to choose her own destiny, she thought on a swell of joy so great it was almost more than she could bear. Her eyes filmed with tears as she smiled up at him. ''I have made my choice,'' she said huskily. ''Wherever you go, whatever you do, I shall be at your side.''

His breath of relief washed over her and his arms tightened around her. Through the thin fabric of the hospital gown, she felt the powerful beat of his heart keeping time with hers. ''In return I promise to love you and honor you as my wife and the custodian of my heart, for as long as we live.''

No woman could ask for more, she thought as his mouth claimed hers again. The kiss went on for a long time, flooding her with desires both sacred and primitive, making her hope that their wedding would take place soon. She chided herself for her impatience. She and Gage had the rest of their lives to be together. ''I never thought I could be so happy,'' she said.

''Nor I, my darling princess,'' he said, sounding as impatient as she felt. ''There's another person who will be even happier, if you feel as I do.''

''Who?'' she asked, puzzled.

''Little Sammy. I'd like us to adopt him,'' Gage suggested.

She knew her cup of happiness was brimful. ''I can think of nothing more wonderful.''

''Other than to provide Sammy with a houseful of brothers and sisters,'' Gage said.

She laughed. ''My parents would consider that my royal duty.'' At the same time, she knew that doing her duty had never appealed to her more.

Epilogue

Nadia felt a buzz of excitement as she took her place beside Samira in the small room concealed from her father's council chamber by a beautifully patterned screen. The palace had many such hideaways. They had been used for centuries by the women of the household to observe palace life without being exposed to the eyes of strangers.

"I was delayed by yet another journalist seeking an interview," she told Samira in an undertone. Since her release from the hospital the previous week, Nadia had been besieged by the world media, fascinated by the story of her adventure and enchanted by her romance with the handsome duke from Penwyck. They hadn't been told the half of it of course, and Nadia had been amazed that her father had allowed her to speak to the media at all. Had he sensed her determination to emancipate herself once and for all, and decided to give her more leeway in order to head off a family crisis?

Her father was a realist, she knew. Before he died, Butrus

had accused Nadia of influencing her father to institute reforms. She was starting to hope it was true.

She smiled warmly at Alima, seated on her sister's other side with her dutiful attendant, Salma, behind her. Their mother was also intent on watching the proceedings.

Alima gestured to the chamber below, which was filling rapidly with delegates to the conference being held to improve relations and trade between Tamir and their neighbors from Montebello. "Look, King Marcus has arrived."

Nadia had no trouble spotting the distinguished monarch. In his sixties, he was still lean and broad-shouldered, his white hair making him look every inch the elder statesman. With her parents' approval, the king had impressed her by calling on her the day before to apologize personally for his role in having her family investigated. Since his actions had led to her and Gage meeting and falling in love, she had seen little need for his apology. Instead, she thanked him, much to the king's pleasure.

Samira nudged her gently. "Your Gage makes a handsome conference chairman, doesn't he?"

Pride and love brightened Nadia's features as she watched Gage take his place at the table. As a member of the royal house of Penwyck, and thus considered impartial, he had been seen as the ideal person to mediate the conference. "Of course."

"Not that you're biased," Samira teased, her sparkling eyes reflecting Nadia's happiness.

Nadia gave her a "who, me?" look and settled to listen to the proceedings.

Her attention was distracted by Nargis bustling in. "Your Highnesses, Sheik Ahmed commands your presence in the council chambers."

"Now?" Such a thing was unheard of in Nadia's experience.

Nargis nodded. "He wishes you to act as his advisers." The attendant also sounded disbelieving.

Nadia looked at Samira, then back to Nargis. "Are you sure he said adviser and not observer?"

"Yes, my princess. He has reserved seats for you directly behind him."

Catching Nadia's questioning look, Alima shook her head. "You two go. I am happy here with Salma for company." Her message was clear. She would do as she had always done, share her thoughts with their father behind the scenes.

Nadia needed no second invitation. Her heart swelled with pride and not a little nervousness as she and Samira slipped into seats behind her father in the main conference room. A ripple of surprise had traveled around the room at their arrival, but Nadia lifted her chin. This would not be the last time a woman of Tamir served in such a capacity, if she had anything to say about it.

Across the table King Marcus smiled a welcome, as did the king's principal adviser, Desmond Caruso. He was standing in for the king's son, Prince Lucas. Evidently the prince was still recovering from his long ordeal. If *she* had crashed her plane, lost her memory and been held hostage by the Brothers of Darkness, she would probably need some recovery time, too, Nadia supposed.

Lucas's cousin, Desmond, had grown up in America, not knowing he was a member of Montebello's ruling family until he was nineteen, she recalled.

Beside her, she felt Samira stir and looked at her curiously. Her sister's eyes were fixed on Desmond. In them Nadia saw the same sparkle she felt in her own whenever she looked at Gage.

Surely Desmond couldn't be the man that made Samira look so enigmatic whenever love was mentioned, could he? Glancing at her sister's vivid expression, Nadia began to wonder. But she had no more time to consider the question, because Gage was calling the conference to order.

His warm look washed over her, suggesting that he approved of her presence. Had he noticed that she was wearing the tiger necklace he had given her? The slight upward curve of his mouth told her he had and was pleased.

She listened intently, offering her father a suggestion when invited, finally feeling as if she was contributing something to her country's future. The time flew past, and soon Gage announced they would break for coffee.

"It feels strange, being here among the men, doesn't it?" Samira whispered as they sipped their coffee. "I could get to like it, though."

Nadia already liked it, and she said so. She felt her spirits lift further as Gage drifted to her side, her father with him. "Thank you for your contributions this morning, my daughter," the sheik said.

Gage's look of love spoke more eloquently than words.

"Thank you for allowing me to voice them, Father," she returned, her tone adding, *at long last.*

The sheik nodded as if he had heard what she didn't say. He took a sip of cardamom-scented coffee. "I have reached a decision concerning your future."

She bristled automatically, but he smiled to disarm her fears. "The choice is yours and Gage's of course, but I have been talking with Ambassador Theodore, and the time is ripe for Tamir to send our first ambassador to England."

Gage, of course, she assumed, as he gave her a knowing smile. The prospect of living in England as the ambassador's wife was attractive, although she couldn't subdue a feeling of disappointment. Was her involvement today nothing more than a token because her father knew she wouldn't be living in Tamir for much longer?

The sheik must have seen the disappointment on her face, because he continued, "How does Madam Ambassador sound to you, Daughter?"

She almost choked on her coffee. "*Madam* Ambassador?" Instinctively her gaze flew to Gage.

He nodded approval. "Sounds pretty good to me."

She could hardly believe it. "You...you won't mind?"

"Why should I? I can operate as well from England as from Penwyck."

"What about Dani, your protégé? Won't she mind you living in England? I was looking forward to meeting her."

He looked pleased. "Dani spends more time traveling around the world with her band than she does in Penwyck, so you'll meet her soon, no matter where we're based."

"Then I accept the appointment with pleasure, Father."

"I thought you might," the sheik said dryly, but his eyes shone with satisfaction as he swept Gage off to consult with King Marcus. Nadia couldn't wait to share her wonderful news with Samira, but her sister had slipped away. Casting her gaze around for her, Nadia almost bumped into Desmond Caruso.

"A thousand apologies, Your Highness," he said formally.

She studied him with interest, certain that he was the man who had caught her sister's eye. He had inherited the dynamic looks of the Sebastiani family, with raven hair, chiseled features and a cleft chin that made him look like a film star. Personality fairly radiated from him. So Nadia was at a loss to explain the unease she felt around him. "The fault was mine for not looking where I was going," she said, struggling to mask her reaction.

He didn't seem to notice. "Are you enjoying the conference?"

She nodded, hoping he didn't know that this was the first time she had served her father publicly in such a capacity. "If it leads to better relations between our two countries, I will be delighted."

He nodded. "That's what we're here for."

A servant refilled their coffee cups from an ornate brass pot. Nadia saw Desmond trying to survey the crowd without her noticing. "Are you looking for someone?"

He dragged his attention back to her. "Forgive me, Your Highness, but I thought I saw your sister, Princess Samira, at your side a few moments ago."

So the attraction was not one-sided, Nadia thought, reading

a certain desperation in the young man's expression. She tried to feel happy for her sister, wondering why she found it such a challenge. "She will return shortly," she assured him. "When she does, she will look for me."

"Then I hope you won't mind if I remain at your side until she returns," he said, his interest unmistakable. He seemed irritated when an aide discreetly attracted his attention. "Excuse me one moment," he said, and turned to the man.

She sipped her coffee, not wishing to eavesdrop, but the aide's voice carried to her ears. He was saying something about a Miss Ursula Chambers from America insisting on speaking with Desmond. Evidently she was refusing to hang up until he came to the phone.

Concern for her sister made Nadia anxious. Did this Chambers woman have a claim on Desmond's affections? Nadia hoped not, because she knew only too well the look she had seen on Samira's lovely face. Since falling in love with Gage, Nadia saw the same expression on her own face whenever she looked in a mirror.

She let her gaze wander over the crowd, pretending disinterest, but listening carefully as Desmond said, "Give Miss Chambers my regrets, but tell her we have nothing to say to each other and I would prefer her not to telephone me again."

Whatever might have been between Desmond and this woman was over now, Nadia gathered. Seeing Samira crossing the room toward them, Nadia allowed herself a sigh of relief. Her sister's happiness meant as much to her as her own. She would hate Samira to give her heart to Desmond, only to have it broken.

Desmond's face lit up at Samira's approach, although Nadia noticed that the smile didn't quite reach his eyes. She decided now was a good time to slip away and find Gage, leaving her sister and Desmond alone.

She hated to think that Desmond might be an opportunist who had decided that a royal princess was more useful to him than this American woman he had refused to speak to, but the suspicion refused to go away.

It was none of her concern, she told herself firmly. In Gage she had found the other half of her soul, and happiness beyond her wildest dreams. Samira deserved the chance to work out her destiny in her own way.

Seeing Gage beckoning, Nadia murmured a prayer that her sister would find a love as all-consuming as hers. A tall order, given that Nadia's cup of joy was full to overflowing. But as she well knew, with love, nothing was impossible.

*   *   *   *   *

Next month, look for

HER LORD PROTECTOR

by Ellen Wilks (IM1160) as

ROMANCING THE CROWN
continues.

Only from Silhouette Intimate Moments!
Turn the page for a sneak preview....

Chapter 1

The chimes above the door rang. Rose tucked her hair behind her ear, turned to the door—and froze.

It was him. The man from the airport. The one who'd been with His Grace, Duke Lorenzo Sebastiani, nephew of the king and head of Montebello's intelligence service. His clothes were cleaner and more casual today, but just as expensive. His face was hard, lean. Not a lovely face, but the sort a woman remembered. And the eyes—oh, they were the same, the clearest, coldest green she'd ever seen.

So was the quick clutch of pleasure in her stomach. "What are *you* doing here?"

"Rose." Her aunt Gemma was repressive.

"Your store is open, isn't it?" He had a delicious voice, like melted chocolate dripped over the crisp consonants and rounded vowels of upper-class English.

Gemma moved out from behind the counter. "Pay no attention to my niece. Missing a meal makes her growl. Did you have something specific in mind, my lord, or would you like to look around awhile?"

My lord? Well, Rose thought, that was no more than she'd suspected, and explained why he seemed familiar. Se must have seen his picture sometime. This man wasn't just rich, he was frosting—the creamy top level of the society cake.

She, of course, wasn't part of the cake at all.

"Quite specific," he said. "About five foot seven, I'd say, with eyes the color of the ocean at twilight and a sad lack of respect for the local police."

Rose lifted one eyebrow. "Are you here on Captain Mylonas's behalf, then...my lord?"

"I never visit a beautiful woman on behalf of another man. Certainly not at the behest of a fool. I asked you to call me Drew."

Ah. Now she knew who he was. "So you did, Lord Andrew."

His mouth didn't smile, but the creases cupping his lower eyelids deepened and the cool eyes warmed slightly. "Stubborn, aren't you?"

"Do pigs fly?" Gemma asked in a rhetorical manner.

"Ah—no, I don't believe they do."

Rose grinned. "Aunt Gemma has a fondness for American slang, but she doesn't always get the nuances right. She enjoys American tabloids, too. And Italian tabloids. And—"

"Really, Rose," Gemma interrupted, flustered. "His lordship can't possibly be interested in my reading habits."

"No?" Rose's smile widened as she remembered a picture of Lord Andrew Harrington she'd seen in one of her aunt's tabloids a few years ago. Quite a memorable photograph— but it hadn't been Lord Andrew's face that had made it so. His face hadn't shown at all, in fact. "I'm afraid we don't sell sunscreen. If you're planning to expose any, ah, untanned portions of your body to the Mediterranean sun, you'd do better to shop at Serminio's Pharmacy. They have a good selection."

"Rose!" Gemma exclaimed. "I'm sorry, my lord, she didn't—that is, she probably did mean—but she shouldn't have."

The creases deepened. "I'm often amazed at how many people remember that excessively candid photograph. Perhaps my sister is right. She claims the photographer caught my best side."

His best side being his backside? Rose laughed. "Maybe I do like you, after all."

The door chime sounded. Tourists, she saw at a glance—a Greek couple with a small child. She delegated them to her aunt with a quick smile. To her surprise, Gemma frowned without stepping forward to welcome their customers.

Her *zia* didn't approve of Lord Andrew Harrington? Or possibly it was Rose's flirting she didn't like. Ah, well. She and Gemma had different ideas about which risks were worth taking. She answered her aunt's silent misgivings with a grin, and reluctantly Gemma moved toward the front of the shop.

Lord Andrew came up to the counter. "Perhaps you could show me your shop."

How odd. She couldn't feel him. She felt something, all right—a delightful fizzing, the champagne pleasure of attraction. But she couldn't feel *him*. The counter was only two feet wide, which normally let a customer's energy brush up against hers. Curious, she tipped her head. "Maybe I will. But I'll have to repeat my aunt's question. Are you looking for something in particular?"

"Nothing that would be for sale. But something special, yes."

Oh, he was good. Rose had to smile. "We have some very special things for sale, though, all handmade. Necklaces, earrings—"

He shook his head chidingly. "I'm far too conventional a fellow for earrings—except, of course, for pearls. Pearls must always be acceptable, don't you think?"

"Certainly, on formal occasions," she agreed solemnly. "I'm afraid we don't have any pearls, however."

He looked thoughtful. "I believe I have a sister."

She was enjoying him more and more. "How pleasant for you."

''No doubt she will have a birthday at some point. I could buy her a present. In fact, I had better buy her a present. You must help me.''

''Jewelry, or something decorative?''

''Oh…'' His gaze flickered over her, then lifted so his eyes could smile at her in that way they had that didn't involve his mouth at all. ''Something decorative, I think.''

''For your sister,'' she reminded him, and left the safety of the counter. Quite deliberately she let her arm brush his as she walked past, and received an answer to the question she couldn't ask any other way.

Nothing. Even this close, he gave away nothing at all.

Rose's skin felt freshly scrubbed—tender, alert. Her mind began to fizz like a thoroughly shaken can of soda, but she didn't let her step falter as she led the way to the other side of the store, away from her aunt and the Greek tourists.

Here the elegantly swirled colors of Murano glass glowed on shelves beside bowls bright with painted designs. Colors giggled and flowed over lead crystal vases, majolica earthenware, millefiori paperweights, ceramic figures and crackle-finish urns. Here she felt relaxed and easy, surrounded by beauty forged in fire.

A purely physical reaction. That's all she felt with this man. That and curiosity, a ready appreciation for a quick mind. She turned to face him, and she was smiling. But not like a shopkeeper in pursuit of a sale. ''What is your sister like? Feminine, rowdy, sophisticated, shy?''

''Convinced she could do a better job of running my life than I do.'' He wasn't looking at her now, but at a shiny black statue by Gilmarie—a nymph, nude, seated on a stone and casting a roguish glance over one bare shoulder. He traced a finger along a ceramic thigh. ''I like this.''

The nymph was implicitly sensual. Rose's eyebrows lifted. ''For your sister?''

''I have a brother, too.''

''No doubt he comes equipped with a birthday as well.''

''I'm fairly sure of it. I'm not sure I want this for him,

though. I like the look on her face. The invitation.'' His eyes met hers then. There was no hint of a smile now. ''Any man would.''

What an odd thing a heart was, pumping along unnoticed most of the time, then suddenly bouncing in great, uneven leaps like a ball tumbling downhill. ''She's flirting, not inviting.''

''Is there a difference?''

''To a woman, yes. I think of flirting as a performance art. Something to be enjoyed in the moment, like dancing. Men are more likely to think of it as akin to cooking—still an art in the right hands, but carried out with a particular goal in mind.''

The creases came back, and one corner or his mouth helped them build his smile this time. ''I'm a goal-oriented bastard at times.''

So they knew where they stood. He wanted to get her in bed. Rose hadn't decided yet what she wanted, but thought she would enjoy finding out....

INTIMATE MOMENTS™
presents:

Romancing the Crown

With the help of their powerful allies, the royal family of Montebello is determined to find their missing heir. But the search for the beloved prince is not without danger—or passion!

Available in July 2002:
HER LORD PROTECTOR
by Eileen Wilks (IM #1160)

When Rosie Giaberti has a psychic vision about the missing prince of Montebello, she finds herself under the protection of dashing Lord Drew Harrington. But will the handsome royal keep her secrets—and her heart—safe?

This exciting series continues throughout the year with these fabulous titles:

Available only from Silhouette Intimate Moments at your favorite retail outlet.

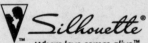

Where love comes alive™

Visit Silhouette at www.eHarlequin.com

SIMRC7

**Where royalty and romance
go hand in hand...**

The series continues in Silhouette Romance
with these unforgettable novels:

HER ROYAL HUSBAND
by Cara Colter
on sale July 2002 (SR #1600)

THE PRINCESS HAS AMNESIA!
by Patricia Thayer
on sale August 2002 (SR #1606)

SEARCHING FOR HER PRINCE
by Karen Rose Smith
on sale September 2002 (SR #1612)

And look for more Crown and Glory stories in
SILHOUETTE DESIRE starting in October 2002!

Available at your favorite retail outlet.

Silhouette®

COMING NEXT MONTH